LUCIA

Lucia

ALEX PHEBY

BIBLIOASIS
Windsor, Ontario

First published in the UK in 2018 by
Galley Beggar Press Limited
Norwich

First published in North America in 2021 by
Biblioasis
Windsor, Ontario

FIRST EDITION
2 4 6 8 10 9 7 5 3 1

Library and Archives Canada Cataloguing in Publication
Title: Lucia / Alex Pheby.
Names: Pheby, Alex, author.
Description: Originally published: Norwich, London : Galley Beggar Press,
©2018.
Identifiers: Canadiana (print) 20190239484 | Canadiana (ebook) 20190239492
| ISBN 9781771964234
(softcover) | ISBN 9781771964241 (ebook)
Subjects: LCSH: Joyce, Lucia, 1907-1982—Fiction. | LCSH: Beckett, Samuel,
1906-1989—Fiction.
Classification: LCC PR6116.H37 L83 2020 | DDC 823/.92—dc23

Readied for the press by Daniel Wells
Cover designed by Natalie Olsen
Text design by Tetragon, London

PRINTED AND BOUND IN CANADA

We sought the opinions of our guides, and set out for an area that had been well documented with no real expectation of a change in our fortunes. That said, there is always an odd sensation in the stomach as dawn rises in the desert, and the last day of an expedition has a superstitious quality to it. So, despite being men of science and exhausted by our previous failures, we made the efforts necessary.

We were taken to a place that had already been excavated, and I was about to remonstrate with the man who was leading the donkeys when I noticed a right angle in an area of ground cleared by a recent sandstorm.

As if he had seen it at the same time, my colleague went for it too. We collided, and confirmed what we were both thinking – that it was possibly the joining of stones that formed the entrance to a chamber buried below.

To cut a long story short, beneath a layer of sand and rubble there were larger rocks purposely piled to block the passage – which is an excellent indication of a tomb shaft – and there was a brief argument over who it was that would file the claim and who would remain behind to guard the find.

Had we known then that we had an intact tomb, complete with mummy, then I don't think either of us would have gone, and we'd have sent for the papers to be brought over.

Pure, Pure!
Pure, Pure!
Pure, Pure!
Pure, Pure!
The statue is washed
with water from the nemset-jars

After death, the body is passed on to embalmers who take it to the house of purification. There it is placed on a low wooden table and the long process of mummification begins. This will take seventy days, the length of Anubis's absence from the sky.

THE FUNERARY PRIEST
NORTHAMPTON, DECEMBER 1982

Nothing unusual – leaner perhaps. Lighter. Bony like a bird. Swan. Long neck. Three and six on the box and half a crown on silk. Save on the wood – no reinforcement. Save on the wadding – no need, can't weigh more than a child – halfway to a skeleton. Paper on balsa wood – like a plane – stretched and pinned at the wrist, at the shoulder, at the knees, at the hips. Tent material pegged taut – in taupe. Never at the neck; tight across the cheeks, but the neck wrinkled and sagging. Like a wattle.

Turkey.

Cock.

—Anything you need?

—No, Madam. The boys and I will be fine.

—Tea?

—No, Madam. And please, don't offer any to the boys – it's hard enough to get them to pay attention to their work as it is. Thank you.

She nods. Nice enough. Hard not to see her as if she was laid out, too – bigger, heavier, shorter, but needing a broader plank. More fluid. This one will barely stink, but her? Vats. Pints. Litres.

No tea.

The measuring tape gives the final tally.

The boys are out there, smoking, laughing. Say something; bad for business, even in a place like this.

Taps on the window bring dust from the frame, sash weights knocking. Heavy lead.

Hand blade drawn across the throat, edge against the Adam's apple, and they drop their cigarettes, grind them out. Fag papers and threads of brown tobacco, guilty looks and the drawing together of jackets. Shuffling.

Back turned, and there'll be smirking.

Not her, though. Time for smirking long past. Time for anything.

The wake then – undress her, preliminaries to the embalming, that job, clothes, teeth, make-up – nothing flashy, the art being to replicate the seemingness of being alive but with the gravity of the hereafter. The lack of movement, of soullessness. Finality. Et cetera.

—Madam!

Down the hall she comes out from another room, a bundle of sheets under one arm, a breakfast tray under the other.

—Open casket?

—What?

—The deceased was a Catholic, you put here. Will the family be holding an open or closed casket wake?

—What?

Puzzled, derisive. Resigned.

—First job here? she says.

It was – the last lot lost out on price. Wouldn't hire Poles.

—Her family won't be holding a wake. Ours rarely do.

Suddenly posh, in the voice at least, bearing still fishwife in the main.

Cheaper, no wake. Easier. Less air to the face: quick glimpse, perhaps, kiss on the forehead and then the grave. Or fire.

One of the boys at the window, hat in hand, forlorn, across his face fat raindrops streaking the glass and the wind rattling. Come in then, mouthed. Rap on the glass. Wait in the hall.

Not much else to do. Look her over for something missed. Nothing – no weight, no width, no wounds, slightly above average height.

Deep breath, check the coat, smooth the brim of the hat. In her mirror – fancy-framed but speckled with black across the middle – a sombre, older man, like himself but more his dad than he remembers; more every day, and his dad remembered more like this man, half father, half son, half living, half dead. One day there won't be a difference between the two of them.

Life in a box.

And out to the hall.

The boys nod and come to a gesture. Hats off, clasped across the chest – good form, no one there to see it, but good form – that's the trick: to do it even when no-one's looking. Isn't that the trick? To care enough to do it when no-one can see? Because it matters, despite everything. That's the art of it. The history. Perhaps it's the dead we should show we know what's right. And don't they look down at us, from the corner of every room? Top corner right, checking our collars and cuffs.

—Got the trolley?

They haven't.

—Why do you think I asked you in here? For a chat? For company? Get the trolley.

Yessirs.

—Not all of you. You, wrap her over – make it tight. No, I've shown you – like this.

A lot in common with nurses – lifting, sorting, caring… if you can care for the dead. A way with sheets. Nice and tight. Mummification. Hospital corners, no wrinkles. Like this, like that, smoothed down, swaddled. Up at one side, sheet under, up at the other, sheet through.

The trolley is in. Up – one at each corner – and over. Momentary doubt that the mechanism will catch, will lock, flash of a body on the ground, limbs askew, hair askew, teeth out and skittering.

It locks…

… and we're off. A smile on departure, reluctant, and a nod, formal, as if to say 'this is the way things are done, aren't they? And they have been done like this, and they will be done like this, for her, and eventually for us, but somehow we are above it all' in this smiling and nodding.

Wheeled away.

★

They can't get far enough fast enough, these boys; still new, still keen to escape the death site, imprisonment, thinking it possible, perhaps. Thinking it still possible, perhaps. They don't know that it follows you, is in front of you, wanting to come before the eyes, to lie in wait, just as you turn your back.

And is it so bad?

That building, heavy and grey, windows tear-soaked in the rain but dry inside, quiet – endlessly reliable. What could happen in a place like that? What could be so bad? It's all done, on death – finished. Like bedtime – warm and done. Blanket under the chin. They'd prefer to rush to something else, to run forward to burial as if that was the way to avoid it, to run past it and away. Wouldn't it be better to sit it out? Live with it? They want to get their jackets off and into the pub and drink and fight themselves out of their fates.

They'll learn.

Ask her.

We stay inside, mostly, except with the children, who we follow to the back of the van and have to be walked away by the elbow, bemused, as if we would have lived with the body, made do, dressed it and washed it forever. Or just held it. With the adults we watch from the window, or return to business – tea, often. Television.

Form must be followed, even if there is no-one there to see.

Nothing weird in this job today. Nothing out of the ordinary – no clingy mothers, no children, no men who punch rather than cry. Get your hands off her! Fucking ghoul, fucking devil. And then gritted teeth and racked with sobs. Apologetic. None of that today. All quiet on the W.F. The crunch of gravel on the drive.

Doors oiled on the hinges slide silently open and the space inside is spotless. Oiled runners, rollers rattling, straps and buckles.

The boys take the car and the van is quiet.

Oil the throat in peace. No scratching the balls, no picking the nose in the presence of the dead.

At the lights, studiously looking forward. What's the alternative? To catch the eyes of passers-by? And then? What common understanding can be exchanged there? Any more than one can communicate with a paramedic at a crash scene, or the wounded, or the jaws of life. Pointless – nothing sensible to be said or thought. No point. And what business is it of theirs? And how to keep that contempt for them secret? – their desire for something of the afterlife, so prurient and formless, peering in the windows hoping for a glimpse of someone else's death, to somehow understand what theirs might be. Neuter it that way.

Stare forward.

No radio, no nuts, no crisps.

The journey is short and then the camaraderie of the office, the going upwards of gravity, easiness of years, impossibility of so much that is sombre being taken so seriously for so long and then its opposite. Just as impossible – the necessity to be light enough for the others in the face of the chest clutching and the gloom.

Better to be her.

Or not. She is less than nothing here. Nothing there, but unique for her moment. Now she's one of a number, one of a class – not many, but more than one. Not centre stage, no solo, part of an ensemble, one of a type, waiting in line for her prompt. Forgettable in the face of even the mundane requirements of the business of the day.

—How did it go?

—Fine. Those lads...

—Give them time.

—But...

—They're cheap, got to give them that.

Coat down. Tea.

—Who's washing her?

—You are. Tea?

—Yes, thanks.

—I'll bring it through.

What's the hurry?

Why wait?

In the pub they talk of wax, snigger behind their hands like young nuns. There is no wax.

Hands first, then feet. Always best to get the big jobs out of the way, dirt from under the fingernails, trim. No need to push the skin back – it draws away of its own accord, tide receding, leaving. Cut further, easier to get at the grime.

Palms white, lines in black – easy to read, this life. No fortune, no future, except the obvious. Palms soft and pale, tending to bunch up, stretched flat, knuckles straightened against the ligaments' twist away from the resting line. Some play in the fingers can be made by stretching. More care and attention paid here than to the feet – the hands on display, perhaps, but professional pride, necessary thoroughness, artfulness. They won't be ignored. Under shoes, under socks, under wood, in the fire, underground – not the attitude.

These feet are twisted little things, bound like a Chinese woman's, toes off at an impossible angle and closed on themselves. Corns. Nails bitten. A small puzzle, but ignorable – where's the need for puzzling? Some needless things are useful, others are not – there's a story there, but no one to tell it, and to what end? The toenails are bitten. Someone has bitten the toenails. She bit the toenails. The toenails were bitten.

Now the flannel to the soles of the feet – flat arches given a turn by the tension in the muscle. The water in the bowl muddies and the enamel greys under it. Only a little – indoor dirt of a woman who died out of the sun. A privilege? Not for her. Who's to say she didn't want to get dirty? Who's to say she didn't want grit and grime and mud, all of that stuff?

No evidence of it. Two bones entwined, twisting from the ankle to the knee, turning in. Two legs entwined, like a shy girl, coquettish, silly, except baggy and lined like an elephant's, brown mottled and white like giraffes are, two long necks, the feet the heads.

—Where do you want this tea?

—On the side, please. Thanks.

—There's more in the pot.

Less care now, with the flannel: less to take care of. At the top of the thighs, nothing, an invisible nothing until the tops of the hip bones, the navel marking the reappearance of the body, visible again and whole, though whole to what? – the question never asks itself.

Skinny. So skinny. Not in the way all corpses are, but translucent and matt, dead to the touch, pliable and inelastic, utterly without substance. A layer of paint, the rice paper of a cheap Bible, the rainbow of a rising bubble, the bones beneath barely beneath the hollow of the hips, so hollow that the mind inserts its opposite, a sphere that will mesh with the absence, make up for it. The pot belly of a long distance lorry driver, taken *en route* and slowing to a crawl on the hard shoulder, cold shoulder, clutch disengaged, engine stalled, choked on a ham roll.

No breasts, just ribs, the finger's width between as present as the rise: the same shape, the same idea, a dishcloth laid over pots and pans and Sunday duties softened by slugs from the bottle above the counter, too high for her to reach. See? Let's hope.

Wipe to the wrists, wipe to the neck, and the sheet drawn up.

Ready for the box.

We had the men remove the rocks by hand, paying them extra for their silence and their speed: often a new find will be met with a flurry of expectant hawkers, experts, and rival teams all alert to any chance they might get their snouts in the trough; we wanted some quiet and privacy to examine what it was that we had.

When we eventually excavated all the rock from the shaft, there was another disagreement as to which of us would have the honour of breaching the chamber; there was insufficient room for us both to be lowered in safely. This was our first indication that the tomb might be unusual, since an adult male's sarcophagus will generally require a wide enough shaft to allow two men to enter at once; perhaps this was the burial site of a woman or a child.

The matter was decided by the drawing of lots, and I won (although as they let me down I wondered whether I had thought it through – he could, after all, order me buried alive and return when I was dead).

I had heard that an undisturbed tomb has a particular odour that emanates from the oils and resins that the corpse and the burial wrappings are preserved in. This, very excitingly, was present in our tomb.

I asked for a torch to be thrown down and I lit it, trembling. A little disappointingly, the tomb was small, roughly hewn, and was vandalised, despite appearing to be intact from the surface.

The statue is censed with the smoke of burning aromatics

First, the corpse is eviscerated. They enter the skull by breaking the ethmoid bone with a metal implement, and stir the brain until it is liquid enough to be drained through the nose. The interior is then rinsed with palm wine and frankincense. Having no further use, the brain is discarded.

THE DESECRATOR OF THE MORTUARY LITERATURE

THE GARDEN OF ████████ █████,
MAY 1988

The box was more a chest, or one of those trunks that first-class passengers' lackeys loaded aboard the *Titanic* – the sort that got pushed up the rickety gangway, with brass at the corners and a double barrelled name stencilled on the side.

It was bloody heavy, and very difficult to drag across the tarmac. His orders were to avoid the house – which was the quickest way – and the next shortest route had steps.

There was nothing for it: brute strength would win the day! Oh, for an abandoned shopping trolley! He didn't care what brand; anything pushed into the bushes would do. There was nothing like that round here, though: it was too well maintained.

Here was Mr ████.

—What are you waiting for?

—Nothing. Just working out a plan of action. It weighs a tonne. I was wondering whether...

—Bring it round the back.

That had already been established. How wasn't yet as clear. His was not to reason why... his was to suffer permanent degradation of the lumbar region at the whim of some bossy, old bastard.

Well, if that was the way of it, then it was best to get it over and done with; then he could return all the sooner to the enforced and welcome indolence of the long summer break, his parents mollified, and the impression of a hardworking and dutiful son restored.

★

It wasn't so bad, once the slope down to the garden kicked in – which was something to be said for riverside places.

—You should set a fire and burn the lot.

That was do-able; the boy scout training proving useful again, despite what everyone said. It was not simply a charitable front for kiddy-fiddlers and retired black-shirts. It equipped a boy for life.

That said, hadn't this ███ heard of shredders? Presumably not.

—I have lighter fluid.

Well, that was almost an insult! The use of accelerants? Cheating! Where was the skill in that? If the old fellow wanted to go that route, why not do it himself? Anyone can pour lighter fluid into a box and light it.

—Thanks. Where do you want it?

—Anywhere.

—Not on the lawn, though?

—Anywhere.

Anywhere. Right.

—Matches?

The old man patted himself all over and went into the house.

Right. Anywhere. He dragged it over, right into the middle of the grass, by the bird bath, away from any overhanging branches and whatever. In his head a scene played out from *Apocalypse Now* – the napalming of a jungle, trees aflame, helicopters swooping. Wagner.

He prised the trunk open and... letters. No wonder it was so heavy: thousands of letters. With ribbons and stamps. There were postcards, too.

—Not there! Down by the compost heap.

Not 'anywhere' then, for God's sake! The decrepit fucker couldn't make eye contact – he was utterly clueless.

Down at the compost heap, ███ produced with a yellowed hand a rectangular tin of lighter fluid, which was also yellow, and then Cook's Matches, the box for which was more yellow.

—I want to keep this trunk.

Really? How was that going to work?

—Well, sir, I can't burn them one at a time, can I?

—Why not?

Because there were fucking thousands of them.

—Perhaps you have an old metal dustbin? Or a barbecue?

—I don't have a barbecue.

He didn't have a barbecue.

—So, burn them one at a time.

His back, like a bag of tennis balls, and his head, just visible behind as he walked away, looked eminently kickable.

—Don't read them!

This was delivered from inside, with old man muttering after.

He wasn't to read them? He was prohibited from reading them. So now, suddenly, he wanted to read them. The interdiction provoked its own transgression. It defined it. Enforced it. Now in his head was a scene, played out not from *Apocalypse Now*, but from a tedious Wednesday morning lecture from his subsid. course – a middle-aged man, bearded and beige, laconically indicating words in chalk, unreadable in this memory.

Fuck it.

Thousands! There would be n hours work, where n is a large integer. Perhaps not if there was a system: perhaps if he lit each letter from the flames of the last, with no pause, no taking of breath?

The first Cook's Match didn't catch on the safety striking strip, but skidded across, ineffectually, damply. He pressed the next harder and the thing flared: yellow – all so yellow. Charlotte Gilman Perkins? Yellow was the most popular colour for psychiatric wards. Was that a coincidence?

The eggshell blue Basildon Bond was as damp as the matchbox, and cold, and reluctant to burn: more reluctant than the matchwood at least. It curled and brittled slowly, flattening and twisting and then surreptitiously burning his fucking fingertips white. He dropped it and the thin line of fire crept along, irregularly jagged, like a scar or a coastline.

He picked it up again by the landmass.

'Don't read' was not, as it turned out, a problem; the handwriting was careful and regular, but in another language: more than one – Italian, French, German – fuck knew. All at once?

As if the heat broke down the paper's resistance, or the pulp suddenly became willing to burn, the letter flared, racing red up to his wrist, and this time he dropped it right onto his jeans.

Later, the ash was a problem; it smudged into everything. One piece floated around and moved as if spiteful, travelling on improbable vectors indirectly towards the old cunt's open French windows, towards his cream carpet, his cherry wood table.

He wondered if he should chase after it? No. That would be too comic, too prone to ridicule and failure. One false step and there would be smudges, recriminations, tedious exchanges – all of it.

It landed, eventually, on the soil of a potted sapling.

He took another match. The system of letter lighting letter needed to work for this afternoon ever to end; moreover, there was only half a box of matches, and once they ran out there would be no option but to talk to the unbearable bastard, which was something that would be... unbearable.

He thought about trying two at a time? Three at a time? Five?

Some letters were older, brittle in their envelopes, antique in their layout, the address so neatly ordered that it spoke of a care no longer paid to niceties. Old letters, old people: they had a respect for, and a consideration of, the convenience of postal employees, a long gone obsequiousness to figures of authority and ideas of proper conduct, however minuscule or manifestly lowly. He didn't have any of that. None of his generation did. Which was progress, as far as he saw it.

Other letters were in different handwriting… the other side of a correspondence? Perhaps they were stealable for an epistolary novel? *Pamela. Shamela. Spamela?* For the modern sensibility?

The flame liked these older letters, though, and *Spamela* was up in smoke before she was ever properly conceptualised. She wavered in the transporter beam, corrupted in the buffer, trapped forever in the quantum flux of the flux capacitor, forever meowing between one state and an opposing state until eventually Newton decided one way or the other, or one way and then the other, that she never existed. Wooo! There she went, like a ghost when the light comes on, sending the cockroaches under the skirting boards.

More letters and the Olympic torch relay undid his reliance on the scarce reserves of matches. June 5th, 1948, was consigned to the flames, June 11th, June 20th, were ash flakes drifting recklessly up and down the garden. Some came down to rest in the still, green water of the bird bath, others made for the safety of the treetops to lodge unwanted in the nests of unsuspecting birds. Choking a hatchling? He hoped not.

█████ asleep now, the old fucker. The glasses on the arm of his chair rested as if there was a second face invisibly staring up, corpse-like and still, prostrate beside him. The Ba? The Ka? The Akh? One of them, willed into its limbo by the insufficiency of the wall paintings of his tomb: no slaves, no ushebti, bushels and oxen absent, brain undrawn through the nostrils, canopic jars unfilled with organs.

October, 1975, was one bundle in another hand, and the heat enforced continual movement, a pass the parcel anxiety to avoid the flame being at rest, the critical skin-scorching temperature avoided by minimal contact. Each bundle was another month.

In an uncovered lower strata were Manila folders and X-ray plates.

He brought them to the light and the plastic caught. Drips fizzed into the open trunk and hissed like napthalene, like Dresden, like toy soldiers lit with Dad's lighter, their arms rendered wax, their legs reddened, bulbs of molten primordial matter swirling with black dust, brought up to the eye.

Too hot to handle.

It was working, but this method risked burning too fiercely. He might burn to death.

The old cunt was asleep, myopically dreaming, snorting in his chair, and here was a terracotta plant pot, low and long and rectangular, empty except for a snail shell, a bus ticket, and some leaves. Fuck it! Who was this ███, anyway? The old must make way for the new!

There was plenty of room in there – end to end there would be at least six months per foot. The job was easy with this new innovation. It was sensible. It was time and motion study-able. On an hourly rate, how much effort would he make and for how much money? This system was amenable to rules. To principles. There was efficiency, Nazi-style. All things were justified if the end was justified. Even if it wasn't. The end in itself was... there was a quote... he couldn't think of it.

He loaded up the pot with a row of paper saplings, trees pulped and resurrected, and the x-ray plates were firelighters. He lit one bundle and placed it beneath the others, the remainder waited their turn, nice and patient, in the box. There was an efficient procession: their muddled proximity formed crowd dynamics in the trunk and in the pot. The possibility of either escape was reduced to zero, chaos turned into queuing, even to the point of ignition. The letter ahead, the letter behind, the similarity of those to each side made this movement towards the fire, towards their destruction, tolerable, manageable. Inevitable. He ushered them forward not eagerly, but inexorably. He had no alternative. Why would he separate some from the others? Bring them forward out of turn, to be next on the pile? Let them wait together, he felt, and hope, vainly, that the fire burnt itself out before their time arrived.

January 15th, dawn to dusk in a cursive hand, scrawled, English, three words to a line; the effort not to read was not enormous, but it was there. He tried not to shift his attention.

But the job needed a certain direction of gaze, or did ███ want the curtains set alight? Ash everywhere?

There were words in a row, but they were meaningless. How many, he thought, would break the law against reading? What makes meaning? One word? Two? That would be too vague, surely. He tried: two words. Nothing. Two words was not reading. Three? This was getting close, but nothing much. Perhaps seven was the magic number. Definitely nine. Then still, what combination of the parts of speech? Nouns and verbs? They'd be dangerous. Look away! Modifiers? Safe, surely, in isolation, but what if they came *en masse*? In sequence? They might be telling – can a story be made from a string of adverbs? A code? Information on this side of the event horizon...

Silly old cunt. If he hadn't made such a fuss, it wouldn't have been a temptation.

His eyes moved by themselves. His eyes moved, your honour, by themselves, and in the fire, curling and agitated, half-fluttering like a butterfly whose wing was being held by an eager child – which will, despite her infinite care, be rendered useless for flight, crushed on one side, the other doing the work of both, neither enough – was a polaroid. It had come free from a bundle, and was now a lone, black square, framed and isolated.

Don't read, he had been told. But an image?

Look away!

Around the polaroid was a sheaf of billfolds, other polaroids, the wrong side of the contact sheet, and a headshot from a black and white film. A random burst of plasma, a release of stuttering gas, and one of the polaroids was on its obverse, its inverse, heads and tails, the one side of a coin, whatever it was called – it had a name... and, and, and in the space in which a word was sought the image propagated even when his eyes closed in shame and his head turned. It was an old woman staring at the camera, hair severe, badly cut round a bowl – like a Plantagenet king – but the eyes staring, one sken, mouth set and small, three dots – therefore – like the finger-holes of a bowling ball, but stern.

A second look and it was gone to black and the polaroid beneath it was already burned, the film still, the billfold beneath it too, and there was embarrassment within him, in his throat: heartburn, acid was behind his teeth, acid was on his tongue.

Now each image was invisible behind her face, her eyes, her pyre. Who would look past it? Shoes and teeth and parcels wrapped in string, certificates of birth and death, all personal effects the property of the state, stateless, piled and shorn, seat stuffing.

Shovel it on, shovel it off.

Diaries and passports, fairytales and ledgers, ration books and exhibition catalogues.

Bedtime reading white as smoke.

The walls of tombs of this period were decorated with pictures and script, so I was expecting to see things of this type as I moved the torch across the nearest wall; and, indeed, there were paintings and engravings, but there were also what appeared to be scratches and excisions all over, places where the images had been mutilated and the funerary texts desecrated. If you've ever seen a photograph after scissors have been used to score out the faces, then you'll have an idea of what it was like.

Time had been dedicated both to the original works, and the process of defacing them.

The more I saw of the walls, the more apparent it became that there had been an effort made to erase something specific, though what was erased was unclear at that point.

From above came a shout from my colleague that echoed down the shaft. Somewhat reluctantly, I told him it was safe to descend, and that he should bring the good lamp, pencils, and paper.

Entering, gazing upon her

The slitter comes and makes an incision in the left hand side of the abdomen with a knife of volcanic glass. Because he has desecrated the corpse, he is chased from the house of purification, and stoned.

THE BA OF LUCIA JOYCE
PARIS, SUMMER 1917

There are many bedtime stories that are suitable for children, and there are many that are not.

Some stories are not suitable because children find them tedious to hear, and while a certain degree of tedium is desirable, at least inasmuch as there ought to be a lack of exciting incident that might otherwise cause children insomnia through overstimulation, a complete lack of engagement will cause a similar restlessness, and not that easy drifting off into sleep that the reader of stories aimed at children prior to their sleeping requires.

Other stories are not suitable for children because they contain content that the child is not ready to hear – for example that dealing with adult themes, or incidents – or contain content that would cause the child distress, such as tales of horror and the uncanny. Tales in which small mammals receive rough treatment at the hands of an authority figure should be avoided. Lucia associates herself with the animals in these stories, even if she is quite content to eat lamb at dinner. The necessary separation between eating and the sympathy-inducing face of an animal is present in the serving of stew, for example. Here, the animal's face is barely in evidence, or is only present in a way that is not recognisable, but illustrations in a book where kittens and mice are given central roles rely on the sympathy that may be induced in a child for a young mammal.

Other stories are not suitable for children because they might provide them with examples in which disobedience to the rule of law is met with positive outcomes. This will make the parents' job all the harder when, in the morning, they are faced with a wilful child who will then not eat her porridge without it being accompanied by a prohibitively expensive amount of honey, or is not at the correct temperature, or will not dress herself and perform her ablutions in a timely fashion, now we are late, smack to the back of the calves, stop crying or I'll give you something to cry about.

Other stories are not suitable because they refer to worlds of which the child has no knowledge. These are disengaging through their unfamiliarity, or are redundant. Also, there is no subsidiary benefit that other stories *do* possess. A morality tale from the Bible teaches as it entertains, for example. Take the one about a mouse who gnaws on the rope that is around a lion's muzzle, or Daniel in the lion's den, or the prodigal son, or Androcles and the Lion. These are all stories which will send Lucia to sleep well prepared for a night of dreams in which proper moral behaviour will be evidenced. Though it is not said that God punishes actions which take place in a dream, why not? Surely there must be some residuum of the self that carries into the dream world? Isn't there some attribute of the heart the actions of which will weigh heavy against the Ma'at feather when the dog-headed god puts it on the scale and throws the offal to a crocodile?

Other stories are unsuitable for Lucia because they put ideas in her head, or reify behaviours that until then were inchoate and unrecognised. They risk rewarding her for doing things she ought not to do by allowing her to *see* those things represented in a form sanctioned by the sanctified ritual of the bedtime reading.

At the beginning of all things, for example, Geb, the goddess of the sky, and Nut, the god of the earth, brought forth between them four children. The names of these children ought not to be mentioned to Lucia at bedtime since they bring to mind the notion that there is not one God, but many gods, and moreover that they have names, which are forbidden. The names are: Osiris, Isis, Set and Nepthys, and while they are predominately human in form they also bear the heads of animals sometimes.

As we have seen, Lucia prefers tales of animals, but the reader must be careful in the tales that he tells her, since the whole business of animals is a little fraught, for reasons that will become obvious.

Osiris and Isis, and Set and Nepthys were brother/sister pairs, which is another aspect that makes the story of their existence, even the very mention of them as facts, difficult and unsuitable for Lucia. They married and had relations together that are neither sanctionable under the law, nor allowable in the eyes of God. Nor are they practical in the Joyce household, unless the Joyces wish to take her often to the doctor, especially after puberty has set in, for the removal of foetuses, and the treatment of diseases, and the raising of feebleminded offspring.

Moreover, it is utterly distasteful and a terrible sin, nonetheless.

And what necessity is there in her for her to behave in this way, anyway? Like some long dead heathen god, or some disinterred pharaoh prior to their interment and death, securing the kingly line by marriage only to his and her own relatives. There is no natural explanation, surely, and no godly explanation, surely, and consequently without either a natural or a theological justification, stories of the incestuous relationships between the Egyptian gods are not suitable stories to tell her before bedtime. Won't she, the minute you are out of the door and your backs are turned, creep surreptitiously through the house to her brother's bedroom and, in a manner that the very mention of these things, even in a story, sanctions, slip beneath his covers and commit heinous crimes such as would have brought the censure of the Old Testament God, priests, and stone-wielding crowds? Drag her into the street and hurl rocks at her until she is dead. Take her to the doctor for the removal of foetuses.

And all the while thinking of it in the same way Lucia approaches any other pleasurable thing – the eating of cake, or sweets, or chocolate, or the opening of presents. The experience of the wind in the hair is pleasant. So also the stretching of the limbs in the park on a sunny day when she has been lying in the grass after a lunch which included cake and sweets and strawberries. So also waking from a dream with her hand between her thighs and a sense of bodily wellbeing all around. After all, there is no difference to her in this, who is not aware of the prohibitions against such behaviour since, in the effort not to bring it into existence, or not to reify it if it be there in a nascent form, no-one has mentioned any of it. And the books on the ancient Greeks and the ancient Egyptians have been hidden. And bedtime stories suitable for children are carefully selected.

Yet ignorance is no defence, certainly not in Irish law, and not in the eyes of God, and that is why we have priests and parents who will put children on the right track. They will pull her hand out from her drawers and will smack the backs of her calves in order that she does not breach God's commandments. Though, if one thinks about it, that is not one of them, and it takes a good while to find it in the Bible if one ever wishes to locate the prohibition. Even then, it's worded so poorly one cannot quite make it out. If it is so bloody important perhaps it would be better to spell it out explicitly, except, of course, that God would then run the risk of reifying that thing which he didn't want reified. Although, if it was so bloody important why not make it so that it was impossible?

Perhaps that is the function of genetics. Mendelian genetics, however, is also not terribly easy to follow, and there is a certain ambiguity in the rights and wrongs here, too. There doesn't seem to be any explicit warning against incest as a means of generating children, so if there is no explicit natural law, and no explicit theological law, is it so terrible after all? And if Giorgio were to take himself to his sister's room in the middle of the night? When she is in a world of dreams with her hand between her thighs and a sense of bodily wellbeing all around? And slip beneath the covers and lie there with her, breathing into her ear and listening, no funny business, just enjoying the warmth? And slip into dreams beside her? And if, by chance, one of those dreams, prompted by the night's bedtime story should take one to far Arabia where veiled women parade? And, like in an illustration from the one thousand and one nights, their stomachs and belly buttons are on display?

The rising up of an unknowable sense of pressure building is not a thousand miles away from a sense of bodily wellbeing, but it is somehow also tension-inducing. It is almost as if one is on the verge of tears, or of passing a motion. And if there is no genetic law that is unambiguous and one has to look very deeply into the Bible and then can only find veiled references, and if one is in a dream, and if one slips one's hand over to her breast, up under her nightshirt, is it such a crime that it should prompt such pleasure?

Her skin as soft as milk, his excitation as pale as snow.

As they made to lower my colleague, I took advantage of my time alone and went over to another wall.

It was given up to a series of scenes, relatively intact. If the reader is familiar with the decorations at Hatshepsut's temple they will appreciate that aspects of the deceased's life are sometimes chronicled in detail – the voyage to Punt, for example. There is a chronological progress from left to right and then down the wall in the same way the text progresses in a book. Hatshepsut appears in each image amongst the people of her life, the gods of her religion, enjoying the spoils of her expedition, and making the necessary offerings on her return home.

So it was on this wall, except that the recurring figure in each scene was scored out. Likewise, in the parts of the wall where the deceased's name would be expected to appear in the symbols, these symbols had been chipped away.

Now, this is not a trivial matter in this religion: if the name of the dead is forgotten it entirely precludes them from taking their place in the afterlife.

As I considered this fact the boots of my colleague emerged from the entrance shaft and, feeling guilty for reasons I couldn't account for, I pulled the torch back from the wall.

Going to the tomb

The interior cavity is emptied with the exception of the heart, which is sewn to the skin. Unlike the brain, the deceased requires this organ – it is the seat of the personality, repository of all deeds, and will later be central in the weighing of the heart ceremony.

THE IB OF LUCIA JOYCE
LES ATELIERS DU VIEUX COLOMBIER, PARIS, SUMMER 1927

She's barefoot in the snow, hands on the glass, breath from her fingertips fogging it, and when she takes one back there's her palm and fingers, their outlines etched into space before the wind blows them away. She leans in, and a warm, humid exhalation obscures everything. She has to wipe it away to see through. She holds her breath, lifts her feet in turn, ice between her toes, grit on her soles.

In the shop display there are living things. Not like her: things warm and animate, hopeful and red, perfect in their forms, so tiny and bright. They are soldiers in regiments, and where there is snow outside there is cotton wool beneath their boots, talc on their gloves, needle prick bayonets, split pin chinstraps in brass, stern, full lips mouthing kisses, made up eyes, blue, with eyelashes like kitten whiskers. There are fifteen soldiers in a line, and two lines in ranks, and her breath hot across them, wiping the window.

The traffic in the road throws up slush. Some of it reaches her all the way over here. It hits her bare legs, her neck, chills her back, seeping through the dress. She feels everything, but she only cares about the soldiers. While she lives this life she can think about whatever she likes. She chooses this display above all other things. She licks her lips so they glisten like the lips of the soldiers. She straightens her back so that she's straight like them. She sets her feet together and the snow melts into a puddle around her.

She raises her eyes, and there's a woman reaching into the display. This woman takes one soldier by the head, lifting him by the helmet, and then two more, one from the end of each line so as not to disturb the distribution. Then they are gone.

The girl's head is untouched, the slush at her feet unmoved, and the soldier is wrapped in tissue paper and boxed for a Christmas gift.

As if he could sense my guilt, my colleague was very keen to see what was on the wall behind me. If I am being fair, I think I would have been equally curious, and he raised the lamp to the wall the moment he reached the ground.

If I had worried that he would find something troubling there, I needn't have; he gleefully identified aspects of the wall painting he recognised from other tombs and from the books of illustrations we had both pored over in the library back home and on the journey over. He indicated the rites and practices of the religion, and while he acknowledged the mutilations, it did not seem to occur to him what had already occurred to me: that if the desecrations were not committed by tomb raiders after the sealing of the entrance (since it was intact) then they must have taken place *contemporaneously with the burial of the corpse.*

*I have seen my mother
in all her outlines*

The corpse is washed
and packed with the
divine salt, natron,
derived from the
Nile Delta. This absorbs any remaining
liquids and fats, and is removed once
the body is dry. Then dried leaves are
pushed into the slit in the corpse's side,
filling it, and preserving its shape.

THE BA OF LUCIA JOYCE
EUROPE, 1907–1924

Italian children are visited on the fifth of January by the ghost of a woman who grieves for her lost son. She is maddened by her loss, and if you see her she will hit you with her broom handle, something she habitually carries since she is busy with her housework. Additionally, she uses it to fly in the manner of a witch. If you have been good she will leave sweets in your shoes; if you have been bad she will leave garlic, and you will spend the year followed by an odour emanating from your feet. You will get a name for yourself among the circle of people you previously counted as your friends, and they will know that you are odd.

If, in the middle of the night before the feast of the Epiphany, you should hear steps in your room and smell the odour of wine, you should keep your eyes dead shut and block your ears for safety. The Christmas Witch is traditionally offered wine to drink, and she reeks of it, having been at all the houses in the street, and when she gets to you she is half cut and breathing heavily. If you hear her scrabbling about, she is looking for your shoes so she can fill them. What sweets do you like, sweetie? Rubbish! Everyone likes sweets. Don't open your eyes unless you want a whack.

Old women will often have bristles on their chins, and callouses on their hands. The first are due to a general inattention to appearance that affects the elderly and the grieving – they simply stop attending to the duty to remain hairless – and the second is due to the hard work that old women must do to earn their keep around the house. They are no longer much to look at and cannot fulfil that function amongst the menfolk of inspiring a desire to keep them without insisting that they also do work. So who cares how hard their hands are now? The two things are linked, clearly. If the old women paid attention to the hairs on their chins they might find that they had less work to do, or work of a kind unlikely to induce the appearance of callouses on the skin of the hands.

The feel of callouses on the soft skin of one's stomach from hands reaching beneath the sheet to draw one across the bed is not pleasant, but it is not supposed to be. Hard skin is rough, but think of it from the other side: calloused skin allows hardly any sensation to carry to the brain, the nerves being under a thickness rather than at the surface. This is why the hands grip so tightly, this is why they pinch, since they must compensate for an absence of sensation with a firmer grip.

One should not chide the Christmas Witch for a hairy chin since she has lost her son and, mad with grief, she searches until she finds baby Jesus. He further burdens her with the motherhood of all the children of Italy, and can anyone expect a woman so burdened to take the usual care of her appearance that her sex demands? And who cares anyway, since she slips unseen between the bedrooms of all the Italian children, and they remain beneath the sheets, eyes tight shut and ears plugged? She draws them across the bed to her wine-ridden corpse on the eve of Epiphany, and so determines whether they have been a good girl or a bad girl prior to the delivery into their shoes of liquorice, or coal, or candyfloss, or onions. If eyes are closed and ears shut, what difference does it make?

When she leaves she does some light housework on the way out, namely some sweeping. This is both a practical help to the mothers of Italy, since it is one less job to do, and also fulfils the function of removing the troubles of the year. This is up to and including any lingering sense of her on the body. And the grating of the skin of her fingers on the skin of the stomach. And the hot press of her lips on the back of the neck, the tickle of her whiskers, the stench of wine and cigar smoke she leaves. And the bruises from the whacking of her broom handle, but my eyes *are* closed, you promised, you promised.

Little bats don't tell.

In other countries, Father Christmas comes earlier. If Italian children are aware of him, from an uncle or another relative, they can expect a visit from him on Christmas Eve to much the same effect. Again, he comes in the night and one mustn't look at him. He has been drinking, whisky this time, or brandy, and he will determine whether you have been good or bad by his methods. He comes with his reindeers though, which are very sweet to look at, and the animal smell that adheres to them adheres to him, too. This is to be expected, because he maintains such close contact with his animals all night long, and he has bristles on his chin. Haven't you seen a picture of him? He has lots of bristles on his chin.

He leaves presents which are in all ways better than sweets. They have a higher financial value, and are also more durable, and are still around many days and weeks and months after they are given. Consequently, Lucia should be more grateful for these gifts than she should be for gifts of sweets. The range of methods for showing gratitude is wider, and may properly be expressed on the opening of the gifts, providing there are no witnesses. Church services are useful for this, since some members of a family are more religiously observant than others, and a sermon takes a good while to deliver. Similarly, the walking of dogs must be done even on Christ's birthday, and while it is being done, here is an extra present, don't tell your brother he'll be jealous, now come over here and count my waistcoat buttons.

Green apples.

On the 13th of December, what do you want for Christmas? That seems like a lot, what a greedy child you are, she will throw ashes in your eyes, come over here, accompanied by Castaldo.

Lord you are wet.

To say nothing of Krampus.

In Switzerland, Saint Nicholas is accompanied by black Schmutzli who will thrash you with a swatch of sticks. Christmases in that territory are particularly fraught, in that the resistant or talkative child can expect blood to be drawn on the buttocks, or welts at least. These welts will cause wincing, and have you ever seen a man beaten with birches? This is a common sight in the forces, and it is done as much to warn those made to watch it as it is to punish the offender. It is impossible not to feel sympathy for a fellow who is striped and bleeding in the way that he soon becomes. If you can't imagine it, do you remember that time you fell in the woods, tripping over an exposed root, and ended up arse over tit in the brambles? It is like that, but much, much, worse and black Schmutzli will do it again and again to naughty children. Perhaps to death. Think how sad that would be. And who would take care of the rabbits? Who would feed the chinchillas?

Still, we need not think of that since there are no bad girls here. That fate is reserved for girls other than us, girls we have seen but do not know, girls who walk poorly shod in the snow, lonely little girls who stare in at the windows of the houses where we live and the toy shops from which our presents are bought, and they hallucinate through coldness and hunger, and it is roast dinner tomorrow.

My colleague's excitement was obvious, but even as I was congratulating him on our good fortune, a nagging thought repeated itself in my head: what would cause the family of a corpse to go to such trouble, having followed the appropriate funerary rituals, to render those rituals useless in this way? Similarly, what could cause the priesthood to acquiesce to such a desecration as they sealed the tomb, knowing that it would consign the deceased to an eternity of nothingness?

*I have come to
seek / embrace you,
I am Horus.
I have added your
mouth.
I am your son, who loves you!*

The incision is sewn up,
and the body anointed
with oils. Once the
scent has infused
the skin, a layer of resin is
added as a sealant.

THE SHUYET SHADOW
OF LUCIA JOYCE
LOCARNO, NOVEMBER 1917

A boy goes about the interesting business of torturing a rabbit in any number of ways, but he must always begin by trussing it with string, as one would with any other joint of meat. It may seem that a rabbit is a docile creature, content to sit in its hutch and press its nose against the chicken wire. When his sister comes to clean out its straw it barely exerts itself, so much so that she has to push it to one side while she cleans out the other. Though it likes lettuce leaves and slices of carrot, it only shows a very restrained species of pleasure. But when a boy, Giorgio, introduces pain into the equation, then it certainly becomes a handful! It will stamp and writhe and bite, so Giorgio ties it to a board, first placing it on its back. Three pieces of string are all that are required, or one long loop. No-one notices the loss. Around the neck and each of the hind legs, and then we are ready for the off.

His sister, Lucia, is brought into the garden, and while she makes the usual faces and puts her hand over her mouth, Giorgio can choose his instruments. Giorgio is a well-educated child and, like all boys, has paid particular attention to lessons at school where the methods of medieval torture were described; he has gone directly to the exhibits in museums where the artefacts of medieval torture were housed; he has taken a lively interest in the excesses of Cardinal Ximenes and the like during the heyday of the Spanish inquisition; he has performed dissections on locusts, mice, and frogs, and compared their innards to the diagram chalked by his tutors on the board; he has played games of scruples and discussed different scenarios which might be prevented by torture, and has considered the most efficient methods to extract information from plotters against, for example, the state; he has considered, alone, whether the public consumption of spectacles of bodily dismemberment might be an effective means of controlling the people. He has, in short, a thorough understanding of the ins and outs, and he chooses Lucia's box of matches, something she has been warned against having, but which he has nonetheless discovered in its usual hiding place beneath her pillow.

While it would have been interesting to choose, for instance, the Pear of Anguish, which is inserted into an orifice, often the anus, and widened by degrees until the sphincter tears, he doesn't have one, certainly not small enough to be used on a rabbit. We have the advantage of Giorgio in that we understand that this object was never used, except in the imagination, but Giorgio still regrets that his efforts to make his own were failures. Similarly, his Judas Cradle, which exceeded his limited skills in carpentry.

Still, one works with what one has, and the good thing about these matches is that they are hers, and this adds a psychological element to the business, since if she had not secreted these matches against the parental edict, he would not have them to hand to use in the torture of her favourite pet, and so guilt along with the threat of future torture can be used to stay her tongue against her blabbing about how he came to her in the night.

She says she will not tell, but who would believe it? The process of interrogation by induction of pain implies, by its very existence, that truths extracted under duress are superior to truths extracted from a person in a resting state. He cannot credit that she is being truthful until she has said it while the hock of the rabbit is on fire.

A rabbit has a very long foot, and the hock is the back of it, and while it may not be particularly sensitive, definitely less so than the eyes, it certainly doesn't like having it set fire to! The rabbit writhes against the string and it becomes clear Giorgio hasn't tied it tight enough on the left, so he props the board up vertically while he ties it tighter.

—You're choking her!

He raises his eyebrow, as if to chide Lucia for saying something that, had she thought it through, she'd see was not really worth the saying. In fact, it might have been entirely counterproductive. Does the torturer worry himself about whether he chokes the victim of torture? Not at all. It may make his job easier, in the long run.

She is very upset, but she is also angry at him; he can see it in the set of her jaw, which communicates to him absolutely clearly that she intends to run to Papa and tell him everything. Anger will do that – hang it all, the angry girl says, this must be punished regardless of the consequences – so it is up to him to sober her up and show her the error of her ways.

The iconic body part of a rabbit, as well as its twitching nose and flashing scut, is its ears, and she loves to stroke these. Indeed, it may be that the stroking of this rabbit's ears is her favourite thing. So – and here he shows that ingenuity that a well-educated boy will show in situations like this – he takes three matches, one of which he places in the left earhole, one in the right earhole, and the third he lights and moves in a figure of eight in front of his sister's eyes.

As younger girl children go, she is bright. She sees what is in the offing and now she is on her knees like a penitent before a bishop. Her hands are held together as if he is someone who will listen to prayers. She pleads to him, 'no', and while he nods sagely, as if he feels his business here is done, his hands do not agree, nor do his lips, which he licks. With one hand he cups the lit match and follows the other as it takes the flame to the left ear and applies it to the phosphorus. This flares in a way that modern users of matches will not quite credit, since the technology was not as sophisticated as it is today, and there was a great deal of redundancy in the materials of the matchhead to ensure successful combustion.

It goes up like a fucking firework.

Tying string is a tricky business, and you must give Giorgio credit, since the rabbit almost breaks its neck trying to escape the pain in its ear, but it does not get free. Lucia shrieks to see it, which he cannot allow, since the garden is too short to ensure someone will not hear. He lurches towards her and puts his hand over her mouth. It is suddenly very like that moment of which she must not speak, they both feel it, which is ideal since it reinforces the mutual obligation to remain silent.

The match burns down along the pinna, making a black trail as if inking a route on a map. He hisses at her:

—You say anything, and I'll light the other one, understand? And worse.

Now when she agrees it is utterly convincing: there is not the slightest edge in her tone that suggests she will run to anyone, and he feels entirely secure in her silence on this matter. He goes to the board and loosens the strings and when the rabbit hops in confused circles this way and that he picks it up and strokes its back. Lucia comes to him. And why shouldn't he hand the creature over? – she will keep her side of the bargain, so equilibrium is restored and he can afford to be generous.

If there are those of you reading this who know Giorgio, you might say that this never happened. But how do you know? How does one ever know what it is that occurs outside the range of one's experience? You may not know that it did happen, but that is not the same as knowing that it did not happen. Perhaps if there were documentary evidence; but who keeps such records? Is it even possible to keep evidence of things that might happen that someone wishes to keep secret? If one has secrets, and then burns the evidence of those secrets on a pyre, one invites speculation, and speculation is infinite in a way that the truth is not. Speculation is limited only by the sick imaginations of those who speculate, where truth is not. Why shouldn't Giorgio have tortured Lucia's rabbit to prevent her from speaking? All things that are possible are, in the absence of facts that have been destroyed that might have proved them incorrect, equally correct.

The moral of the story is: do not destroy documentary evidence of the truth, since it will come back and bite you in the arse.

A chinchilla may be tortured in ways a rabbit may not, since they are smaller, more timid, and have longer tails. They are also more affectionate than rabbits are likely to be, once they have been habituated to handling, so the range of secrets that the torture of chinchillas can silence is different to the range of secrets the torture of rabbits can silence, and the torturer must know his trade. Giorgio should pay close attention not just to distant historical instances of torture, such as the Brazen Bull, but also to modern day usage, and carry out his own fieldwork, following the rules of scientific empiricism.

It is very easy to come by flex, and electrification is all but ubiquitous, so, Giorgio, why not carry out a series of experiments to test the effects of the application of electrical current to small mammals on the willingness of sisters to remain silent about matters of incestuous sexual activity within the home? A transformer will be required, since the voltage of a mains electricity supply is likely to kill a chinchilla, and while its death will like as not appear natural (providing no combustion occurs) it will affect the results of the experiment. Additionally, chinchillas are not cheap, nor will their repeated deaths go unnoticed, and no parent will repeatedly buy pets that are likely to die spontaneously, since it will have a negative emotional impact on the children, did you see her crying? she was inconsolable.

If you are afraid of electricity then take one of James Joyce's cigars, light it with your sister Lucia's matches, take a surreptitious puff so that you can brag about your smoking habit to your friends, cough until you retch, far more than is manly, even for a boy, since you are such a nancy, and then, in anger, apply the lit end of the cigar to the openings of the chinchilla's vagina and anus. You will need to pull back the fur with the thumb and forefinger of your left hand as you apply the lit cigar with the right, then test to see whether your sister can be induced to remain silent on the matter of your Uncle Stanislav's affairs not only with her, but with all the slags in the area, he's known for it, it's a disgrace, why don't you talk to him?

Index the results and collate a table by which the progression of methods of violence against the body and soul of a mammal can be made to induce silence on specific topics, and in this way do the world a favour. Make something known. If, Giorgio, history decides that you have committed a crime, rest assured that the actions of all men through time will be seen to be crimes in the end. A world is coming in which all actions are seen for what they are – crimes against the state of the world as it was in the beginning, Nu, from which comes right, Ma'at.

He who transgresses its ordinances will be punished.

It is not enough to claim ignorance of the forty-two laws of Ma'at, since ignorance is no defence even when the lore that describes the laws is lost to you. Do you think that is of any interest to God? He sees and knows all things, and if you find his word contradictory that is because it exceeds your ability to parse, since you are, as you know, inadequate to the tasks put in front of you. This is why you act so viciously in the world, through shame, and the vicious shall be punished according to their sins.

Please prepare to receive as you have given, and I don't want to hear any more moaning about it, now back to sleep, it's late.

Perhaps I am exaggerating or misremembering, knowing what I now know. I certainly felt excitement along with these misgivings; this, after all, was the culmination of long years of work and preparation, and made right the many disappointments we had both experienced up to that moment. Moreover, the decorations that survived were very beautiful; the artisans responsible must have been amongst the most proficient of their time. At the very least I must have bitten back whatever qualms I was experiencing, since I remember the sense of exhilaration that followed my colleague announcing the presence of a passageway into a second room.

'Come, smite my
mother for me!'
'Let those who smite
your mother be
protected!'

Then comes the
overseer of mysteries,
wearing the jackal
mask of Anubis, to
supervise the wrapping of the corpse.
Strips of the deceased's clothes are
bound around the head, the limbs,
and the torso, while the reader-priest
recites the prayers.

THE IB OF LUCIA JOYCE

LES ATELIERS DU VIEUX COLOMBIER, PARIS, SUMMER 1927 (*CONT.*)

And later there is a bear, thin-tufted and long-snouted with eyes like raisins, eyes like pinheads, black and shiny, tacked in twice, holding together the seams of white thread. On his muzzle there is a ball, striped, divided in four, red and white, and beside that a ballerina, white-legged, tutu-ed, arms angled and mirrored, all mirrored, framed in white leaves and red petals.

They both turn, these objects, one clockwise, the other anti-clockwise. At first it seems that they turn at the same rate, the arms making a plié, the ball making a day in a few seconds. Thin, high, plucked notes from within the boxes beneath make a discordancy at the same meter. As they turn and the tunes play it is clear that the ballerina turns more slowly, the bear seeming eager and energetic, its world keen to pass the day, for the past to be present. The ballerina is sluggish in comparison, enervated by her key sticking on its gear teeth, sticking on the notes, until it sticks entirely. The bear's song takes over, clear now, a solemn anthem in red and white and gold fur. The ballerina, immobile, is made to watch its triumphant progress round.

She has dots for eyes, red diamond lips, a daub of brown – one single brush stroke, enough to stand in for the thousands of strands of hair, pulled back and efficiently tied, of her ideal. She shows no sign of envy, or of recognition of the joyous victory the bear revels in, spins in, and the whole scene is faintly ridiculous. They are overlooked by the guards, bayonets to their shoulders, protecting what, precisely? Against whom, precisely? Something that a bear could not handle? Which would be what?

Wooden blocks in yellow and blue and red – an archway, triangular roofs, a viaduct of them make a fort under which these soldiers shelter. Now it is obvious that they defend against the bear, against the ballerina, against the girl outside, palms against the glass, lips bitten, against the snow. They defend against the whole world that exists outside as it presses in. Against encroachment into the world of which these soldiers are defenders – jars of marbles, towers of wood, little dresses, peg women lined up in boxes, lying side by side waiting to be washed, small tins in which there is nothing, waiting to be filled with pins and odd lengths of thread and offcuts.

Someone enters the shop – the girl sees her back, broad shoulders under thick worsted, fibres catching silk at the neck, the wrists and the calves. There is a moment when an invisible cloud of warmth finds the girl's skin. It is such a difference from the cold that it has a presence, a front. It is an almost violent assault, and when it goes it is worse than before, the edge of numbness replaced by the sting of ice, ice in the heart, ice in the bones, in the fragments. She goes to follow, but she has been standing so long that her feet will not obey – they are frozen in place, become ice, become snow, insufficiently alive to allow for movement. She strikes a match, but it does not catch. She lets it drop to the ground where it does not sizzle and hiss but lies sullenly, half hidden beneath a cliff of snow.

The woman who went into the shop comes out, and with her the warmth again. The girl is wary of it, leaning back. How frequently would this door have to open to save her life? If there was such a rush of patrons to this small shop that the door never closed, would that be enough? Or would the draft eventually make the shop as cold as her fingers are? Her neck. What then? Would they all die – the bear, the ballerina, the soldiers, the shopkeeper, the peg doll women?

Corpses in ice, drowned in frigid air.

There aren't enough customers for this to be an issue.

Once the woman is gone, the door remains closed. The little match girl stands in solidarity with the others, all the toys that have insufficient interest for the world to draw its attention. They are equally lifeless things with no life invested in them through sympathy, except that which they have for themselves. Perhaps that which they have for each other. Can we bring each other to life? Can dead things recognise life into each other? Doesn't a fire burn from the smallest spark? Doesn't it burn the coldest, dampest kindling if only it can be made to catch? Surely.

She presses her face to the glass, her cheek scalded by the cold. It feels like warmth to her. She concentrates on the soldiers as if her spark-less matches can make them live by force of her will, in the absence of flame, despite the bitter cold in her ankles and knees and the backs of her teeth. On cue, the soldiers move – they dance like the ballerina, they spin like the bear, they perform a loop on a track like a small train of wood does when it is pushed. With her eyelashes, she taps on the glass.

The soldiers drill, unaware of her tapping, unaware they were never alive until she made them live. It is as if they had been interrupted without their knowledge at the final moment of their training, and now continue without recognising the break. If they could only see and feel her. They do not.

The bear though, they see him, constituting – as he does – a more obvious threat to the security of their fort, to the shop, to the others, and the ballerina. Her threat is equally grave, though obscure: a dancer's freedom, her discipline, her feet, the toes on which her weight is balanced, are so different to their solid planting on the ground, and might undermine it. As if in response, bear and ballerina move, dancing together, though at a chaste and respectable distance.

He entered first and stood obstructing the entrance to the second chamber so that I had to push past him, but there in front of us was a stone sarcophagus, richly decorated. On the sides were protective spells and inscriptions, and across the top surface of the lid was the most exquisite depiction of the deceased, her arms crossed. So detailed was the image of the face that in the flickering lamplight it seemed as if she might be alive. Her eyes were open and she stared at me, and the shadows played across her lips and I felt as if she might speak, or might already be speaking, but so softly that I could not hear her.

My colleague rushed forward, clumsily, and it was then that I saw that paint had been daubed, red, across her breasts and between her thighs, like the childishly obscene graffiti a schoolboy might carve into a library table during detention... and the lid was not properly closed.

'I am Horus and Seth;
I do not allow you to
make the head of my
mother white!'

Onto the wrappings, prayers and spells are written, and between the wrappings amulets and charms are placed. Providing the necessary recitations are made in the chapel above the tomb, these will serve as protection for the dead in the underworld.

NEARBY MEN
EUROPE, THE YEARS AFTER THE MENARCHE OF LUCIA JOYCE

There are so many ways it is possible to act improperly without realising it.

You must try to understand what it is like for us, we creatures that are driven by our needs and for whom there is constant goading from our groins. Glands... we are affected by them terribly, constantly pumping chemicals into our nervous systems. They fire us up, changing what we see. We see red mist. We become slavering, rabid bears. Is it any wonder we sometimes do things we ought not to do, and don't take account of the feelings of others? You should feel sorry for us, really, and not mope about the house in a mixture of resentment and self-pity – what good will ever come of that?

Can you imagine what it is like to have the testicles of a monkey inserted under the skin, or to be at the beck and call of the same urges that drive a rutting stag? From the moment one wakes, to the moment one sleeps? It is a wonder we get anything done at all! Puffing and panting, and everyone we see a threat, or someone to dominate. It is we who deserve the pity, not you. And to expect us to know which side of the line we ought to stay on, under the circumstances? You will learn.

Let us say that a father is drunk – James Joyce likes to drink. He wanders the bars of whatever city he is in, partaking of the local specialties one after the other until he can scarcely see straight, and why not, since he has done his work for the day? Can he be expected to exercise the same degree of control that he can when he is sober, over the urges his endocrine system exhorts him to satisfy? He is very short-sighted, too, James Joyce, and visually fixated, which is an unfortunate combination, because he finds himself aroused not just by those things he finds attractive, but also those things which may be mistaken for those things he finds attractive, since he cannot differentiate between them at a distance.

Say he is sitting in the living room and there is the proper object of his affections – his wife, Nora – and he is aroused by her, but then she leaves while he is reading the paper, and you, Lucia, replace her in her chair. When he puts the paper down he sees you, in his state of arousal. Is it any wonder, in the blurry world in which he exists when he has his reading glasses in place rather than the glasses he has for distance, that his arousal is transferred to you? This is the kind of thing that happens ten, twenty times in a week, such are the comings and goings in the house, and so, like a duckling who has imprinted on its mother, in the same way James Joyce imprints on you, in error. And this is when he is sober! So think what it must be like when he is stinking drunk.

Is it any wonder?

Also, remember that a certain type of man finds himself attracted to women who bear a superficial resemblance to his mother (although, equally, there is a type of man who desires the opposite of his mother in every way). If, then, he has a sister, and that sister bears a resemblance to her mother, one also should not be surprised when that man, Giorgio Joyce, finds himself attracted to his sister. In a house where there is a lot of play between the children, where horsing around has never been discouraged, unless the father is writing, and where space is at a premium, rooms must be shared since there is no money for anywhere bigger. Brother and sister are often in close proximity, and during the rough and tumble of everyday play, especially during puberty and adolescence, it is not surprising that you will sometimes find him on top of you, Lucia, panting from your rough-housing. There is a sudden shift in the mood. Remember, he is surging with the hot-bloodedness of his sex, and if a line is crossed, if your blouse has become open at the breast, and your slip is revealed, and perhaps more skin than is proper, and he leans forward, or quickly dismounts, then this is no surprise. This will happen ten, twenty times in a week, and like a duck, et cetera, it can become a behaviour that is reified, purely by accident, and nothing should be said about it.

Also understand that a man's brother will often have an unspoken desire for his brother's wife, and what could be more natural? Two males of the same brood, James and Stanislav Joyce, for example, will have similar tastes, particularly if they are of the type of man that chooses for his wife a woman who bears a superficial resemblance to their mother. There are lines to be crossed in this department too, and, like the brother, he is a big drinker, so it is not unusual to find him breathing over the mother's shoulder when she is cooking chops. That he then slips his hand around her waist and asks whether there is anything she needs should surprise no one.

Here also the question of mistaken identity comes into play, since if the daughter resembles her mother then the husband's brother might also find himself attracted to the daughter by substitution. As she grows into a lithe and troubled young thing, and bearing in mind that a brother can never come between his brother and his wife... perhaps the girl? And can she be induced to remain silent on the matter? Such are the thoughts of a drunken man, filled with the urges that a bull satiates on a harem of cows in any field in Ireland, regardless of which of them was sired by whom, and you should not take it so personally, you will learn.

The flat is so small, with everyone pressed up against one another, and the nights so hot that it's unfair to make anyone wear bedclothes. The customs of this country require one to drink a great deal of wine and smoke cigars and be hospitable to guests, offering them every consideration, and where are the lines drawn anyway? And aren't you at least partially to blame, Lucia, being a volatile little thing? You stand there in the doorway to the bathroom, splashing water onto yourself in the humid past-midnight, lit from behind so that the outline of your stomach and your chest and your buttocks could not be clearer from this angle. Don't you know the story of the sirens, who lured sailors to their fates? Or the selkies who did... whatever they did, and can you blame a drunk man for his indiscretions when he is hot and confused and wakes in the night with an erection borne of too full a bladder? He finds you there, dousing yourself, in a piece of cotton that barely covers your arse? Or a brother the same, rolling over onto your side of the bed since Uncle is in your room, with an erection borne of a fever dream of mermaids? Your cotton slip is pulled up since you've always turned in your sleep and your belly button is visible, like the women in far Arabia. He's never seen a breast, let alone touched one, and don't you need to show some empathy? To understand what it must be like for us?

It's different for girls; they are driven by love. But boys? We are slaves of our gonads. You can smell it on us, that reindeer musk, and we don't really have a choice. Once we have a head of steam up a girl can easily fail to see where she crosses the line between childish horse-play and prick-teasing. Between wearing clothes that are comfortable, and revealing too much thigh. Between affection for the men of the house and driving us to distraction, particularly since her menarche.

Women and girls give off a chemical like that which attracts insects to each other, and in such a small flat, with the windows closed against the oncoming winter, the concentration of pheromones is overwhelming for a healthy man. It can cause him to sleepwalk, so that when he is dreaming of his wife he finds himself in the bed of his daughter. When he is dreaming of his brother's wife, he finds himself in the bed of his niece. When he is dreaming of a woman who bears a superficial resemblance to his mother, but is not his mother, he finds himself in the bed of his sister, with an erection borne of his dreaming. Once he has a head of steam up, it is unfair to hold him to account for that, and you will learn.

Indeed, if a girl wishes to avoid the attentions of the men that surround her, and this is a good lesson for life in general, she should not go to so much trouble to make herself beautiful. Some say that, to the old, all young women are beautiful, but there are degrees. One only need consider the existence of spinsters in the world. Or women who have been left by their husbands. Or widows who cannot remarry. Or women who expend all their energies in compensatory activities, such as work. Understand that some women are less attractive to men than others. So perhaps cut your hair short, since men prefer long-haired women. Dress in clothes that do not cling to the body, since men are attracted by a woman's secondary sexual characteristics. Keep boyishly thin, since men who find boys attractive will have their hands too full with boys to have time to seek out boyish girls.

She should also not display personality traits that men enjoy, such as an easy, relaxed, and unpretentious attitude. She should be reserved and nervous in the company of men, and thereby not draw attention to herself. If spoken to, she should then make shrewish and sarcastic remarks that do nothing to make the man she is conversing with feel as if he has a high place in her affections. She should not be constantly giggling and holding onto his sleeve as if in apoplexy. She should not grab his shoulder as if to support herself and drop her head, laughing. This will cause him to imagine her mouth around his erection, even if he has not imagined it already. Indeed, she should not laugh at all, or speak much, since the open mouth is very like to the spread vulva. The sight of it glistening, lips parted, is too much for some men, and they will seek to press any advantage they feel they have. If she speaks, she should show her teeth often, and so offset any desire that may be building with threat of castration, which is what we fear most.

She should not discuss matters which men find interesting, such as sport, gambling, or the news, since we will then feel as if it might be very acceptable to have a partner in life who is so affable. We long for a woman who shares our preoccupations, so that the entire evening can be spent in conversation before we take her to our rooms and undress her. If she wishes to be left alone she should show a strong desire to discuss laundry, or recipes for bread, or childbearing (though this itself can come perilously close to topics that will cause a man to imagine intercourse, her uterus, and by association, his sexual domination of her, later, in the hotel room, slap her, put a pillow over her face).

She should never drink, since she will need her wits about her. Does a fox drink before a hunt? Not if it wishes to stay ahead of the hounds! Dogs will tear a fox to bits, and while this is a sobering thought, alcohol deadens the senses and dulls the mind. If she has taken none, while we have been helping ourselves to the bottle freely, with money behind the bar, this will even the playing field. She should not give up this small advantage. A drunken letch can be seen coming a mile off – our gambits are as clumsy as our fat fingers, and the grasp of both is easily avoided.

Some girls believe they can do away with men altogether through lesbianism, but this is wishful thinking, since for some men the more distant the prize, the more effort we exert to achieve it. The thought of two girls together, sweating beneath the sheets at the heavy work of defying nature's intentions for their bodies, is tremendously exciting. We will do almost anything to interrupt your exertions and show you girls how it is properly done. We will often bring our friends in numbers, to watch or help out, and what was intended as a means of avoiding the issue altogether brings it front and centre.

We will not be told.

Girls should hope for war, provided the campaign is prosecuted in another territory, since then men are occupied with it to the exclusion of all else. The only men left behind are those who are relatively easy to fend off – the elderly, the very young, and the infirm. During wartime, the nerve-fire that our glands secrete is spent on the exciting business of killing each other, or on waiting to kill each other, or on training to kill each other, or on thinking of ways to kill each other. If there is any goatish behaviour it is carried out at the expense of the women of the territories in which the war is raging. God help those women, certainly, but things go much easier for those left behind – wives are left un-harried, children unmolested, and lesbians may go about their business without fear of being barged in on. Girls may then read the papers in the public library with interest for news of how the war is progressing, and watch newsreels in the cinema, and luxuriate in the knowledge that many miles lie between them and their tormentors. The only way back is in a coffin, or through time-consuming and heroic traversing of enemy territory. In the meantime, if hands are slipped across thighs in the dark they will be owned by people whom they wish would do so, not by those they dread doing so, which is so much more relaxing.

Say the man comes home, then, injured and requiring care. You should provide it, gladly, knowing that it is you who are in control now. If you spit in his soup while he is upstairs, bed-ridden, and cannot see you, then that is your privilege. If you have your friend round, you can finger each other on the threshold of his bedroom door, and, if he hears you, you can deny it. Act as if it is *he* that is losing his mind, that *he* gets it from his *father*, and does *he* expect there are *women* out there who will put up with this kind of paranoia? From a cripple? Think again and count his blessings.

Not you personally, of course, Lucia. None of this is to do with you personally. But stop seeking out the company of men; nobody likes a girl who only likes men. Other girls are suspicious of her, will expect treachery from her, will not include her in their small talk, will stop speaking when she enters the room of things that are common knowledge to everyone else. At some point one has to stop being so bloody doe-eyed and roman-tic about everything and come to terms with the world how it is – it is a shithole. More so than you imagine, since you have been sheltered all this time. If you had to live as your mother lived as a girl, then you'd know why it was you moved around so much and never went back. If you think your mother had it bad, then you should think of your grandmother and grandfather and the stories your mother could tell you would make your teeth chatter, make your hair curl, would widen your eyes.

Those stories might make you think twice about your attitude, which is ungrateful to a degree that is startling, and your mother would have given an arm to have been brought up in the lax and slovenly environment that you constantly complain about.

There is no telling people, though, and consequently, you shouldn't go crying to her when you get what you deserve. You were warned, and she cannot live your life for you. If you refuse to take good advice when it's given to you, then what do you expect her to do about it? Men are men, and whining about it isn't going to help – you get your jabs in when you can, how you can, and learn to take a punch.

When you are old enough you will stay out late and come home as infrequently as possible. You will walk the streets, which is easy enough if one has money since the bars never close. When it is raining one can sit under the canopy and smoke and wait for men to buy you drinks, which they always will, until you lose your looks, which will happen eventually, but not for many years. Things will be different then, the world will be different, it will be more to your tastes, more in your image. You will rule it, decide who does what when, and then they will see.

Just wait.

Again, the nature of the desecrations was not appreciated by my colleague. He ran his fingers in awe through the air immediately above her image, tracing the line of her nose, her shoulders, her hands and then back up, along the crook and the flail. He was breathing as heavily as a man who had run a mile. I found his excitement vulgar and out of place, and I had to look away from him. Here were more of the erasures, in those places where she was represented in the funerary spells on the sides of the sarcophagus.

The crook and flail are symbols of royalty, and the precision of the decorations was so perfect that the sense of unease and, I don't know how else to put this, *wrongness* was very strong. Why was the tomb vandalised? Why was the name removed? Who had disrupted the protective magics?

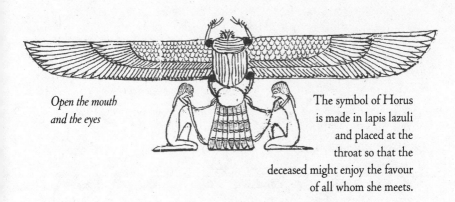

*Open the mouth
and the eyes*

The symbol of Horus
is made in lapis lazuli
and placed at the
throat so that the
deceased might enjoy the favour
of all whom she meets.

GIORGIO JOYCE
FRANCE, SUMMER 1925

Giorgio waits on the grass verge.

A gnat buzzes at the periphery of his attention, but he is under no obligation to turn his head. On a late afternoon walk in summer, after the bar has shut and the old sots wander slowly home for bollockings from their wives, clouds of midges gather above the drought-stagnant brooks and rills that follow the road. The insects sense a young man and want the sweat that gathers on his forehead, his wine breath, and as he stands still to appreciate the views they mob him. He isn't able to swat them all away. They are too small to have the sense to avoid his hand, too numerous as a race to need to develop that intelligence, but they swarm recklessly and get what they are after that way.

When he resumes his progress, he passes through them as if they are nothing, outpaces them, and though they follow for a while he is soon away, up to higher ground.

Gnats and midges are not the same thing. Gnats live solitary lives, and their wings make high-pitched screams an inch from your ear. They are less easily put off than midges, who are content with the company of their own kind, generally, and don't stray far from their territories. A gnat will follow you for miles, craving you, sometimes resting on your shoulder, or in the small of your back. When you think you have left it behind it will appear again, distressingly close, shrieking in your ear when it's quiet and dark.

From the top of the hill he takes in the surrounding land and what is cracked and brown close up – wilted, yellowing – from up here is almost as verdant as one might expect it to be, despite the incredible heat and the prolonged dry spell. His eyesight is not good, and this is one of the few benefits – he has an impressionistic appreciation of the landscape, a sense of the whole of it undistracted by particulars, and fields and trees are daubed in, the boundaries of farms scored with the edge of a palette knife, an outhouse a fingertip of grey.

Giorgio puts his hands in his pockets and walks on.

If there are hedgerows either side of the road, you hear animals long before you see them: cows and sheep. Birds have to be sought for – they are almost invisible through the tangle of twigs and branches even if the leaf cover has died off. Horses are tall enough to peer at you, but horses are rare round here. There are other walkers, but there is a pact that ensures that few words are ever spoken – an identification of the time of day – and that even those can be replaced with a nod. He is alone.

Except for the gnat.

He is wearing a wax jacket since thunderstorms are predicted as soon as the day cools, and he hates carrying things. His shirt is soaked down the back and under the arms, but he is stubborn and several glasses worse for wear. He suspects, though he doesn't know it, that the gnat is somewhere on his jacket, in a fold. Where the collar is, there are places that are dark, shadowed and cool. It is probably in there. He runs his fingers around, but a gnat is wise to this. It watches for objects that come within its range of vision and launches when it recognises one, landing again once the object has disappeared.

These tiny creatures live at a faster pace than he does. He is slow and lumbering, a great moving mountain to this agile speck. If it sees his hand coming it is at the pace of a glacier carving out a valley, or the shifting of the tectonic plates – easy to avoid, no bother to it at all. Giorgio is cleverer though, and if he puts his mind to it he could trap it, with luck: scare it with one hand, slap it with the other, and have an end to it. But putting his mind to it is precisely what he does not want to do. It is hard to ignore something when one has to think of it. There will come a time when he has to do what he is avoiding – when he finds the gnat on the back of his hand, for example, biting at his skin – but this is not the time.

On hot days like this, when a thunderstorm is predicted, there is a build-up of pressure in the air. He is susceptible to it, feels it as a headache, as an encroaching irritability, and these are effects that too much or too little wine has on him, too. If he notices these symptoms he will look for external justifications, since he does not like to think of himself as sensitive, or drinking too much, and these justifications will either be to do with the weather or the tension induced by not thinking of things he does not wish to think of. If he puts these feelings to the back of his mind they will build, like the electric charge builds in a thunderstorm, and when he sees Lillian later these feelings will find an outlet. As electric charge builds in a cloud the chances of lightning approach one hundred percent, and as his tension builds the same can be said. He'll snap at some arbitrary flash point, and she will wonder what she has done.

She won't have done anything.

The problem is this gnat.

The hedges are too high for him to see what is in the field behind them, but he imagines there is a horse in the field. He overheard, coming downstairs into a room where they were listening to the radio and drinking, other women describing Lillian as horsey. What they meant by this was that she has a long face, big teeth, and a tuft of dry hair for a fringe. There was some talk of her having whiskers like a horse does around its mouth, but even they admitted this was unfair. He doesn't like to think of his lover as a horse, so he forgets what they said, but now when he sees a horse he can't help but look for her face in its features. When he sees her, if he has seen a horse in the recent past, he can't help seeing the features of a horse overlaid onto hers. This sounds comic, but he finds it infuriating – he is angry at the women who put the idea in his head, he is angry at himself for thinking it, and he is angry at her for looking like a horse, despite the fact that he had never noticed before.

If there is a horse in the field beyond the hedgerow this would undo whatever good work he had done in not thinking about how she looks like a horse, but now even the presence of a hedgerow over which a horse might look is edging horse thoughts into his mind.

As the humidity grows, the clouds precipitate out of nothing and the promised storm gathers above him. And always the gnat, hovering and unavoidable.

What is it that a gnat needs? What will it be satisfied by? Only his blood, clearly. It will drain him dry if it can. Its appetite for him is endless, as if it has no resources of its own to rely on and can only exist if it is within his presence. It can only breathe if it breathes his breath, can only find pleasure if it is through him. Why can't it understand that he has his own life to lead now, independent of it, and that it is its constant presence at the periphery of things that is putting the mockers on everything? It is such a strain to have it constantly in the background, its needs to be understood, its behaviours to be dealt with, their shared history to be the defining condition of his life when he wishes to make something new of everything, to get out from under the yoke. If it doesn't have a place in this new world, that is very unfortunate, but it is unavoidable. A man cannot be accompanied by his sister everywhere he goes. He is his own person and eventually the ties have to be cut. He knows it's hard, but that's no reason to make everything so difficult. A gnat can suck the blood of any host, and there is no shortage of hosts for it to buzz around. It should know that better than anyone.

Who knows, it might prefer someone else in the end.

The road leads down into the town, and there Lillian will be waiting, expecting him to have arrived earlier than he is going to. She will not be pleased to find he's been drinking, or that he hasn't broached the very important issue he was supposed to have broached with his father, and that he is going to have to return to town before the week is up. She will not be pleased with any of this, and it seems as if a constant state of not-being-pleased is her usual mood nowadays. So unlike the way she used to be. Perhaps this is the way of things with older women: once the excitement has worn off they become motherly, and a man has to spend all his time engaged in the occupation of pleasing her and doing what he is told and playing second fiddle to another man. Yes, this works quite well – her husband is the father, she is the mother, and he is the son who must do what he is told. Quite the stable.

He is just like the old sots, walking at a drunken snail's pace to avoid a bollocking. But what's the alternative? He could go home. Confess everything? That would certainly be one way to release the pressure. The storm will inevitably break and why not let it break there, in the place where so many storms have broken that thunder and lightning are the expected weather? The broken barometer in the hall always points to stormy. This is surely preferable to beating a married woman because she looks like a horse, and he has a headache, and she thinks she has the upper hand, and at some point you have to show these women who is boss. There is no arguing with the back of a hand, or a fist to the guts since you can't bruise her horsey face since the husband would see and we can't have that.

Would he do that?

Why not? This is the prevailing orthodoxy in matters of this kind, so much so that a woman who is not beaten considers her lover effeminate, and providing he does not make too much of a meal of it, and saves it for special occasions, it can be an aphrodisiac, particularly if he handles the apologies well.

But the gnat. There is always the gnat. It flies so unpredictably that there is no telling what effect an early return and stories of affairs with older married women, known to them all, will have. There will be bloodsucking, that much is certain, but affectionate or angry? When the storm has died down, what will be the aftermath?

He has been standing halfway down the hill for five minutes, easily, and while the sky isn't lowering it is no longer as bright as it was. If he wishes to take the train back he will need to do it soon, since the service is infrequent. Otherwise he'll end up sleeping in a hayloft.

Perhaps this will be one of the days when Lillian will surprise him with an easy cheerfulness that will wash him free of all sin. That is possible. She is not predictable herself, this woman, and she has a complicated life of which he has no real understanding: the husband, the business affairs, the friends; they are all unknowns to him. What's to say that these unknowns haven't combined to put her in a wonderful mood, and she will simply smile and rush him off to bed, as she often has done? Who is he to question her motives at times like this? One should never look a gift horse in the mouth.

This thought almost makes him laugh, but more it accentuates his headache, which is building as the clouds darken, by degrees, and he turns to face back up the hill.

No one likes to backtrack – it shows weakness. There is an exhaustion inherent in going over old ground, but if he carries on into town and then decides to return he'll have even more backtracking to do, and probably in the rain. Can he let the weather decide? Test the wind direction with a wet finger and follow it? To walk to an uncertain fate with the wind at one's back, there is a romantic aura to that, while struggling against the oncoming...

When did he become so ridiculous? Women, they drive you insane! If this was sport he'd do what had to be done. When he has the ball he knows in which direction to run it to the touch line, and he does it without thinking. There are rules. Who knows what rules women set for men, in their heads? This is the source of all his problems, the reluctance of women to make themselves clear, though they know clearly enough when something has been done wrong.

For heaven's sake... He goes down into the town, walking with quick urgent strides, setting the church tower in his sights and making for it, manfully, having a mission and executing it. In his head, behind the determination to get where he is going, he knows that he can veer off at the last. He can find a place to drink, get someone to drive him to the station. So he has not really taken a decision, but this is something he does not admit and will not admit until he sees the door of the cottage she has rented for them. In the meantime, he feels better to be doing something.

Since he is distracted, the gnat makes its way over the wax jacket from the elbow where it has been lodged in a crease. The breadth of his shoulders is a walk in itself for something so small. The swells of the hillsides through which its host walks have been tilted vertically, and the land ripples like a sheet on an unmade bed.

When it reaches the collar it meets the wisp of curls that grows where the barber's blade ends, and there is a deep and shadowed canyon formed between the neck and the jacket. Down there, in secret, it can feed. It pierces the skin, raising a welt, but in private, since the spike it inserts is anaesthetising. It is only when this wears off that he will feel anything, and only then if he is not engaged in activities that distract him. If Lillian pulls him in by the hand, smiling, barely letting the door open, since, as he finds out, she is entirely naked behind there, he will not notice a gnat's itch until he has scratched an itch of a different sort, upstairs on the bed. The bedroom has a faintly old-fashioned quality about it even as it attempts to be neutral and modern – there is still a white enamel jug there, and a white enamel basin in which that jug rattles as they wrestle together on the bed. The gnat makes its way from his neck down the hill range of his spine, the tickling of its feet against the small fine hairs of his back so slight that it is impossible for him to notice it.

At intervals it inserts its proboscis, if it has one, into his skin, in spite now, since it is full of blood. When he is in the bath later, leaning back into Lillian, both of them facing the taps, she will run a finger over the welts in turn, joining the dots into an image made from histamine response. She will comment on them, and whatever sense that he had made the right decision, here on the hill, will be undermined by this bringing to his attention of things he was hoping to ignore.

Regardless of what happens this afternoon, the whole mess is coming to an end, if he has anything to do with it. It is all too complicated, and he will find a way to reduce that complication.

For some men, all they want is peace, for things to progress in a logical fashion without too much thought. They hate rousing themselves against endless crises. There are ways for men to find peace for themselves in their choice of women, of where they live, of their profession. He has control over these things and he'll damn well exercise it, since what is the alternative? He has seen what it is like to live under the rule of women, and while he feels the temptation to live his life like his parents lived theirs, he has seen what it does to people. He is determined it will not do it to him.

Domestic life is like a war, factions struggling for victory, innocents sacrificed to the greater good. Daily battles, territory won and ceded. Brothers, sisters, mothers, fathers, aunts, uncles. Lovers. Even animals. It is a war he has determined to win and there are always casualties in war: boys, girls, soldiers, animals, dancing girls.

My colleague stepped back, placed his lamp on the floor in front of him, and made one slow inhalation. This done, he buttoned his jacket, and returned to the other room, where the rope was still hanging. He shouted up through the gap that one of the guides should return to the camp at a run and fetch Mr Pfeffer, the gentleman who had made our travel arrangements out from England and on whom we had come to rely for the various practicalities of the expedition.

I was grateful to my colleague for this – whatever else, he was meticulous and calm in a crisis. I listened to him as he tried to make himself understood in shouts, first in English, then in French, and then in his very basic Arabic, and there was a comedy in this that undercut the pain in my stomach. While I listened I let my eyes rest on a shebti statuette three or four inches high that had been placed near the sarcophagus. I don't know why – I have a daughter and I thought it might make a good gift? – I slipped it into my pocket. It was of a soldier or bodyguard – someone who might protect the corpse in her journey through the dangerous hinterlands of the underworld.

*'I smite her for her mother,
so that she bewails
her. I smite her for her
consorts'*

Over the heart is bound
a green stone amulet
in the form of the
resurrecting scarab
beetle. Onto this amulet is
carved the name of the deceased.

Up close these toys were odd in the vagueness of their detail. The single daub of the ballerina's hair, which from a distance barely drew the attention, was, up close and reached for, stroked, so hard and uniform, so raised like the meniscus that forms on liquid in a tube, that it was difficult to read as hair at all. Similarly the eyes: lacking whites, lacking irises, two huge and dilated pupils that stared. And so the bear. So sparsely grown was its fur that it seemed rugose and mangy like an old street dog, matted about the eyes. Only the ball was as perfect at this scale as it was from the other side, geometrical objects having the property of scaling without loss of definition.

The girl's own hands, too. The fingers were fused, the nails forming one line of black across the fingertips, the thumb flush to the palm and unmoveable. Across the knuckles the hand folded in exactly the same way, right and left, as if perpetually sheltering a small flame. Where her arms met her dress there was a divide as her flesh ended and she became gingham. So, also, midway up the thigh, where her legs emerged from her white bloomers. Her shoes were perfect – glossy black with a brass button on each, a heel carved on the sole, and ankle socks. If her feet were cold now they didn't feel it – there was nothing to feel but a steady calm content-edness, and on her face was a simple line in red that matched her cheeks.

The soldiers: they were gruff and correct in their orderliness, confident in their platoon, sure of their duties, unflappable, indefatigable. The bear, even in the indignity of his clowning, exuded a perfect at-one-ness with the world.

On the other side of the window the snow fell; it was visible in the colour and tone of the light that came through the panes, one row of them only, the nearest, while the others disappeared into a darkness the weak light couldn't illuminate. On the ground, the snow would gather, certainly, and on whatever lay there, but that was hardly of any concern to her. Hardly any at all.

In one corner was a box, and on that was a latch so made that one would need to slide the bottom of a hook aside to allow the lid to come off. Should such things be of interest to a doll? Why not? What else, in fact, would be of any interest if not a painted box like that? To a doll like she was?

To the extent that she could move she did, tentatively and drunkenly as though she was suspended by strings and her puppeteer was inexperienced. Anatomy should have dictated that she remain still. She had no bones, no muscles, nothing, but movement was possible nonetheless. The clack of the porcelain shoes made music on the wooden window sill, and so did her hands. On all fours she climbed down until she found herself amongst the things of the shop. She crossed the train tracks, warily stepped over chains of coloured paper. She left a wake through the desiccated coconut that made the snow in this world. Any hunter worth their salt could have followed her, but she didn't care. She made her way to a box which filled her attention so completely that, as she neared it, the soldiers coming to arms went entirely unnoticed.

Her hands were not made for fine discrimination in action, but the freeing of the clasp was achievable nonetheless. It was stiff and wanted to return to the locked position, and it slipped back to the beginning. With both hands it was easier. After a few attempts she brought the clasp around and left it hovering, suspended above the lock, balanced at the point to either side of which it would fall.

She moved to find some purchase, set her shoulders, and made to open the box, but there was no effort required. At her slightest touch the lid sprang up and back, and in the dark space it seemed to leave, a figure appeared, emerging at speed, almost instantaneous, gesturing with both arms high and a look of hilarious surprise on its face. It flopped forward, as if its back was broken.

She leapt in shock, her arms swinging up from her sides and her hands coming to rest on her cheeks, framing her mouth.

Such are the reactions possible for a doll of her type – such are the proscribed preoccupations: small boxes, desiccated coconut. Such is the range of experiences which, for dolls, are relevant. There is no ice, no frost bite, no hunger, no blistering, no matches. Death, envy, and justice are not for dolls. There is curiosity. There is surprise. There is, to an extent, loneliness, but of dolls one must speak, more properly, of the forms of movement, the manner of hinging of the joints, the shapes in which the limbs are held, all of which make more sense than talk of feelings, and ideas, or longing, or slavery.

The body of a doll is an idiosyncratic object, and while it would not be true to say that each is unique, as those things created by God are unique, they are certainly not all perfectly of a type. Some dolls are all of one thing – wool, for example – and more all in one way, as a snake is, or a wooden effigy. A porcelain doll may or may not have a skeleton of pipe cleaners, but either way it must move with proper attention to the fragility of its china parts – it must move as if it fears breakage.

A wooden soldier has no such concerns – it must move as its courage determines, its *métier* – but it will be stiff; that is its nature. A jack in the box is dictated by its spring and the potential energy stored in its tensioning. Its motions are momentary and abrupt. If it is possessed of intelligence, of sentience, of volition, it will find itself frustrated. It will seek ways in which it might be capable of drawing the objects of its interest into the scope of its attention without the need to move the position of the box. It will twist its head, swivel its eyes, cry out in a high pitched voice as a means of attracting an object to it. Its spine will be as flexible as rubber and its movements random, except inasmuch as they tend toward stillness. Each of its movements will be less than the one before it, until it is left facing in the direction it finally stops. If this direction is not facing the audience then other members of the cast will need to make a show of directing it so that it faces the front, without fearing the breaking of frame, or its lines will not be delivered visibly and the movements of its lips will not be caught by the lens and the scene will need to be reshot.

Verity – one should not be a slave to it.

There are times when beauty trumps truth, but these are very few, for truth is beauty and even in the fantastic there are forms of truth – fabular truths, allegorical truths, wider human truths – that are beautiful in a universal manner. In this, a dancing puppet can exceed any philosophy in approaching both universal truth and perfect beauty – who could say otherwise after a visit to the Louvre, or to the Musée D'Orsay, or the ballet, or the countryside, or the, or the, or, all the others?

The dancer Lucia Joyce, daughter of the famous writer James Joyce, performed for the famous director Jean Renoir at Les Ateliers du Vieux Colombier, Paris, France, in the summer of 1927, and her performance was filmed. She had been commissioned to perform for a role in Renoir's *La Petite Marchande d'allumettes,* based on Hans Christian Andersen's *La Petite Fille aux allumettes*, but her dance was cut from the final edit. She was removed.

This is apt.

Truth and beauty, perhaps they are inseparable, and so lies and ugliness. Looming down, weighing on the shoulder, wiping the mouth and the nicotine-stained fingers, putting aside the glasses, folding them first and pulling up the nightdress, moving aside the sheet. Fingers on lips. Hands on heads. Line up in the playground, cane to the palm, slipper to the arse. Pull up the skirt, pull down the knickers, face the front, face the corner. Gym shoes, gym shorts, gym knickers. Hands out, hold still, pull yourself together. Hit the mark, proceed slowly to stage left in a stiff and wooden manner, obedient as a soldier. And break now.

Costume.

More paint to the cheeks.

Stop crying; you're making it run.

When my colleague returned, the guilt of my theft was still on my breath, which was perhaps why I acquiesced to his contradictory requests: he argued both for making every effort to ensure no aspect of the tomb was disturbed, but also wanted me to assist him with the lid of the sarcophagus, suggesting that we should lift it to ground and inspect the condition of the mummy, if there was one.

By now I felt that there would be, but in our excitement we had either overestimated our combined strength, or underestimated the weight of the stone lid – anyway, there was no way we would be able to lift it safely. Generally, these sarcophagi were made so that the lid fit into grooves in the lower container, but this one was different (perhaps this related to the fact that it was open rather than sealed), so we were able to slide the lid to the side enough for us to see within, but not so much that we risked the lid smashing to the ground.

He brought up the light to the foot of the sarcophagus, and there were the tell-tale wrappings. Her precious body was still in situ, left where it had been centuries before.

*Find the son who loves
her and bring him
within the tomb*

To ward off curses,
they include the
Wadjet eye.

ARTHUR HUBBELL
PARIS, SEPTEMBER 1930

It is the afternoon of a dreary day in Paris, late autumn, not raining, but rain isn't far off in any direction. Arthur's Hubbell's mood is low, but it was low before he opened the bottle. Outside on the rue de Bellechasse there are the usual Parisian goings on, so familiar now that he has given up noticing them: the wandering, well-dressed tourists skirting isolated islands of the French, who bellow at each other across the rivers of delighted spectators, spit in the street, and discuss illegal business full in the face of everyone, Francophone or otherwise. He is standing looking through the netted window, but he's not seeing anything. His eyes meet at a point so far distant it doesn't exist on this continent, and perhaps not anywhere.

He places the wineglass down on the table, edge of its base first, and then leaves it to keep itself upright. There are two or three clumsy revolutions before it settles into a safe position a hand's breadth from falling and smashing on the tiles. He's in the rooms he rents from a widow everyone believes to be a madame, but who is, to his eye, just a particularly hefty old woman with a vulgar turn of phrase. He doesn't care, anyway. She is cheap, and the rooms are clean.

The armchair beckons, and an open book, cigarettes, but he goes instead to the mantelpiece. There is a clock there, hers, and candlesticks, hers, but between and around them are photographs unframed, his. Six or seven – scenes of the French countryside, the imposing facades of small rural churches, details of days out, taken very close up, so that their formal qualities replace their context. They can't be mistaken for tourist snaps, and are clearly the work of someone who has pretensions to artistry. Undeserved.

There are sketches, too, avant-garde in a way he recognises, but which hasn't yet acquired a name. Perhaps he wasn't present for the naming – it's so easy to miss out on these things unless one lives one's life in the bars, drinking until sunrise and never sleeping. If he was one of these people he wouldn't need a hotel.

Behind the sketches there is another picture, turned to the wall and hidden. Not that hidden. Hidden? No, of course not! Why do you say that? What's to hide? It must have fallen behind the others, that's all. So suspicious! But it is hidden enough. He takes it out and holds it six inches from his face. Stares at it.

It is a portrait of her. His love.

He is aware that he can't do her justice in the way that a Man Ray or a Steichen does her justice, but it's not for anyone else, it's only for him. While he's no slouch, photographically speaking, he's also not that hard to please. Anyway, she would be beautiful in any picture, an idiot could see that. Even if she put out her tongue and ruffled her hair, crossed her eyes, she'd be beautiful. It would be pointless to deny that, even if it's hard to see the beauty in her features all the time. Her perfect stillness in an image is disrupted by his living memories of her in person in as many situations as a man can imagine, good and bad. Experiences have a tendency to overlay an image, like nylons on the lens. Or Vaseline.

He's staring at her now, and is drunk enough to move his whole body backwards and forwards when he wants to see her clearer, keeping the image still, rather than moving the image and keeping himself still. He blinks more than he needs to, and swallows. The bottle is empty, but there are more bottles somewhere, and he'd drink them too if it wasn't for the need to see her now, to study her features. He doesn't know what he is looking for that he hasn't seen a thousand times. Whatever it is, he's not finding it. Once or twice he turns the picture over and stares at the back, on which is written a date, and then turns it frontwards again.

It's not a matter of beautiful or not beautiful anyway. If it was that simple there wouldn't be a problem, but it never is that simple. God, if they could just remain silent, just stand there in their beauty, preferably naked, and simply exist then that would be wonderful. But they don't. They have their wants and their needs and their opinions and they must, absolutely must, make those known to the world. Didn't he have his wants? Didn't he have his opinions? Didn't he have his needs? Well, if he did, they weren't causing anybody any sleepless nights. Whereas she...

It occurs to him that he needn't stand by the mantelpiece any longer. One of the advantages of a photograph is that it can be carried around. It goes where you want to go without much fuss being made over it. It doesn't insist on being consulted and having its desires taken into account.

He takes her to the kitchenette, where there is some casserole left and three or four already opened bottles of wine that he can finish without having to do anything that might bring himself to his own attention, such as making the effort to find the corkscrew and going to the trouble of opening a fresh bottle. Either of these actions would demonstrate the very obvious fact that he is making unseemly progress through a finite supply of bottles, and that he is drinking too much for his health.

He spoons food into his mouth and uses its reluctance to go down his throat as an excuse to help it on its way with the last third of a stale bottle of Merlot. The food can chaperone the wine, which shouldn't be out on its own at this time of the afternoon.

There is a small table in the kitchenette, more use for preparing meals than for dining, but there's enough room for him to prop his elbows either side of the photo, hold his head in his hands, and rest his forehead on the top of the bottle. He tilts it a little and then puts the full weight of his skull on it.

Her nose, so perfect.

People will tell you that noses must be straight, but that's rubbish – there needs to be a curve, a concavity, only a little or the whole thing gets like a caricature, but a definite slight concave curve. Otherwise it is too masculine – there is something masculine about perfect straightness, something mathematical, whereas the curve is more feminine, more natural… are breasts triangles, after all? They aren't, and neither are her lips.

The same people who will tell you that noses should be straight will tell you that a woman's lips should be full and red, but the best lips are barely there unless you get close. They've got an anaemic blueness to them, and their contours are only visible to you when you're close enough to have earned them. Same with the nipples: subtle and pink and formless, not great brown teats.

Red lips are a whore, and dugs are animalistic.

The back of the kitchenette has a window onto the small yards where people empty basins of water and have long and private conversations in loud voices in front of their neighbours. There is such a conversation taking place now, and it disrupts his ruminations on the perfection of her face.

When he gets up to pull the sash, a bottle spins across the table, circling like a compass needle, erratically following the dictates of whatever magnetism determines the motion of spinning wine bottles before they eventually drop off the table and shatter. That is what this one does.

His grasping hands only grasp in retrospect, clutching ineffectually above the fragments of green glass. One is huge, half a bottle in size, and the others are increasingly small until they become so small they will only be found by the next tenant of this place, becoming invisible to Arthur forever.

And the window is still open.

He sits back down and between his feet are vicious shards like daggers, and in his ears is an argument about a woman's sister and why it is that she is able to afford dresses that the speaker can only dream of. Another voice makes suggestions about possible ways women can come to afford expensive clothing, and whether it is worth it all, in the end. In front of his eyes, there is the photo of his love, lodged in his heart like the fragment of mirror is lodged in the eye of the boy in the fairy tale, colouring everything and making it different from the way it ought to be. Making him think and do evil.

Another bottle with wine in is just out of reach, and what wine was left in the broken bottle is now on the floor with the glass pieces. He looks at her while he shifts enough to reach the new bottle.

She was always so beautiful and he never used to drink so much.

He sighs and then a part of him that is disgusted to see how low he has fallen, all over a woman, picks him up and marches him to the sink. He puts the dirty dishes on the draining board and then fills the sink with cold water, right up to the brim. In books, the villain's head is dunked into freezing water before the hero extracts vital information out of him. Ostensibly this is to bring the miscreant to his senses, but there's also an element of punishment in the dunking, and both of those things seem to be at play as Arthur pushes his face down until the water threatens to go into his ears. It's something he's always been sensitive to. He holds his face under, and then opens his mouth and attempts to drink the water in the sink, as a means of diluting the wine.

This is not the best idea he's ever had. The water catches in Arthur's throat and chokes him, forcing him to rear up and shake himself about like a dog. While he coughs he soaks the floor, the surfaces, his clothes, with water.

He can't now consider himself sober, but he certainly feels more sober than he did. The combination of the cold, the rallying of his autonomic nervous system, and his own self-loathing all kick in to undercut his self-pity and the dull, maudlin indulgences that come with Paris in the rain in the late autumn.

The telephone rings. Will this be her? Can one person's concentration on another cause them to become aware, across a distance, that they are being concentrated on? It would be nice if that was the case. Despite his wetness, he goes to the phone, his drunken feet ignoring the glass, and the water, and the remnants of wine spilled which will surely stain the carpets and result in a stern letter from the fat, vulgar widow who is probably a madame. It will be worth it if this is her, if she plans a reconciliation, something she has always been able produce out of a hat, like a rabbit.

He picks up the phone and he can tell straight away it is not her. It is the bloody Irish girl, Joyce's daughter, and, too drunk to think of any other way of putting her off, he gingerly replaces the handset in the cradle. A little later he removes it and leaves it nestled in the leaves of his book while he goes to take a bath.

By now another basket of supplies had been lowered to the tomb entrance and I ran to get a second lamp. It is good practice when entering a tomb to make a record of its disposition before too much else occurs, so I brought pads of paper, paints, and pencils too. When I returned, my colleague was sitting cross-legged on the ground, sobbing. I thought he was unhappy at first, that he had seen something that confirmed my worrying feelings, but in fact he was laughing so hard that tears were rolling down his cheeks. I asked him if he was feeling well, and he replied never better. I passed him a pad of paper and told him to make himself useful while I shone my torch into the gap in the coffin lid.

To my dismay, I saw that the binding linens that should have protected the corpse had been slit in numerous places and that the skin was visible beneath. I moved the light up to the face and her head had been pulled to the side and the same red paint that had been splashed on the lid was splashed here too, where the lips would have been.

'I bring you your loving son, that he may open your mouth for you!'

They position the arms crossed over the abdomen and wrap the corpse again, finishing with a shroud of fresh linen.

THE SHUYET SHADOW
OF LUCIA JOYCE
PARIS, CHRISTMAS 1930

There is a good story by Chekhov called 'The Lady and the Dog'. In that story a woman goes on holiday with her dog while her husband is left behind, and she has adventures. It is set in Yalta, which is by the seaside, and the lady parades herself up and down the sea front, looking forlorn, in the hope that some roué or rake will take her for a vulnerable case and move in on her. Her dog is a help in this, for she can pay it too much or too little attention by turns, and thereby indicate her desire for company, or her intense sadness and introversion, and all from a distance. This is rather like what a fly fisherman does, making his lures and then flicking them about on the surface of the water to represent something a pike likes. Or a chub: a mayfly landing on the surface and spreading its legs so that it can balance on the surface of the water like Jesus. It skates here and there like a little girl does at Christmas when the lake is frozen over, and she deserves a treat, good girl, that's the way.

The dog is little and white and has been trained to perform many minor tasks for the amusement of its master (who remains at home) – such as sit, stay, roll over, play dead and lick the vulva, scrotum, and anus while he watches, good boy, have a biscuit.

When she needs to carry a parasol, she keeps the dog on a lead, but when she can she picks the dog up and brings it to her breast, like she would if she were mothering a child. This it is acceptable even in public, since that is what is done with dogs. It is also done, but less often, with rabbits and chinchillas. Those do have the tendency to wet themselves and earn their mistress's censure when later they are indoors and there are all sorts of items at one's disposal for the punishment of such crimes, major and minor.

Up comes a bounder and a cad, the kind of man who would make free with her and thereby ruin her reputation. He has a goatee and devilish eyes and in his ignorance imagines himself evil in the way that the Devil is, having only the desire to corrupt her in his heart. This is hilarious, since she is corrupted in advance of his arrival to such an extent that whatever corruption he hopes to add would be very minor, if noticeable at all. What does he intend to do? Make love to her outside the legally sanctioned unions of his country? This doesn't even register, any more than the mating displays of a spread-legged pond skipper register to the perch or the bream that hopes to snap it up. It registers as little as the hunger in a freshwater fish registers to an angler, who may or may not return this fish to the water after he has raised the specimen up and held it thrashing in his hands as he smiles at it, makes a rough estimate of its weight, and then places it in the net to determine its fate later, when he has had his fill of sport. Or to the eel, who, once its teeth have been removed with pliers, will slip half inside and writhe there until it dies, to the sickened fascination of onlookers.

Up he comes and he applies his wiles to her, which are so obvious in their intentions that there is no way they could work on anyone but a child. On a child they would work very well, no doubt – he flatters, then becomes dismissive; he smiles, then frowns; he reaches to touch, and then pulls back, all the time showing his faces. He has a face that is pretty, one that is stern, and one that occupies an intermediate place between the two. The aim, although he may not realise it, is to engage the child in a world in which he is at the centre, rather than those tedious things of her own childish life. He aims to occupy her with the business of pleasing or displeasing him, which he will eventually take indoors, by which time she will not know whether she is coming or going and will have to take her knickers down either way.

But she is not a child, had not been a child even when she was a child, since she was corrupted and evil in the way that Eve was, or her Egyptian precursor deity, or the Babylonian one. She was made to be the focus of evil acts, whether they involve men, or dogs, or eels, and it is because she is evil that she recognises in him the desire to be evil, though, frankly, he will be incapable of it. He earns her derision in the first instance, and makes it so much easier for her to do what she intends to do, and what she intends her little white dog to do.

In Japanese mythology there is a demon who is a whore and also a spider. While the whore aspect plays you plangent and somehow also seductive tones, and flatters your arrogance, the spider aspect wraps you in silk so that later it can play with you. It will put its sting in you when the lights are out, and the liquor is poured, and mother has retired to her bedroom with a migraine. Eventually it will go so far as to appal itself, at which point it will kill you and suck out whatever is inside.

You will feel a strange warmth when you think of this demon, which the dog notices, and this is how you know you are wrong, and what are you going to do about it? What can you do about it? Can a spider demon divest itself of the demon? Or the whore? What would be left? It is up to the victim to be wary of such creatures, since demons have no alternative. You, on the other hand, can steer well clear. If you see a whore, or a vulnerable woman parading on the sea front, or an insect in trouble having broken the surface tension of the water, you should resist the temptation to pounce. You will thereby avoid being wrapped in silk and submerged in a net and made subject to knife play while a little white dog fucks you in the arsehole to the appalled amusement of onlookers.

The action is very slow for her, and she has long grown tired of the simmering build up to festivities, but also she knows she must punish herself. Boredom is now the greatest punishment since, in the longueur, she has too much time to think. Even in the evildoer there is the memory of the time before the evil was done and seen to be integral to the self. There is a time in which the child is of the opinion that they are simply existent, rather than existent in a world of evildoing of which they are the prime mover. During periods of intense boredom, when the body does not supply enough excitement to quiet the mind, it is possible, indeed likely, that the mind will revert to this period of the child's life and therefrom will they experience the world as an innocent will experience it: as horrific, and frightening, and very sad. To the evildoer, this is not ideal, except as a punishment that the weak-minded must suffer, and which can only be alleviated by greater acts of evil that the strong-minded will bring to mind when some act requires greater fortitude of will than such acts usually do. This will be something particularly awful that truly sickens even as it delights. So, she suffers the boredom, knowing that it is what she deserves, and it is constructive in the end anyway.

After what seems like an eternity of this, of sitting on the river bank, flicking the fly a couple of inches at a time over the surface of the water, he kisses her and she reciprocates, guiltily, one eye always for the arrival of her husband, who waits at home.

Now there is a pleasure in waiting, since she knows she has him, regardless of whether he realises it or not. She knows his heart, and while he is no saint, he falls on the side of the line that dictates whether love is possible for him, and it is. This line is clear and obvious to those who are on the other side of it, but it seems not to exist at all to those who are not, and he is not. It is like the surface of the water, or the division between this world and the underworld: one side has no use for it, the other spends its life walking it, looking for people to drag across.

There is an accumulation of events in a life that will prevent the heart from loving, and these events are all of a type – the use of love to commit crimes against the person. Once there are too many of them, then love itself is revealed to be a crime, and it can no longer be seen as anything else, since it exists only to facilitate these other crimes, and hence is a form of entrapment. Similarly, drink or strong drugs. Once they have a hold on one, it is impossible to see the world in the same way, and not simply through intoxication – the world becomes a place which facilitates more drink, more drugs, and those who do not understand this fact are like idiot children to her – they can be used, since they do not have the wherewithal to resist – and are consequently an easy meal.

He will come to love her, since he still has the capacity, and she will use this to commit crimes against him for her own satisfaction, and for the amelioration of her condition that dragging others into it brings. The drug addict revels in company – she will induce others to become addicted and thereby make it easier to facilitate more drugs (company may have money, and company provides a world which sustains itself in the way that many sparks together may sustain a fire, but one alone doesn't catch, even on the driest kindling).

Now when he returns to Moscow and she loiters wherever she wishes, on the periphery of his life, but at the centre of other people's lives, where she enacts whatever horrors she may, he will pine gradually for her. He will see her seductive face and body in his dreams. He will see dogs in the street and remember her dog, and think back to the time in Yalta with fondness. The longer this goes on, the more deeply felt will be his pining love for her, and she can entertain herself however she wishes in the meantime.

Eventually they will meet again at the operetta, *The Geisha* (which is appropriate since there is a woman who loves a goldfish in it), and she will lead him away from her husband. He is in the audience, so they go up and around staircases, she seeming to be unwilling, but really only enjoying the preliminaries. When he claims, as he must, that he loves her and cannot live without her, then she inserts the hook into his lower lip. The hook is barbed, so that even if he has the will to get free, which she is reasonably sure he has not (though one can never tell), he will tear when he pulls away, and rip when he pulls close. She can take pleasure in that, at his little squeak when he realises that actual damage is being done to him, and he might even weep a little, which is delightful!

She will spin some tale which will result in them meeting at an unfamiliar place – a party, perhaps, which she cannot miss, but which he can attend without drawing suspicion. There she promises to retire with him up into the room which has been set aside for some other purpose and ought not to be occupied. There she will give herself up to the desires that she too has been feeling. When he arrives, she will get him down to his pants and socks, and restrain him with ties to the bed post, and gag him. Then she will leave and give the signal, and in will come the other partygoers, who are all dressed and having drinks, and most of whom are utterly unfamiliar to him, except a few, but he is not sure; has he seen them at the shop? He hopes not because now it is obvious that it is all a trap, although he still can't believe it. She will step back and pull aside her mask and there will be the face of a spider, slit eyes, eight of them, and distended jaws, but speaking French as well as any native. She will come and pull down his knickers and pull off his bra, at which the crowd will applaud, their rings clinking against their champagne glasses. She will give a short speech about what a good sport he is.

Is there a world in which this is acceptable: a world in which, later that night, or tomorrow, she will be surprised to discover this was not what he wanted, was not what he had intended, something that, had his mouth been free, he would have begged them not to do? Surely not, and now she is whistling for the dog, who needs no encouragement. It has done all this a hundred times, a thousand times, so quickly does it go about its business of mimicking the attentions of a considerate lover. His desperation to be free looks entirely like the writhing of a woman in the throes of passion, and all this is bad enough until, at the clap of his hands, it comes up to her face, where it writhes around on her. The crowd finds this much to its amusement, clapping and laughing, and once this is done, the animal's thick scent so strong that she would gag if she weren't gagged already, it returns to the other end, where it does what all men do.

A spider demon would do this, must do this, since this is how it makes its living, but it is also a wonderful reversal of the natural order. Chekhov is to be admired for recognising in this story of modern mores the desire for revenge that lies in the breast of a woman who has been mistreated by men. It is not only that he writes a vengeful woman in this way, but also that he writes for his audience, who are women that are vengeful themselves. It is not easy for a male to empathise with females in this way. He has a reputation for writing situations that accurately represent the modern world, of which women are certainly a part, but it is here, surely, that he surpasses himself in the creation of a demonic champion for all those women who have been spurned, or made to do things that they do not wish to do, or who suffer at the hands of their fathers and uncles in childhood. Cousins, brothers even. He has made a fantasy which allows them some vicarious revenge, though it be nauseating and uncomfortable to read for those of us who have never had cause to wish for the painful sexual humiliation of our foes. Still more uncomfortable is it for those of us who have not come to have our own erotic preferences inscribed in this manner through poor handling as a child, as if one were a duckling who followed by accident a fox rather than the mother duck, and who has the image of it imprinted where the image of our mother ought to be.

We have committed awful crimes ourselves, and so must offset the pleasure we feel in seeing our enemies reduced to the level of objects of sexual mockery against the pleasure we have received in doing precisely those things that we wish our enemies to be punished for. It muddies the waters when one thinks that perhaps those who victimised us were victimised in the way we victimise others, and so won't someone one day humiliate us, sexually? The only resolution to this being that we could experience it as a form of pleasure if we so chose, and later close the circle by self-immolation, such as that done by Brünnhilde in the ending of the *Götterdämmerung*.

This was the route taken by the gods as Wagner saw them, which is noble (although a little unfair on the horse) and much more fitting as a subject for opera than whiny songs about goldfishes, with rhymes and word play and jokes about things we don't understand.

The Egyptian religion is not coherent – contradictory things are believed simultaneously, the same gods appear in different forms, with different functions, rituals are doubled, tripled, to ensure efficacy – they take many routes to the same place, so it is not unusual to see strange and confusing things. But it is coherent in some things – the body, the name, and the protections for the deceased in the afterlife must all be preserved. With this tomb, care had been taken to undermine all that. Though I was squeamish, I reached in and parted the cut linens and there was no sign of the talismans and amulets that would always be placed inside the mummy bindings to protect the corpse – specifically, and I reached in to confirm this, there was no scarab over the heart. Those things necessary to maintain the body intact into the afterlife had been removed.

Carry out the opening of the mouth and eyes, first with the djedft-implement, and then with the finger of electrum

So that the face of the deceased is recognisable in the afterlife, a mask of beaten gold is made in her image, finished and coloured with precious gems. This is laid atop the wrapped body.

LUCIA JOYCE
PARIS, AUGUST 1930

What on earth is Sandy up to now?

He brings in two of those trunks that first-class passengers' lackeys loaded aboard the *Titanic*, with his name painted on them in white. ALEXANDER CALDER. One is full of heavy stuff, and has two belts strapped around it to ensure it doesn't fall open as he drags it up the stairs, and send everything everywhere. He's very precious about it, this foolishness, more precious than he is about almost anything else, and certainly more precious about it than he is about you, Lucia – you are an audience, and an audience is a wonderful thing, but interchangeable with any other audience. One may find members of an audience almost anywhere, particularly in Paris, which is a city to which people travel in order to be the audience for things, whether buildings, or street performers, or artists, or combinations of the three.

The things in these trunks are unique. That is better and consequently more worthy of the attention than being simply a person who can see and appreciate unique things that someone has spent an awful lot of time over (seemingly for no good reason).

The first thing he pulls out is an elephant. Its trunk is made from the piping one uses to connect a gas supply to a small machine that uses gas – a Bunsen burner, for example, or a portable stove. Unlike the ears, which are a naturalistic grey, the trunk is orange, which does somewhat lessen the effect of verisimilitude. But that isn't what he's after, for God's sake; could you just wait until he's got the fucking thing set up before you judge?

The second thing is a phonograph, on which he plays some god-awful racket.

There's a red piece of diaper material and some segments of the arc of a circle – he lays the diaper on the floor in front of him and places the arc segments around it – they are painted with blue triangles, which is pretty. In the middle he puts a ringmaster made of pipe cleaners. The ringmaster is wearing a tuxedo and a tall hat, and has one huge hand. Sandy does his voice in French, introducing the audience to the forthcoming. He says, 'Mesdames et Messieurs', which is wrong because you are the only one there, and you are a 'mademoiselle' if you are anything. He moves the ringmaster's hand with string, which, again, is visible, and spoils the effect. If the effect is to make the audience believe that the ringmaster is moving by himself, which of course it isn't, then it is ruined. Why trouble with the string at all? He marches the ringmaster out of the ring, and it seems as if this is in response to criticism, but apparently it is always like this. You shouldn't think, Lucia, that your fleeting role as audience to this performance, which he has spent the best part of the evening setting up when you could have been doing something much less focussed on him and his silly games, is pivotal in any way.

Which is the problem.

Once the ringmaster has cleared the arena, burlap is put down, and then a sweet little white horse is brought out. It is made to process the arcs of the circle in a manner much less obtrusive than the way the ringmaster was made to move. There is a handle that gets turned out of eyeshot and there must be some kind of gearing beneath the burlap, because the horse canters gaily around. Then a girl acrobat rides on his back. There is something very affecting about this, but art? You should keep your comments to yourself, or are you being provocative? If so, then he should move this wine out of reach, for both your sakes.

Now there is a negress in a white dress, who is terribly elegant and she has a funny dog, whom she has trained to walk on his back legs. Clever thing! Which? Both.

She has a Pegasus who rides in, and directs, his own carriage. The negress watches imperiously and takes credit for the work of her animals, before making way for two clowns, one of whom is incapable of playing the tuba well, despite a shock of red hair. It is, though, more than capable of smoking a cigarette, which Sandy lights for him with a match from a matchbook. It is the kind of matchbook that you find in a glass bowl on a table in a restaurant or bar, and which you have a habit of taking multiples of, even if you don't need them. Are you starting a collection? You have no idea what he means.

He smokes the cigarette through the orange tube, and if you don't look at him, but only at the red-haired clown, it is very funny – almost worth the price of entrance alone. Now he is blowing up a balloon, which you find inordinately amusing, to the point of apoplexy, but when you see Sandy's face – which has an expression which suggests he is a little put off by your reaction – it sours your pleasure very quickly. You then adopt a studiously bored expression, and urge him to get a bloody move on.

The clown now blows up the balloon, and blows up the balloon, and blows up the balloon, and all the time you are unhappy. The other clown, who it now becomes obvious is a woman the first clown is trying to impress, watches on dispassionately, as do you, until the woman falls over, which is rather typical, doesn't he think?

Now there's a great deal of fannying around with string which interrupts whatever momentum the performance had up to this point; is that how he always does it? Sandy? And don't people get bored waiting? And he understands that there are real circuses people can go to?

A net is strung in silence beneath what are now trapezes, and a little trapeze artist is brought on. He swings back and forth by means of a string and leaps from trapeze to trapeze using magnets until he is chopped to the nets with a flat hand.

A man of metal wire puts his head in the mouth of a metal-wired lion, who has wool for a mane. The lion allows the trainer to live, and the trainer repays his kindness by forcing the lion to stand on a small platform. Is there a rule in life that says the beautiful and magnificent things of the world must always be cowed by the cruel and the ugly? Sandy? He does not know, and it's coming to the end now, whatever you think. The trainer makes the lion rear up under threat of a whipping, and it dies of sadness while charioteers lurch to the sound of a bell.

You like the horse best, though you will not tell him. You like it even more when the cases are packed and closed, and his attention is reserved for you, and not for idiotic confections of wire and string, which is rarely. It will become rarer still, because, despite the fact that you love him, Lucia, he will leave without warning and return to his fiancée and take his stupid little circus with him.

It was as if the funerary priests had meticulously followed the proper procedure and then, at a time after that (but before the sealing of the tomb) they had returned to the corpse, knowing where the protections had been bound into the wrappings and, with a knife, cut them out.

Now, Egyptian mortuary rituals were a notoriously expensive business and the priesthood associated with it was held in high regard. Would they have done this without payment? Would they have done this without influence being placed on them, knowing that the desecration of a tomb was a crime against their gods? I could not imagine that they would.

'I clean out your mouth;
I open your eyes for you'

At her feet are placed
the four canopic jars.
In these are her
mummified organs,
preserved to serve her in the afterlife.

THE IB OF LUCIA JOYCE

LES ATELIERS DU VIEUX COLOMBIER, PARIS, SUMMER 1927 (CONT.)

The spoilsport makes its first appearance, unseen, but always there. Its presence is assumed from the change in atmosphere, a shrillness as if somewhere above a glass is rung, a wet finger around the rim, teasing out sound. Its trembling is visible in the image cast by its contents and shadowed on the table top. It is a vibration in the doorway, light creeping through the keyhole from the lines of shoddy joinery. It is the cracks of untreated, unpainted wood, dried and separating, pulled apart and left gaping, light coming in and not, as a body passes on the other side.

It pauses and passes, both their breaths held, sharing the expectation of something but hoping for different things.

Needing different things.

Back to the mark, please.

This wooden soldier does not feel the presence of the spoilsport, could never feel its presence, would never be spoiled, even, even if it was taken and broken and its parts fed into a pencil sharpener and turned into shavings. One long curved curl, blond wood at the centre with a ribbon of red at the edge, the longest curl, the whole pencil taken in one turn, a new blade and new pencil turned slowly, slowly, but never pausing, never letting a splinter catch. Hand holding, fingers in the grooves, the hexagon imprint on the fingertips ever flatter. The lead is painfully sharp, sharp as a compass point, sharp enough to blind, jabbed in the lens, inserted into the lens and pulled down into the iris so that it never recovered. Slit like a goat's eye, a vertical stripe of black, demonic, Satanic, drawing the round eyes of all the others to it, school friend, employer, lover, forcing them to look and look away. Grind this soldier into sawdust and scatter him in the backroom of a butcher's shop. Put him into the sausage machine, into the sausages – rusk, blood spots on fabric, on the apron, in the knickers, on the sheets. Toenails catching against the linen, whisky on the breath, pigs slaughtered, pigs sighing, half carcasses hung from hooks.

A puppet moves very jerkily, but not like an epileptic. Such are the directions of Jean Renoir, who knows more about dancing than the dancer Lucia Joyce knows. The elbows are held high, the wrists too, and the knees are perpetually half bent – there is no gracefulness to it, the opposite, and this poses a problem. Lucia's instinct is to form lines of beauty, to create unity of form, to act in consonance with some underlying order, or method, or aesthetic, but the puppet is imperfect – stop jerking like an epileptic!

Not like that!

The limbs flow to the ground when the string is relaxed, the head slumps to the chest. When the string is made taut again the flow only gradually returns to the horizontal – it's the knees that cause the problem. The puppet is poorly constructed – it doesn't joint in the way God made the body – it's perfectly possible for a puppet's knees to go in reverse, like a dog's. It has a characteristic angularity on rising that is hard to recreate.

Not impossible!

Perhaps a puppet can be captured first during its rising, but then the real woman can take its place and perform its dance, waiting at the end for the real puppet to be brought off, a brief cut and the seams stitched and the effect is created. Easier certainly than bending the knee back on itself, the elbows and the neck.

This is not about ease; try again.

Relax the joints, relax the ligaments, relax the things that we know, the expectations, relax the self. Let it bend back, relax into it, relax. Not possible when you are so tense. It's not that bad. Relax and enjoy it. The knees won't work against themselves, but they can be put to the side to give the impression of inversion, and so the spine, laid straight, and the neck, in contraposition. Place the limbs both on the same side, both left, like an

Egyptian in an exhibition receiving the benediction of an animal-headed Jesus, all the rights wrong.

Much better! Wonderful. That's it. That's it. Good. Good girl. Pig squealing, blood sausage, weight crushing out the breath, the Ba, the Ka, the Akh, emerging from the sinuses, organs in jars, panting horses at the last race. 4.30.

Are you getting all this?

No, the lighting is wrong, all wrong.

Go again.

This time is too much like the last time, too similar, trying too hard for something lost, aiming to recreate the absent thing. Gut feeling.

Having begun the preliminary sketches, my colleague put down his pencil and drew my attention to a scene on the side of the sarcophagus. In it, the deceased, obvious in that her likeness had been chiselled out, stood before the figure of the *sem* priest at the weighing of the heart, both overlooked by Meskhenet, the goddess of childbirth present in her form as a brick with the head of a woman, and also as a goddess from whose head a stylised cow uterus sprouts. Representations of Meskhenet are not at all unusual in tombs of this period, but what was strange was the presence of the *sem* priest, whose function is funerary, and who is generally only depicted in scenes of the funeral preparations. It was as if the deceased was presenting herself to him rather than to the goddess (who would outrank such a priest). We exchanged looks and I directed his attention to the inscriptions, but these were nearly nonsensical, referring to a song or liturgy that neither of us could understand.

'Take the Eye of Horus, may your face not be devoid of it'

Each of the jars is made in the form of one of the sons of Horus and has a tutelary goddess. Qebesenuef, the hawk, overlooked by Serket, protects the intestines of the deceased.

THE SHUYET SHADOW
OF LUCIA JOYCE
IN A LECTURE, 1930

In an abattoir it is not uncommon to come across tapeworms of ten meters in length – when one eviscerates the slaughtered animal and cleans the offal for sale they are flushed out of the gut. Tapeworms of pigs are of one length, tapeworms of cows are of another, but if length is disregarded it would take an expert with a microscope to tell the difference between them.

Rather than a head, like a mammal might have, the tapeworm has a scolex, which contains the sucker, a ring of barbed teeth, and a primitive cerebral ganglion which manages the autonomic functions and the limited senses a creature who dwells in the bowels of another creature requires.

In order to reproduce, the tapeworm finds another tapeworm inside the digestive tract and they exchange spermatozoa via their genital pores. One might imagine the love life of these parasites as they thrash around inside the bowel, and there are some parallels with human romance, the worms having a concentration of nerves of sensation around their genital pores through which pleasure is no doubt produced in the scolex.

Once it is pregnant with fertilised eggs, the tapeworm migrates to the anus of its host, where it finds egress into the world, there writhing, white and seeking, until it sheds the proglottid containing the spawn onto the pasture, where it is eaten by a new host. The eggs lodge in either the stomach or the brain of the new host, where cysts may be formed which cause aberrations of behaviour.

A woman wishing to lose weight who finds herself unable to do so by the exercise of willpower may ingest the eggs of a tapeworm in the form of a small pill and, once pregnant with the parasites, will vomit and pass – through diarrhoea – a great portion of that which she eats. The rest will be eaten by the tapeworms, allowing her to maintain a shapely figure simply by taking an anti-parasitic preparation. After the tapeworms die, regardless of their own state of pregnancy, they will be passed in the stool, gorged on the chocolates, Turkish Delights, and fatty treats that are served at dinner parties to which the girl is not invited, but of which she avails herself once the adults are in bed and she can sneak around unwatched.

If a tapeworm infects the uterus it can lead to miscarriage, either via the worm eating the blastocyst, or the worm drawing on the resources properly produced by the placenta for the foetus, depriving it of them at a vital stage and causing it to wither on the branch. It is possible that the tapeworm will be purged when menstruation forces the shedding of the cells by which it is attached to the wall of the uterus, but it is also possible that it will not, at which point an anti-parasitic should be administered and care taken that the uterus does not become a locus of infection.

If a girl comes to you with the intention of inducing a miscarriage via tapeworm, she should be discouraged, since other more reliable methods exist. If a girl comes to you having attempted to miscarry by tapeworm, she should be chided in the strongest terms to prevent her doing anything so damned stupid in future. Tapeworm cysts may migrate anywhere in the body, including the eyes and the brain, where they will cause blindness and aberrations of behaviour and necessitate long and difficult treatment, up to and including surgery. During surgery, areas of the skull will need to be removed to give access to the cyst in which the parasite now resides, putting pressure on the brain. Perhaps this is why there is such a thing as trepanning, which might, if you think about it for a little while, have been why it was attempted at all. Certainly, if one wished to relieve the symptoms of a tapeworm infection of the brain, or neurocysticercosis more generally, then drilling into the infection site would certainly offer the possibility of a cure, though not for the reasons the ancients imagined (bad humours, spirit release, et al.).

If one's dreams were affected by the residence in the part of the brain responsible for the generation of dreamscapes of a tapeworm, or a culture of tapeworms, then would one dream of tapeworms, or dream as a tapeworm dreams? Or would the tapeworm dream as a man dreams?

There is in the animal kingdom ample evidence of symbiosis between species, so would this be another example? The tapeworm would seem to benefit here, having use of the superior facilities of the human mind to expand the possibilities of its dreaming, but it may also be the case that a man might benefit from the clarity of focus that the primitive ganglia of the scolex provide for the tapeworm. A tapeworm is not constantly bothered by drifting ruminations on this or that matter of which it has read in the papers, or vistas culled from memories of visits to Bavaria. Nor does it feel anxiety bubbling up from its unconscious, nor the requirements of its place in the collective unconscious of its race. A tapeworm's culture is little more than darkness and the pleasure it receives from the stimulation of its genital pore, and the urge then to pass to the anus and shed the proglottid engorged with eggs. As a hermaphroditic culture, there are not even archetypal genderings to pull it in one direction or the other. So might a man's dreams be freer of weight if he dreams as a tapeworm allows him to dream?

What if he should write down his dreams? Would there not be something in this tapeworm-inspired material that would be useful for others to read, if only as a relief from the terribly mannered and intellectual writings his readership is used to? What can a man tell another man anyway that he does not already know using words in an order he recognises, in a form he already recognises, on subjects he already recognises? By definition, if he already recognises these things it is because he knows them already.

Would he know the thoughts of a tapeworm? Only if the writers of works he has read were also written by men whose brains were infected with tapeworms, and who were also inspired by the thoughts present in the scolices of tapeworms living in cysts in the areas of their brains responsible for the generation of dreamscapes. Which raises the possibility that all the writers of the past were writing in this manner, and that the literature we take for canonical is not of our species, but is the literature of tapeworms, and what should be done about this?

First, we should apply an anti-parasitic to writers of note like those provided to women who wish to lose weight but find they cannot stop stuffing their faces with cake and butter all day long and half the night. While the worms will not be passed in stools, they might bleed out of the ear, or be absorbed by the body, or purged through the lymph after having first been destroyed by defensive white blood cells. Then we must prevent the transmission of the tapeworm cysts into the brains of writers by encouraging them first not to have intercourse with girls who have attempted to induce miscarriage by tapeworm. The migration of the tapeworm to the mouth of the cervix and the shedding of the proglottid engorged with eggs might well result in the proglottid being transmitted through the meatus, up the urethra, and by turns to the brain (via the circulatory system).

Also, writers should avoid undercooked pork and always wash their hands.

If this is not sufficient, then all contact with girls and pork must be prohibited, at least for as long as it takes to determine whether the canon is a function of the mind of a human, or the scolex of a tapeworm. A survey must be carried out in which writers who are known to be free of parasitic infection are induced to write on whatever topics they prefer and the results read by learned critics, and then that these writers be forcibly infected with tapeworms and induced to write on whatever topics they prefer and this work handed in too.

It must also be determined whether the critical function displayed by learned critics is itself unduly affected by the thoughts of tapeworms, since critics are integral to canon formation. Children must be raised who are, firstly, free of tapeworm cysts, and, secondly, riddled with tapeworms, and these two groups of children raised in a very literary culture, with books of all sorts, or only books produced by men who are riddled with tapeworms, or only books produced by men who are not riddled with tapeworms (if these are found to exist), and then allowed to generate critical faculties, and then allowed to read the books from the writers engaged in the survey.

It should be noted that this is a rather time consuming procedure.

If, in the meantime, the daughter of a writer whose writing is suspected of being produced by the scolex of a tapeworm – James Joyce, for example – should come to you, Carl Jung, for the treatment of neuroses, there are several considerations that must be taken into account. Firstly, is the presence or otherwise of tapeworms in the mind of the father relevant to the treatment of the daughter? It is perfectly possible that there is no intersection of the two issues, though this is unlikely. Secondly, is the presence or otherwise of tapeworms in the mind of the father central to the treatment of the daughter? It is perfectly possible that there is an overwhelming intersection of the two issues, so that if one were to draw a Venn diagram of the intersection it would almost appear as if there were only one circle present, rather than two. You would have to take an eye-glass from the drawer in the writing table, such as the one that is used to consult the dictionary produced in two volumes rather than twenty-four that was received as a gift from your father long before he died, this must have been forty years ago now, to see that at the very edges of the circles there are two more lines only a fraction of a hair's breadth separate, but separate nonetheless. Thirdly, is the presence or otherwise of tapeworms in the mind of the father only marginally relevant to the treatment of the daughter?

You must also ask yourself whether the daughter is infected with tape-worms, since if the father is infected with them, and the father lives in close proximity to the daughter, might the daughter not also be infected? It is not an easy matter to determine infection *in vivo*, but inspection of the anus for proglottides might be one way, or to ask if proglottides have been noted in the stool. The presence of diet preparations in the handbag of the daughter might also answer this question. If she leaves the bag unattended while she answers a call of nature, it is not improper to peek inside if it is open, and only a little improper to undo the clasp and look around. Place the tip of your nose an inch or two away from the slit, and the scent of violets will fill the nostrils. If she returns unexpectedly, then adopt a surly indifference to questioning and urge her to return to the point and stop changing the subject.

If the daughter is infected, then the question is raised as to which direction the transmission occurred. Did the father give the girl tapeworms, or did the girl give the father them? There is no way of knowing by looking at them, so instead you must question both parties rigorously in order to establish the facts, since no independent cure can be attempted on the daughter until the question is resolved. Indeed, the resolution of the question will be pivotal to the diagnosis and consequently the cure. If, for instance, the proglottides were shed at the mouth of the uterus following the daughter's induction of the removal of the foetus against the necessity to raise a feebleminded child, and then they invaded through the meatus and made their way up the urethra and via the circulatory system to lodge in the brain of the father, then this is one thing. If the transmission was made in the other direction, by poor hygiene in the preparation of food, and/or the undercooking of pork, then this is another thing.

It is a simple matter to ensure pork is thoroughly cooked through: simply purchase a cook's thermometer and establish that the temperature of the meat is between 145°F and 160°F before serving. This will ensure that any tapeworm eggs are destroyed before consumption. In a dish like *cassoeula*, this temperature will not be difficult to achieve, but with something like *arista al latte* a reluctance to overheat the milk (since it will catch) can result in the temperature not reaching the required level, regardless of how long the dish is cooked. Once consumed, the eggs will migrate across the body and infect the brain. Inserting a thermometer into meat is not an onerous task, it takes only a few moments. Similarly, washing the hands thoroughly will prevent transmission from the anus of the infected father to surfaces, door handles, and shared books should a proglottid migrate there and rupture. If both these requirements are met, the treatment of the daughter for her neurosis can continue after a course of anti-parasitics has been administered without fear of remission on the grounds of reinfection.

If, however, the transmission is from father to daughter via the route described, then all such transmission vectors must be addressed prior to treatment since there is significant risk of re-infection during the treatment. The same holds true for other members of the family who may similarly run the risk of infection, or who are infected already, brothers or uncles included. This holds also for friends of the family who visit the household, or whom the daughter meets in the streets, or at parties, or at bookshops. Unless such transmission vectors are prevented, the risk is run that many more infections of tapeworm will be caused, and that the entire social circle of the daughter will suffer the aberrances of behaviour that are noticeable in the daughter. Such aberrances are self-replicating and auto-reinforcing when evidenced in a closed population, and it will be very difficult to effect a cure.

If the daughter has been riddled with tapeworms since early childhood, there is little chance of a cure in any case, since she will have been dreaming the dreams of parasites and speaking the words of parasites and thinking the thoughts of parasites during the period of her development and can more properly be thought of as a symbiotic hybrid of daughter and parasite than she can be thought of as a woman. A child requires a certain amount of pure and free space to develop her own self and to come into her human inheritance and if she has been raised in a jar of squirming worms this space will not have been given to her. Also, the tapeworm can infect the eye causing visual disturbances and a sensitivity to light and in the mind this causes a tendency to see nightmarish things of the everyday world, to seek out dark places, remain in bed during the day, and only come out in the night. The daughter will wander the streets looking for experiences that reify the darkness she feels in her visual field and in her heart, which is melancholic and gloomy.

To a tapeworm, though, this is like pleasure. It feels good to a tapeworm to reside in the bowel where it finds its mate, and even from its birth as an egg its only desire is to find darkness, to be consumed by another, to fester within them, drawing whatever it needs from the dark and private realms of the inside. To attempt to bring light into the situation is a mistake, since photophobia and hypersensitivity to ultraviolet rays can be fatal, and the patient should instead be taken to a place in which they can remain undisturbed and undisturbing and there live out their life in the manner of their kind, which is to thrash about in shit outside of the range of human experience, and there to take pain for pleasure, day for night, death for life.

Fire is the one solution.

Writings that are influenced by the scolices of tapeworms can be burned, as can the criticism that is produced by critics grown from tapeworm-ridden children. The eggs of tapeworms can be destroyed by introducing them in a skillet to a flame and taking them to a high enough temperature. A tapeworm removed from the body can be killed by throwing it into fire, or by heating a needle and applying it to the body or by burning it with matches. Care must be taken on removal since the proglottides are easily detached. If you intend to take a pencil and twirl the tapeworm around it like a Chinaman twirls a noodle around a chopstick then you must do it slowly and never tug, since the worm will separate in two and the free end will retract into the anus before you can grab it. Be sure to wash your hands thoroughly, since it is easy to pick up eggs on your skin if the proglottides rupture.

If one wishes to purge oneself of tapeworms one can immolate oneself, neatly solving two problems with one stone, since the tapeworms will die and their host will also die, ridding the world of one more disturbance and ridding the disturbance of the world, which is nothing but a jar of wriggling tapeworms always seeking ingress so that they might lodge within one's bowel and there suck all the nutrition, replacing it with a permanent stomach ache and migraines behind the eyes.

And again, in the subsequent scene, there were strange additions and omissions – the presence of figures, symbols and images that did not fit the standard forms (as much as these are recognisable in what is often a bafflingly complicated and contradictory iconography). What was clear, and this brought the feeling of dread and unwholesomeness back to me worse than it was before, is that something terrible was being represented. All the symbols were negations, violence, destruction and chaos, where what should have been present were spells ensuring the opposite: peace, creation and order.

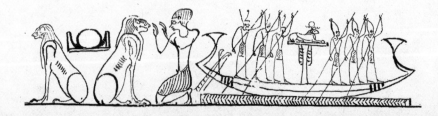

O Osiris of Lucia, your mother has given birth to you today!

Imsety, in human form, overlooked by the goddess Isis, protects the liver.

THE BA OF LUCIA JOYCE
LONDON AND PARIS,
1932 ONWARDS

It is painful to live within the pages of a book, and/or to be recognised only by one's attributes, for example to be a pair of eyes removed from their sockets and placed on a dish. Would you like it, Samuel Beckett?

No matter how wonderful the artist, or how prestigious the gallery in which one hangs, it is no substitute for a life to be a pair of disembodied eyes staring uncannily at passers-by, even if one is considered a masterpiece. Better, infinitely, to be allowed to walk free in the summer, or to comb one's hair, or to stretch, none of which are activities available to two dimensional representations of the facility of sight, done in gouache. If these eyes grow from the stalk of plant, that is no consolation, and is more like rubbing salt into the wounds – one would enjoy picking a flower, although not, perhaps, if it had eyes on it.

Similarly, to be represented under a pseudonym in a book some consider obscene is also tiresome. Would you like that? To have your character dissected and the ins and outs of your behaviour commented on, and your secrets revealed? And always the sexual material?

That you are described as beautiful and perfect to look at is nice, but then there's all the rest of the stuff, and if someone brings your good name into question then calling you beautiful while they do it, that isn't any consolation, even if the name they call into question isn't your own name. You and your friends would know.

And so what if it is never published in your lifetime? – there are plenty of very widely read books that are never published. Only those who are completely ignorant of the way literature is produced could imagine that books aren't read before they reach the shops. The book is already dead by the time it reaches the shops, like a cow is dead when its meat is portioned for sale by a butcher. The life it had frolicking gaily in the fields, walking free in the summer, and being passed from hand to hand between some of the most well-regarded readers in the business is all forgotten by the time the shillings are handed across the table. Everyone who matters has already read it, and do you think literary people buy each other's books? Of course they don't: they pass them from hand to hand as manuscripts, prior to publication. If you are *in* the book, and *in* the room when the book is passed from hand to hand, to your father, then it is no good calling a person beautiful and then exposing their sexual behaviours to the world, even if it is under a silly name, which is so bloody obvious, don't you think everyone knows who the saints of Syracuse are?

Even if it isn't then published at all.

Worse if it isn't published, because then all the damage is done and only to those people who have a specific understanding of the party being libelled and for whom this represents evidence of a side to that party's character previously only rumoured at. The general public might take a character study from a novel and see it in the round, bringing to it their experience of the general run of things and thereby understand it generally, thereby diluting any particular significance. They might even take your side, and so provide a counter perception of the events. But stuck in a box in an attic, or held in a library, or in a drawer in a publisher's office, or in the studies of all the writers in Paris, then this is like a prison.

When one is dead, it is only those things that remain that constitute one's existence, we can all agree on that. For the ripples one makes in the pond of existence to lessen with time until they are vanishingly small, then this is also the way of things. But if someone has gone around erasing all trace that you ever existed, burning your letters and suppressing all word of you, and then there is a great rock with or without your name on it thrown into the water, it is no solace that you are dead, and cannot answer for yourself, when waves wash about you and hit the shore. That it was published *post mortem* is an irrelevance.

And that Bohemianism is dead now.

Think of the Egyptian pharaohs – not Akhenaten, who himself was erased from history and therefore might be the first pharaoh you think of, and his beautiful wife, who might also be a factor. Those who were buried with proper attendance to the rituals would secure their afterlives. Tuthmosis III will do as an example, despite the unusual style, his tomb was filled with ushebti and his walls decorated with hieratic and hieroglyphics and depictions of the hereafter. He was content to live in the representations of himself *post mortem*. This was his dearest dream, in fact, and he hired artists to come and paint him wonderful worlds, and write him wonderful lives that he could live out in perpetuity.

You would want that for yourselves after death, as would anyone rational if they could believe it was true.

And then what if some idiot came in and tore it all down? Shipped it off to museums in different countries? Exhumed you from your sarcophagus? Undid your bindings and peered at your naked corpse? Slit you with a scalpel, splayed you open to be seen by one and all? And then *this* was your afterlife, for all eternity. Slaves gone, wives gone, oxen gone, bushels gone. In their place the gawping wax-faced idiots who drag themselves past your body because they think it is the thing to do on a Sunday afternoon, or because they read about you in the paper, or because they have an interest in the conditions of the dead. They watch through the glass, their desire for something of the afterlife, so prurient and formless, peering in the windows hoping for a glimpse of someone else's death, to somehow understand what theirs might be.

There is a journey the dead must go on before they reach the Field of Reeds (which is roughly analogous to the Christian heaven), and this journey through the Duat is perilous and filled with terrors – horned snakes, crocodiles, devils – it is the journey the God Ra takes in the solar chariot during the period the sun is beneath the western horizon before it rises again in the east. The Egyptian dead are provided with magical assistance ensured by the tomb decorations, and by the rituals performed in the shrine that accompanies the tomb. Here, each scene depicted the opposite – the surrender of the deceased to the jaws of ravening jackals, or the depredations of underworld gods.

You have been made into one who knows what was not known

Hapy, the baboon, overlooked by the goddess Nepthys, protects the lungs.

THE IB OF LUCIA JOYCE
LES ATELIERS DU VIEUX COLOMBIER, PARIS, SUMMER 1927 (CONT.)

Understand, there is no flamboyance in a role like this, no individuality – it is written into the part. The director, Jean Renoir, can read it in his notes, they are specific on the matter. That is the point! That he should be one of a sort, a soldier – to obey.

This is the dancer's role also. Also the actor – not to have one's own thoughts or feelings but to be perfectly that thing that another wishes one to be. The self must drift out of view, even that part of the self that first attracted the attention of the producers, the casting director. Lucia Joyce must disappear entirely, and then only exist inasmuch as someone must perform the motions, someone must fill the space that requires filling, someone must be able to do what the notes have written them to do. Generically this is true of all roles, but specifically so here.

Move like a wooden soldier, articulate like wood, drill like the others. Not so far from the orders given to living soldiers: be as nothing except what you are ordered to be. Do not exercise judgement in anything. Train in the manners and modes of your trade and execute them by reflex when prompted. Spasm as muscle spasms when an electrical impulse is received. Wear the uniform, exercise the frame into its correct shape. Place your face behind the mask, your head beneath the helmet, hoist the bayonet to your shoulder and learn to relish the abandonment of individuality as a pack wolf bitch learns subservience from the most vicious dog. Invisible the self, cover those brittle hands with white gloves, relineate that jaw with the face straps, cover the gradual erosion of the teeth.

Stop sucking matches – are you crackers? Poisoned, match strike girl. Phossy jaw. Regardless of that taste of tobacco, of fireworks, of a metal strut, rusting, a bedframe, the wood splintering between molars, splinters on the tongue and gathering in the edges, where the glands secrete saliva, can't be swallowed, must be spat out. Where gather the pieces, drying and brittling, until discovered under the bed, beneath the bedstead in a little pyre waiting for their Guy? Who's it to be? Who likes fire that much? Little match girl, stealing a box of Swan Vesta from a pub garden table.

—Let her have them, I've got more.

—Not the point.

Slap on the back of the hand and face to face, nose to nose. There'll be words about this when we get home. Glass to lips and smiles for everyone else, but not for her. A hand slipped under the table to a bare knee is rebuffed with bile in the throat, heavy on the neck and shoulders, pervasive sense that the world is over, that death is the only solution. Shrink into the earth and dissolve back, seep between the grains of soil, let capillary action redistribute your water, re-use it for some useful purpose, something warranting of God's infinite grace. Not some whiny, thieving, sken-eyed slut – a show, an embarrassment, an inconvenience.

Not now, the door is shut.

Not now, important work.

The way a person moves is very particular to them – try watching silhouettes on the wall, or through frosted glass, or projected on a cinema screen before the film begins – you can tell who is crossing the stage, if you know them, by how they move. There is something in the way a person holds themselves and how they progress through the world that is tantamount to a depiction of them, and in combination these things are recognisable to the eye.

Also, the person feels themselves at odds with the world if they are prevented from moving in the way they are conditioned to move, and of which the body is capable. To be made to move like a soldier, and to adopt the gender of a soldier, it is a kind of unkindness. For that to be filmed, and for that film to achieve some level of success, due, partly, to the labour of one who has been treated unkindly, is an offence against natural law.

In the same way, it is an offence to spice up the depiction of an execution in a play by beheading a criminal, even if that criminal has committed a capital offence. Or if one wishes for verisimilitude in the depiction of a horse race, of a charioteer race, and hires for the week a number of horses from a stable, and one of those horses, or several, falls in the action and breaks a limb and must receive a bolt to the head: it is wrong to allow these scenes to remain in the film, because there is something in art that cruelty is inimical to – is there not? – and it shouldn't be done. Too close to revelling in the pain of others that civilised society does not allow itself, particularly when no screen credit is given.

So it must feel, even if the best work is cut out. Particularly as it was performed during a period in which the artwork as a whole was produced, it has an influence, though only a very minor one. A professional should know this, and she should also know that no amount of huffing and puffing and stamping and weeping will matter for anything – that is the way it is, the conditions of the industry, the material conditions of existence, for only a few of those involved in the making of something will be rewarded. To them all the credit should go, not only for those things for which they deserve credit for and over which they had close control, but also for all those things that happened outside their purview, and for which they do not deserve credit.

Does the soldier deserve credit for the successful prosecution of a campaign of war? When territory has been seized and the corpus of the army advances, to whom does the credit accrue? To the general, correct, and the soldiers must console themselves with the spoils of the conquered territory – its wine cellars, its sausages, the bodies of its women. On the converse side, who has to fall on his sword if his decision results in defeat? If there are mounds of corpses steaming and crow-pecked in the morning, dew on their beards and moustaches, dew on their eyelashes, long and stiff like kittens'. Like Kitten's? Ha, ha. Who is it that must answer for the error? Not the soldier, no indeed, miss! Not she. Unless of course she be dead, heaven forbid, and answers in that way for her failure.

And when her whole scene is disposed of, decided against, then does the soldier have the right to question her officer, to insist on a rationale? – no amount of chest beating or hair pulling can force a man to explain to a girl the dictates of his art.

I looked at my colleague, hoping to see in his eyes some understanding of what we were seeing that was lost to me, but he was as baffled as I was.

We did differ in one important respect though – he thought this was all enormously wonderful, and outlined the benefits to our expedition and reputations that a discovery of this sort would bring. There is nothing the papers like more than a mystery, he concluded, and this mystery would be the making of us if we could only play it correctly. Providing we kept this find to ourselves, jealously guarded the tomb's secrets and, after sufficient study came to some easily understood conclusions as to the function or provenance of the tomb, it would be worth a fortune to us, just as the discovery of the boy king's tomb and the mysteries associated with that made the fortunes of Carter, et al.

Geb at the head of the corporation of the Great Ennead has healed you

Duamutef, the jackal, overlooked by the goddess Neith, protects the stomach. The uterus and its associated generative organs are redundant in the afterlife and, like the brain, are discarded.

THE SHUYET SHADOW
OF LUCIA JOYCE
PARIS, 2ND FEBRUARY 1932
ONWARDS

Under what circumstances may James Joyce beat his wife? No doubt there are many. He may beat his wife since she acts shrewishly, and is always ready with an insult the husband does not deserve, such as that he pays too much attention to his work and not enough attention to her, so that she, like an untended garden, goes to seed in the absence of his affections.

James Joyce may beat his wife since she is inadequate to the tasks that are allotted to her, and the house is rarely dusted, and the surfaces remain covered in crumbs even when he has been out for several hours. When he comes home for his lunch and pours himself a glass of water his sleeve is covered with jam from where he has leant on a countertop. The floor crunches when he walks on it, because something – perhaps eggshells, which would be appropriate, given the saying – has not been swept up from breakfast, and what's the point of having a broom if it is never used? And he chases her from room to room like black Schmutzli, giving her the benefit of the birch twigs against the buttocks and upper thighs.

He may beat his wife also since he is drunk, a condition he induces in order to be less sensitive to the shrewishness of his wife, and less aware of the poor standard of cleanliness, of which his mother would not approve, and to allow him to sleep at night against the sobbing of his beaten wife who will not be quiet, but keeps the bedclothes pulled over her, even if it is very hot in the house.

Under what conditions may James Joyce beat his daughter? These are also numerous. He may beat his daughter since she is wilful and will not do what she is told, and shows surliness when requested to do even the simplest of tasks – such as sweep up discarded eggshells and wipe bread-crumbs and jam from the work surfaces. She is growing up to be a right madam, which she gets from her mother, that much is clear.

He may beat his daughter for coming home late having been out God knows where, with God knows whom, doing God knows what. What time do you call this? You'll be getting a name for yourself.

A father may also beat his daughter, though barely, at her menarche. She comes to him confused, brow furrowed, blood on her fingertips with not the slightest idea what has occurred, since the selection of proper bed-time reading for a child has been rigorously achieved. At that point the father may deliver one hard slap to either cheek of the face in order that he draw blood up from the uterus to the head, and so lessen the menstrual flow and prevent undue soiling.

This slap has a symbolic function, also, of bringing the girl to an aware-ness of herself. It forces her to understand what she must do in the future, which is to leave the world of children behind and prepare to enter the world of women. This world is characterised not by that easy and surly resistance to work that she has so far evidenced, but is primarily a thing of pain, duty and anxiety. She ought to get used to it now rather than later.

If James Joyce wishes, he may deliver a kiss to Lucia's forehead, to bal-ance things out, though equally he may wish to leave this to the mother.

Under what conditions may a daughter beat her father?

None at all.

Regardless of what the father does with a broom, or how much he resem-bles black Schmutzli, the evil Christmas elf, or how irritating the newly menstrual daughter finds him, she may not lay a finger on him. He is the God-sanctioned authority in the household, and if one does not believe in God then he is equally sanctioned by the state and by general opinion in all the civilised parts of the world. Certainly, if one wishes to read the entirety of the encyclopaedia, or spend time amongst isolated tribes in the

Amazon, or in Papua New Guinea, one might find mention of matriarchal societies, but does the girl live in one of these places? By God she does not, and so she should treat her father with respect in his own home lest she induce him to go to the broom cupboard, or take off his belt, or have a fourth or fifth tumbler of whisky, after which all bets are off.

Can, then, Lucia beat her mother? No, she may not, since Nora Joyce (née Barnacle) is the father's representative in household affairs when the father is not in the house. Should the daughter beat the mother then she is delivering a beating to her father, by proxy, which we have already seen is forbidden. If the mother displays her jealousy by repeatedly smacking the daughter on the calves, or demonstrates favouritism toward her son by ignoring the daughter until the daughter acts up, and then pushes the daughter away, even so much so that the daughter falls and bangs her head against a low table and raises a bump the size of a songbird's egg, this does not give the daughter the right to enact violence on the body of the mother. If she has a complaint, then this should be reserved for when the father returns home from his place of work, or a bar. It should then be uttered in very mild and plaintive tones out of earshot of the mother. The father, should he give the complaint credence, can then beat the mother himself, when he has had a skin-full, and the wife complains about the daughter's behaviour and what exactly is he going to do about it? He's been told a thousand times.

If, many years later, the mother puts any number of obstacles between the daughter and her chosen career – let us say dancing, which is more of a hobby than a serious attempt to earn a living – that does not give the daughter the right to pick up a chair and hurl it at her mother, even if it does only strike her glancingly on the ankle. This can really hurt, as anyone who has caught their elbow on a pub bar will attest, the joints being singularly prone to knocks of this kind. It can send a person hopping round the room in an odd mixture of giddy, almost good-tempered, delirium and excruciating pain.

So what is to be done with a daughter who attempts violence on her mother? She should be taken to a sanatorium, where she can then be treated for the disorder that afflicts her. For a father to enact violence is understandable, and by association also a mother, since she is the father's proxy and his rights devolve onto her in this regard, but for a daughter to attack a mother, or father, is to break any number of laws, including the biblical law that one should honour one's mother and father.

Nor should that girl be allowed to interfere with the life of her brother, Giorgio, even if his wife is many years his senior and it is the scandal of the year, though no-one will say as much. The bohemian set in which this brother mixes thinks nothing of it, but what of the older generation with which everyone is obliged to live? He might not care, but he doesn't have to put up with the snide comments of Madames X, Y and Z, or the sniggering of a Monsieur whose surname is represented by the Greek letter gamma, or sigma, or mu. Even so, Lucia has no right to deputise for the mother's indignation and make trouble with this new wife. Nor should she, in an attempt to regain the high opinion of the daughter that was previously evidenced by the brother, make extortions with menaces against him, the exact details of which are shrouded in secrecy, obviously, since to make them plainer would be to do the work of the extortionist, and why is she asking? Please leave it.

I could not deny the logic of his points. He was a Cambridge man and a great intellect in his way, but the speed with which he had come to his conclusions I found troubling. I am slower than him, that I admit, and where he leaps to conclusions it would take me days to conceive of by myself, the scaffold of his thinking, if you'll accept the metaphor, is often rickety or non-existent, whereas I will tend to build an edifice on first principles, each block firmly placed on the ones below it. The first principle here was that there was something wrong, and that the nature of this flaw should be examined before any further consideration of the future.

Also, I think we differ in our ethics – I would not want to profit from a crime, even if it is committed by another. Further, my first feeling is for the victim of the crime, not for my own advantage. My colleague took an entirely different, more self-interested position.

Joining your head to your bones

Now mummified, the deceased is taken from the house of purification and returned to her family. Seventy days have passed, and the preparation of the tomb is complete.

MYRSINE MOSCHOS
PARIS, JULY 1933

Myrsine takes the satchel from the counter, gives instructions to Hélène, and leaves. It's so hot outside that the shutters are all closed against the sun, and she has to hold her free arm up to shield her eyes in the crook of her elbow. Like home, today.

There are an infinite number of ways to get where she's going, some of which will be shadier than others, but unlike Hélène, who is so pale for a Greek, her skin can take a tan. It looks good on her, so she walks the direct route to the river where she rolls up her sleeves, puts her empty satchel over her shoulder, and crosses the Pont des Arts to the Rive Droite, which seems appropriate.

The Joyce's apartment is on rue Galilée, and while she has been there many times she doesn't often go from the shop – that's her sister's job. Today she'll kill two pigeons with one shot, or one stone – however they say it – and she'll 'take the post' by whatever routes she feels like. Past the Tuileries, through the Tuileries, wherever.

It's not unpleasant work this morning, but it is work – she enjoys Shakespeare and Company, enjoys the feeling that she is indispensable, enjoys being the sensible one amongst so many deliberately impractical protagonists of their own melodramas. All the while so unselfconsciously beautiful! This side of the bargain, though, is more of an imposition. But why not? Shouldn't work be an imposition? If it was all *une partie de plaisir* then she oughtn't to be paid for it.

She exits through the Place de la Concorde – it is the quickest way, and even if it weren't, the sun is high and why walk in the shadows?

The heat brings out the tourists, like ants from their nest, and they swarm past her. She sighs like a Frenchwoman, and though she catches herself, she doesn't let any hint of her awareness of the hypocrisy of this show on her face – she's been here long enough; she's earned it. Anyway, isn't she part of a more international crowd? Travellers have little in common with sightseers; they gather together for camaraderie and the shared commitment to their art. She can sneer at the crowds from that perspective instead, and if anyone picks her up for the fact that she's not French, she can claim a better, broader, more intellectual community. And if that doesn't work, then she gets to sneer by virtue of her bohemianism, which she is on her way to demonstrate, while they huddle in their bourgeois little tribes eating stale bread and bland cheese on a chequered tablecloth on the grass on their holidays.

And she does all of this so effortlessly and without having to consider it! Silly, really, the things we think. Still, the unexamined life…

Suddenly she feels she's had enough of being in the sun, so she cuts left between the high apartment blocks, into the streets where one side at least is always in shade. Here she doesn't feel as if she is on display, and the consciousness of her self-consciousness can give way to the everydayness of everything that it's almost impossible to experience in the avenues of history. Who can truly feel as if the Champs-Élysées is their home? With all that grandeur?

In the side streets there are doors opening, people on bicycles, tobacconists shouting, backfiring engines – the scale is reduced, and a person need not constantly live up to the impossible. Architecture, it has a lot to answer for. It dwarfs the soul and makes everybody feel insignificant. Which is why it's better to live in the poorer parts of town, where the dishevelment of the everyday removes the burden of posterity, and where the real work gets done, where real change is made, where real experimentation takes place, out of view of the giants of the past. Which is why they all crowd into the shop… couldn't be more dishevelled. Her fault, though, perhaps. Still, makes a nice justification for not dusting.

The longer she spends in the back streets, the more she forgets the river and the more she realises that even the underside of the right side is still too much – the shops are so expensive, the people arguing so much better dressed... even the vagrants have an air of superiority. How much is she being paid for this? Anyone who catches her eye seems to see straight through any pretence she might adopt on her own turf, and looks inside her, to a place where she feels uncertain. Or perhaps they judge her on her skin, since they are all so pale here, while she is like patinated copper. Her skin is like tanned leather, like a Turk's. She rolls down her sleeves, hitches the satchel onto her shoulder, and lets her eyes follow the cracks on the paving stones.

Myrsine should have come by bicycle – there's something about pedalling that calms the mind, and the shorter journey time means there is less chance that one's fragile and delicate mood will change between travelling to a task (which implies some kind of willingness) and arriving at it (when reluctance has gradually won out).

She stops at a drinking fountain, and approaches it from a number of angles, hoping to find one that doesn't risk getting her dress wet. Any angle will do, don't be so ridiculous. Stalling now? Why? Coy, now? Embarrassed? Ridiculous! Doesn't she live amongst people for whom modesty is anathema? Especially governing this kind of behaviour. And if there is one thing she is not uncertain of it is her body. She has seen enough nudes to know that her body is something to be proud of. Enough people have said so. Artists, for God's sake. Is it Lucia's body that disturbs her? No, not at all. Anyway, perhaps there will be none of that. Often it's a sisterly chat, or a game of cards. Sketching.

There is a bar run by Moroccans that she has been to. They know her there and like her, sensing a kindred spirit, and they don't raise an eyebrow when she wants a drink or two, so she slips in before it's too late.

There are rounds of cheerful hellos, chefs brought out to see her, curious looks from patrons. Generally, she would sit outside, but today she doesn't want to be overlooked, so she sits with the men playing games and smoking. They bring her a coffee, very bitter, even with sugar, and spiced. She orders pastis, which they don't have, but unusually they do have arak, which is fine.

Sitting alone she is the object of staring, but she has the protection of the staff who have sat her near the counter and who make slow, halting, but consistent conversation. This keeps the other men at bay. They ask her about the shop, about the authors who come in, and whether she knows of a string of writers whose names she cannot translate into words, let alone recognise. One of the waiters goes into the back and returns with a book, but it's in Arabic and she can't make that out either. She smiles anyway, and they press the book on her, waving away any attempts for her to give it back.

She pays and goes, to a mixture of cheerful farewells and suspicious stares, and on the street it is very bright again, and hot. There doesn't seem to be any point hanging around, so she goes to the apartment building and rings the bell.

After, on her way out, she meets James Joyce. He takes notes from his wallet with the manner of a man who has been waiting: he seems stiff and too focussed, his pleasantries are rehearsed, safe. When she comes across a busy man he's often too preoccupied with what he was doing before, or flustered by not expecting to see her, to be completely on his guard. She likes times like that, when things are said, or gestures made that are truer in some way than at other times, even if the meeting as a whole is more awkward. This meeting with Joyce is awkward, but more because he is playing out a scene, and the lines he's written for her are so banal and predictable that she can scarcely deliver them with any sincerity. Warm, isn't it? Yes, very. How are things at the shop? Fine, thank you. Any post? Not today. Thanks for this, we really appreciate it. It's nothing, and thank you.

In comparison to what she's just been doing, the exchanges suffer.

She's not a prude, but she's not a whore. When the money changes hands she does rather feel like a whore. Is one paid, after all, to visit a friend under the pretence of delivering post? No. Is one paid by one's friend's father to remove her drawers? No. Is one paid by one's friend's father to allow that friend to kiss her breasts? No. And, if one is, then what's to say that one isn't a prostitute to one's friend?

She wants to feel that it can't be prostitution if there aren't any men involved, but he is a man, with his pirate eye-patch and the nudges to the shoulder. Admittedly, he isn't in the room at the time, watching from a wardrobe, cock in hand, stroking, but he is somewhere nearby, drinking until his breath smells, and writing little plays for them both to act out.

Do they make the same bargain with Hélène and the others? If not, what is it about Myrsine that is so special? She is known for her charm and her efficiency – perhaps that is it – an excellent combination in a whore, charm and efficiency – nice and quick, cheap when paid by the hour, without sacrificing any of the fun.

He looks utterly guileless, though. Either he is a great actor, along with his other skills, or he simply does not know. Perhaps it is customary to pay for friends to keep lithe and troubled daughters company where he is used to living, and that the fondling and slipping in of fingers is a side issue, an agreement between two girls with nothing else to entertain them between ten and one daily. That is certainly nicer, more in keeping with the world as she wishes it were. Let it be that, then – terribly old fashioned to think of it in any other way, terribly reactionary, and she is neither of these things.

When his wallet is back in his jacket he is away and down the stairs almost instantly. Blown kisses farewell, and he leaves the odour of wine processing through his system and out in the sweat, and of cheap cigars.

She returns to the bookshop, past the Moroccans, but this time she crosses to the Left Bank as soon as she can, where the unease drifts away as if it was a function more of geography than morality.

I listened to him and kept my own counsel; after all, our first duty was to the recording of the find, and whatever secrets the tomb contained could be puzzled over together regardless of any differences in our motives. I took a pad and pencil of my own and began a brief sketch of the east wall, where instances of the deceased's life were combined with representations of various rituals carried out on her either before or after her death.

Then he speaks to you, and the Great Ennead

The body is placed in its coffin, which is in turn placed in a catafalque, protected by goddesses at the bow and the stern.

THE IB AND THE BA
OF LUCIA JOYCE

LES ATELIERS DU VIEUX COLOMBIER, PARIS, SUMMER 1927

This world is numerological, numbers having such great importance that they are counted every day. They are divided so that they are easier to manage into very small divisions for constant appreciation. There are larger and larger units so that more subtle sensations of numbering are catered for: the passage of an hour, that time between meals, day and night, menstrual cycles, tides and moons, religious observances, the progression of the seasons. These numbers are all measurable and relatable to each other over the course of a life. They are placed on top of the coursing of events, and are celebrated most loudly on the most numerical day of them all – the passage from one annual numeral to the next, and the beginning again of all things at the beginning, at the strike of midnight on New Year's Eve.

At this time, snow will fall on the slums and the numbers will mark the progression towards heaven of a slum child. She is close to death, and the excited reiteration of the numerals in sequence across the whole day makes inaudible her gradual and increasing deathliness. Those numbers rise in inverse relation to the numbers measured on a thermometer falling, if inserted rectally, indicating the gradual reduction in her core temperature, or, if mounted on a wall, the ambient temperature of the air.

Down snow falls in heavy flurries to drift and gather against the walls of her shack. It forms a rather picturesque scene not unlike that which would decorate a tin of biscuits, or a festive advertisement for cough syrup. The contrast between the presumed coldness of the snow, its pretty whiteness against the damp black wood, and the presumed warmth of the wan, yellow light coming through the window somehow evokes the Christian virtues of faith, hope and charity, and the pagan ones (now forgotten) simultaneously. All this is an illusion, of course, because there is no warming fire within this shack. How could there be? Any warmth would certainly cause the snow drifting against the poorly insulated walls to melt. It is only the fitful flickering of a candle stub, itself threatened by the girl child's laboured breathing as she attempts to instil in herself enough courage to leave the shack and attempt to sell her matches.

She is obliged to do this work for a number of reasons.

Firstly, one must work. Such is the number fetish of the culture that each participant in it must substitute their worth and effort for numbers allocated in fiat currency. The promisors of that currency oversee the distribution of those numbers on a largely arbitrary, though practically inescapable, scale depending on the historical prestige attached to various forms of employment, movement, or physical/mental activity.

Secondly, she works under duress – her guardian will beat her if she does not return with money, in coins and notes, sufficient to allow him to buy enough material to satisfy his requirements. These vary between drink, food, and the payment of debts for the late payment of which he will be beaten.

Thirdly, she has always done it, as far back as she can remember, so she will do it today.

Fourthly, she has been conditioned to believe she has no ability to question the way things are.

Fifthly, she no longer cares.

Sixthly, she will be dead soon anyway, so what difference does it make? Let it happen, for God's sake. There is only so much a child can bear, and if this is all the world has to offer then to hell with it and let her die in the street and the rats can have her.

When she opens the door the shack almost collapses – the joints were never properly fitted, the wood never properly cured, and her guardian is not the kind of man to pay attention to the remedial work a property requires to keep it in good condition. Quite the opposite: the effort required to make a single stitch and thereby save nine is more effort than he is prepared to make. Moreover, he is insensible to the world around him, dizzy through drink for the best part of the day and always on the verge of some terrible bodily emergency, whether it be the unwilling passing of motions, or the regurgitation of blood and bile, or some other ailment that causes him to grip the back of the chair and gasp. His situation is too pressing, certainly, for him to worry about the fitting of the door in its frame, or cracks in the glass window panes, or whether girl-children in his charge are this or that distance from death by starvation and exposure.

Once outside she is cold, but there is still a beauty in the falling of snow. She appreciates the way it lies on the streets and covers up the shite that covers up the mud that covers up the shite that she usually walks over. She has seen biscuit tins in the past, like we all have, and she has seen Father Christmas and his elves, like we all have, and she knows how closely this kind of precipitation is related to the giving of gifts and the being of good cheer, jingle bells, jingle bells, jingle all the way. Even if she has rarely experienced it, there is in her no less, probably more, appreciation of the wonder of it all.

Even as she teeters on the brink of collapse, the matches she is obliged to sell in a tray are suspended by straps across her shoulders. Her shoes are made of slum detritus – cardboard, elastic bands, scraps of rubber – and no use whatsoever against the snow.

We might imagine her catching a snow flake on her tongue, if we wish. We might imagine her smiling.

We might imagine also that she is not a starving girl, but a well-fed girl. She acts the part of a starving girl, not starving herself, but trying to seem starving. She is not hopeless, but represents hopelessness. Thus we alleviate any guilt on our part, replacing the question 'what should I do to help this child?' with the question 'is there any help I need provide?' and 'am I being hoodwinked?' We replace a starving child, who is deserving by any definition of the word, with a mythical undeserving child who has been put on the street, for example, by her gang master, to extract the charity of passers-by in a confidence trick it would be idiotic to fall for.

Both are true of this child in any case. She is starving, and any charity would be given to her gang master. Either way she will die, and the passers-by are little more than silhouettes to her – coiffures and hats, cigarettes and handbags, cossetted dogs held to the chest. They are all in shadows, lamplight drawing them against the walls as they pass. They are cold themselves, hungry themselves, hopeless themselves, differing from her only by degree, and there but for the grace of God go we, and all the sooner if we waste money we don't have on matches we don't need for children who misrepresent themselves on the street on New Year's Eve, when the numbers reach the end and begin again.

It is hard, though, to misrepresent death.

It is equally hard to represent oneself as having a conscience when one does not.

She cares about none of this: neither that they do not care for her, nor that they might be induced to care for her once she is dead. It is a condition of care that it comes after the event, when one can be sure it is merited and after there is any practical requirement on one to do anything except feel appalled. Feeling appalled is a very trivial matter, and something that can be done whilst going about one's normal business without it impacting too much.

When a man who has found himself without any matches – his daughter has surreptitiously taken them from the box, chewed them, and spat their remnants into the corner behind the bed – and now has no way of lighting his cigarette, comes to buy her matches then she is not paying attention. She is distracted by his opposite, by the people who pass by and do not want to buy her matches. She turns to follow them, looking for any sign that they might want the matches, determined not to miss her saviours through inattention. In striving so hard for their attention she misses the man who can save her. He is always behind her, pantomimically, when she turns. When he tries to attract her attention he fails because she is whirling about like a dervish after people who wish to ignore her. When he taps her on the shoulder she is so numb with cold that she doesn't feel it. He gives up and goes to a nearby bar, where it is easier to get a light.

He goes into this bar and he goes into his own hell, for he, despite his almost saving this girl, or almost contributing to her saving, is in trouble himself. He has something that someone wants, something they are willing to take by force. Or he does not have the thing he is supposed to have, and for which he has already received money, but has gambled it away. Or he has lost the thing that was given into his charge and no amount of hiding in bars and smoking cigarettes is liable to save him. It might even bring him to the attention of the men he is hiding from, and they will torture him, something that this girl cannot complain of. She has nothing, her guardian has nothing, so they will be allowed to die in peace and will not have to suffer thumbscrews, and kneecappings, and threats against their children.

So, if this world of numbers is cruel, it is cruel in a largely even-handed way, and the starving girl need not think she is alone in this.

There is justice, then, of a sort, and here is a policeman, amongst the men in hats and women in coats and toy poodles carried to the breast. Against the panes of lit glass which separate the starving girl from the world of warmth behind them, there is an officer of the law. His attention is turned to the match girl.

Is it a crime to be a seller of matches? Is it tantamount to vagrancy to be close to death and unable to convince others that they need matches and might buy them from her? The statutes and bylaws are mysterious even in one's own country, and who is to say what is and what is not prohibited in this land, which is like ours, but also different. It is different in the uniforms, in the architecture, in its attitude, possibly, to cold, starving girl-children.

He does not seem to be intent on arresting her, so perhaps this is a more liberal regime than we imagine. Perhaps here the agents of the state roam the streets looking for unfortunates to rescue, rather than miscreants to bring to book. That would be a great thing, if it were true, we will all agree. If we, as a people, could turn our resources to the rescuing of starving children it would be wonderful, but he is neither rescuing, nor arresting – he hovers, watching from a distance, then drawing close, as if considering the possibilities before settling on one.

She, as with most things, does not notice him. Now she presses her nose instead against the glass, frosted already on one side by the gathering of the water vapour from the warm breath of the people within as it meets the cold glass. It is frosted now by her own breath, which she wipes away with stiff fingers. The glass is obscured by the breath on both sides, opaque as if she has cataracts, equally blind are the people inside, to whom she is nothing but a shape. She could be anything – a pile of boxes, a sack of coal, a shadow of some smaller or larger object lit from behind and at a distance. She need not be a child, certainly, who has substance in the world, even when she is frail and dying.

She switches to another pane and here, by some fluke, she can see in. When the rag with which a pane of glass is wiped is greasy, this grease can transfer to the glass. If that grease is clear (if it is linseed oil, for example, rather than lard) it can both go unnoticed and also prevent the gathering of water vapour. It prevents the fogging that might otherwise obscure the movement of light. If she keeps wiping off her breath as she breathes, she can see in now.

Inside there are wonderful things – beautiful men and smiling women, dresses and jackets, cossetting of dogs, drinking from flutes, pampering by servants and slaves who have been conditioned to smile through their servitude, and who exist in a regime so lax that, once their masters turn their backs, the slaves can snigger and offer their low opinions of the assembled to each other without it resulting in their torture, or expulsion into the snow. The monocle is particularly frowned on, and laughed at, though amongst the rulers this affectation is a sign of great status, providing it is not undercut by contradictory indicators of low status, such as poorly polished footwear.

There is an excess of cake, and this draws the starving child's attention. So hungry is she that it isn't the sweetness of the thing that particularly entrances her, despite that being what marks cake out as desirable, it is the amount of it on offer. She is attracted by the presumed mass of it, imagining what that amount of food would feel like in her stomach. In reality, to fill a starving and empty stomach with food of this richness would certainly result in vomiting, perhaps even hypophosphatemia in the long term, but there is no reality in which this child would be allowed access to the cake, so the question is moot.

Now the policeman is over her shoulder, attempting to see what she sees.

When they have seen the same thing, the policeman finds something in her behaviour that is actionable by an officer of the law – she should not consider stealing those things which do not belong to her, not unless she wants to get on the wrong side of him. With this warning he withdraws to a distance again.

She returns her eye to the glass, hoping for one more glance of the food, as if its nutrition is transmissible optically, but before she can see it she feels the chill and light concussion of snowballs, which have been aimed at her and thrown by two naughty boys.

A child, even a starving one, is like a kitten: it is wont to play given the opportunity. Play is a kind of reflex. It may be that a child will play at snow fighting up to the point of death. We can certainly imagine such a situation, even if it isn't one we can empirically prove, and the girl's reflex is not yet so dulled that she can ignore it. Consequently, she picks up powdered snow, wads it together, and returns fire.

This might provoke a pleasant scene in the mind: children playing in the snow. Let us imagine squeals and laughter, mock indignation and mock aggression, all in the context of a good natured expression of high-spirits. If we wish, we might see this as an outpouring of the dying girl's humanity, irrepressible even under the harshest of conditions.

This is certainly a supportable reading.

However, we must remember that snow is formed from solid water, and that the body temperature of even the coldest living child is capable of melting snow back into liquid. We should also remember that, once wet, matches are useless for their primary function; they will not strike and go alight. We should also remember that when powdered snow is balled it does not remain balled on impact, but rather scatters about.

Bearing all this in mind, we can see that the snowballs will disintegrate into the tray of match boxes that the girl has close to her chest. We will understand that it is impossible to sell wet matches, and that the girl's life depends on her selling her matches. By wetting a proportion of the matches (not all, as we shall see later) she thereby reduces the chances that she will live out the night.

We can see, then, that her playfulness is also fatal, and that along with the other factors that combine to see her dead, her childishness in this regard is not without its consequences. It is tragic, in fact, and/or ironic, that her childish nature should result in her death as a child.

The game causes a nuisance to passers-by and the policeman returns to issue a ticket for loitering, a ticket for littering (a certain number of matchboxes were dropped in the game) and a demand that she move on.

Move on, black lips.

Move on, dancer.

In the next window, Chinese dolls. Dance for him with your hands clasped behind your back. Spin in the way a carousel spins. Horses impaled through the sternum with a spiral gold rod. Ride at a gallop. Names calligraphed, illuminated at the initial, soldiers and drums, soldiers and beards, strings of gems like the curtain that separates the front from the rear of a butcher's shop, horse meat smoked and salted.

—You have on the wrong shoes for this type of weather and consequently must go home.

Is there a law against inappropriate footwear? If so, to whom is the law
addressed? Which party is punishable under it? Is it she that wears the
inappropriate footwear, or he that provides the inappropriate footwear? To
whom is recourse made, under the law? There is certainly no point going
to a dying girl in the snow – if she had appropriate footwear she would
wear it, and there is none at home. If she returns home without money she
will have what little remains of her life beaten out of her. The question of
who wears what shoes will not arise under any circumstances, regardless
of any citation written, since her guardian cannot read. Even when sober.
He would not read anything provided by this girl unless it were the date
stamped on a coin, or the promises printed on a bank note.

She moves on.

In one panel the deceased was shown surrounded by priests. Egyptian paintings, while figurative, are also ritualised, and their ritual function outweighs any overweening commitment to verisimilitude; expressions are always neutral, the better to preserve the likenesses of individuals, and types are all depicted the same so their function is recognised in the afterlife. So, these priests all appeared the same and all expressionless, and on the surface the scene was innocuous enough. The face of the deceased, of course, was scored out, but the positioning of her limbs was unusual. There are certain gestures and poses that symbolise certain emotions and the deceased was depicted in a supplicative, or fearful, pose, as if she was resistant to the attentions of these priests. If she had committed a crime and was called before an authority for her punishment she might have appeared like this, but she was surrounded by those who would have been paid to attend to her needs in the afterlife.

*Among the living
hears it on this day*

The coffin is inscribed
with texts helpful to
the deceased in her
journey through
the Duat.

STAFF OF THE INSTITUTE
OUTSIDE GENEVA, JULY 1934

It's been a nightmare ever since Miss Joyce moved here. I know we made mistakes, but then we didn't know what we were doing. You can't expect to get it right first time, or really know what went right and what went wrong until you've seen it done properly.

We'd only read it in books.

We used the wet room, which was where we bathed and showered her, and sometimes where we laundered the sheets. It's about the size of a decent dining room – twenty by twenty, something like that – and tiled in green.

The bath is a long concrete trough, not too high. It takes a lot of water to fill it, so the taps are like old-style pumps, something that you might see at one end of a horse trough in a western. They don't need pumping – one is on the mains and the other draws from an immersion in the room above – this was a godsend, so we thought, because it meant we didn't have to heat the water and bring it in.

There are showers at one end, sinks, and the whole room drains into a grate in the middle so that you only have to sweep the water from the sides with a stiff broom to do a decent job of drying down. There are no windows to open – light comes from electric strip lights in the ceiling, and the steam goes out through vents. It smells a bit fusty most of the time, but we bleach it regularly and it never gets too bad.

We planned to do it in the afternoon – morning and evening would be too busy, and it was a quiet time for most of us, being when they'd have their after lunch nap – which was another consideration – you've got to feed them eventually or it affects their mood, and the book said no food for two to three hours before, and to make sure she'd evacuated her bladder and bowels.

The aim is to get their temperature up high as if they are in a fever – the book the doctor read was very praising of a fever's ability to cure almost anything. A fever burns away bacteria and viruses, it purges toxins through the skin, carries them away in the sweat, and it puts the body and mind back to square one, letting it build itself back up to normal when the fever goes. It has a kind of sense to it, though we all wondered what use that was likely to be to a mental case.

In our experience, mental cases aren't caused by viruses or infections, but by problems in the person themselves. No amount of getting hot is going to sort that out.

The book said to fill a bath with hot water at a temperature of 95°F and then slowly raise the temperature to 105°F and to keep it there for an hour. This wasn't too difficult since you can dial a temperature on the immersion and the thermometer in the tank turns the light off when it's right. We left one of us in the boiler room – so to speak: it's more like a glorified airing cupboard – so they could sit there and keep an eye on that side of things. That was a cushy job, we all thought.

If we could have filled the bath in one go with 105°F water that would have been easy, and if water didn't naturally cool down, that would have been easier still, but as it was we had to start with 95°F water and then raise it and keep it there. What we decided on was to leave the tap running on a bath of water at 95°F and keep refilling 105°F water until it was done. Rather than let the plughole drain the bath, which would have caused problems with it running out too fast or slow, we bunged the overflow pipe up with cloth, left the plug in and decided to let the water spill over. One of us was there to broom it down the drain.

We started off with the three of us: one in the airing cupboard, one with the broom, and one to take care of the bath, but as soon as Miss Joyce came in we got an inkling that this wasn't going to be enough. She was in her bathers, so we didn't have to strip her at least, but she did not want to get in the bath. It was too hot, she said. Right enough it was hot: the hot tap had been running for a while, but we hadn't thought that it might be too hot to get straight in. Fair enough – that was a mistake. Some people prefer to get in the bath when it's luke and then add the hot until it gets to the right temperature. Anyway, she put one foot in and then wouldn't come near again. She went over to the corner and pushed herself back against the wall, staring us all down like she was going to fight if we came to put her in.

This was only a couple of minutes in.

We know enough, from hard experience, to understand that there's no underestimating a patient when she gets it into her mind that she doesn't want to do something, even if she is as skinny as a handful of pipe-cleaners, so I went and called for reinforcements.

When they arrived I slipped the lock and let them in.

—Can't they give her a sedative?

Possibly they could, but bathing patients is our job and most doctors don't appreciate writing a script out just to make our jobs easier. And I didn't want to ask since the doctor on the rota had a reputation (as it turns out, he would have been fine with it – he certainly was the next time – but there you go). So we rounded on her, one from the left, one from the right and I went down the middle.

It's best to be polite and pleasant in matters like this, and you can avoid a lot of wrestling with a few nice kind words. It's like when you want to get a horse into a horse box, or a child into its bed – there's no point shouting at them.

Not all of us feel the same way though, and each to his own, but I always put a stop to any cursing and rough treatment on my shifts and everyone knows that well enough by now. That said, this was one occasion when I was tempted myself to have words with the madam.

Whether she was doing it on purpose or not, she had an uncanny knack of finding sensitive areas with an elbow, or knee. She wasn't making it easy on herself, and though we are professional enough not to let little accidents affect the way we carry out our duties, we certainly weren't of a mind to let her wilful behaviour win the day.

Once we'd got her out of the corner and into the bath, that wasn't the half of it. Putting her in the bath spilled a good quantity of water about the place on its own, but she thrashed like a cat in a bag once she was in. We had her by the shoulders and knees, but the bath was half empty in no time. She kept making waves, and when we tried to keep her still and hold her beneath what water was left it made her face go under, which she really didn't like… more so than anything else.

Soon there was barely any water in the bath for her to be held under and we were soaked and also very hot and bothered – the place was like a sauna – so when there was a lull we let her sit up while the bath filled again.

She was much quieter for that time; whether she'd seen the error of her ways, or was exhausted from the struggle, or whether the hot water was doing its job, we didn't care. But as far as the treatment went, this was another mistake – we didn't get her to a temperature of 95°F and then gradually raise the temperature to 105°F. Whether this was important in terms of its medical effect we weren't qualified to judge, but it was the first thing we were asked to do, and we hadn't done it. All the water was coming in at 105°F and there wasn't a great deal we could do about it. Actually, it wasn't the first thing we were told to do – she hadn't had breakfast and lunch, we got that right, but now was the time that one of the others pointed out that she hadn't evacuated her bladder and bowels – she'd been asked to, but said she wasn't ready.

Anyway, we'll draw a veil over that.

When the bath was filled with fresh hot water we were already in there for half an hour and some of us were getting overheated – they went out, leaving me and one other to carry on.

Now, the treatment requires that the patient lies beneath the water with as much of herself under as possible – all the body from head to toe, except the nose and mouth, and then only the minimum necessary for breathing. Whoever's idea this was must only have been thinking of doing it to people who, by and large, are co-operative and who don't mind having their face under water. I don't like having my own face under the water, and I know lots of people who feel the same. I think most people would get panicky if they had to lie for an hour in boiling water with only their lips and nose poking out.

So, I can understand why she wouldn't like it, but we had our orders and this is what we were ordered to do.

By now she was a bit drowsier than she had been, and a bit more compliant, but she was also slippier and anyone who has seen someone having a nightmare will know that no matter how drowsy you are, you can still thrash about. I made the decision to get in the bath with her, to straddle her, and, with the help of the other attendant, to hold her head and face mostly under the water. I stripped down to my underwear, which was the only sensible thing to do in the circumstances, and, while my colleague subdued her a little bit, I climbed in.

Now, one of us was supposed to rub her skin with a hard brush and so bring the blood to the surface where it could pick up the heat and thereby create the fever that was going to make her better, but no-one had a hand free. It would have been hard in any case to get it rubbed on her, and she was still in her swimmers and neither of us felt right getting them off her, so we left out that part of the treatment too.

The water was very hot, as I've pointed out, and the parts of me that were under were red as a lobster and this seemed to amuse my colleague enormously, and though it's easy from a distance to say that this was unprofessional behaviour, it was also a very farcical situation, and we are only human.

Most people are not required, in the run of their daily jobs, to strip off and get in the bath with mad women and hold them until they go into a fever, so a certain amount of leeway must be given. None of us had done any of this before; we were given orders and we tried, to the best of our abilities, to follow them through with the equipment we had at our disposal.

We did keep her there for the hour, and for most of it she was very well behaved, very still, and even if we must have looked ridiculous, as I freely admit, and that the things we did were unusual, the treatment itself was unusual and that if the doctor had any better suggestions he should have given them to us before we began, when they would have been useful, not standing in the doorway to the wet room an hour and a half after the procedure started and when I'm in my pants and the other attendant was soaked through.

It's certainly not right to suggest there was any funny business going on – I'm a married man, in the eyes of God, and no-one should think that either of us were doing anything other than what we were paid to do, and if she says any different she is either lying or has misremembered. Or she is too mad to understand what was happening to her. If there's any issue with my honesty being called into question then I suggest the authorities look into my record, speak to my manager, and remember not to jump to conclusions.

Anyway, from this point on no-one will be using that technique. None of my colleagues will agree to cover that work, and if the doctor tries to insist then he will need to find qualified staff in that procedure, since he clearly doesn't think we're qualified to do it.

There are alternatives, too. Having spoken to colleagues it would be better to raise the temperature by using electric blankets – that way the patient could be kept restrained in bed, where she no doubt prefers to be, and an electric under-blanket put on and then sheets, then a plastic sheet (an incontinence sheet would work well) on top. The patient should be dressed in warm pyjamas, socks, and a woollen hat, then another electric blanket put on top of her. It would be much easier to monitor the temperature that way too, without the attendants having to do it via the water, and also her pulse – something the doctor should have had us do the first time round (it shouldn't go over 140) but which he forgot.

If she struggled it would be much easier to hold her down in bed rather than in the bath, and there would be no need to get undressed at all, unlike in water where you can't just get into the bath with your clothes, shoes and watch on. You have to strip down, regardless of what that might look like to the unsuspecting onlooker.

You'd have to look out for the flex and make sure it didn't pull the plug out of the socket, but that's easy compared to a water bath, and the doctor, if he's so good at watching over everyone, as he makes out, could watch to make sure the plug doesn't come out while the attendants are busy making sure his precious patient keeps hot. It's no doubt the kind of job a doctor is suited to, one which means he doesn't have to get his hands dirty and instead can just give the fruits of his enormous wisdom to everyone around him and do what he does best, which is to know it all without having to do any of it.

If electric blankets are too expensive, another way is to give the patient malaria and let the fever raise her temperature. None of us knows how that would work, but you can get the malaria bug and inject it into a patient and then let them have the fever, then cure the fever with quinine. No doubt the doctor will consider this far preferable than to rely on us, who he doesn't seem to have any faith in. He prefers to believe in the ramblings of a mad woman than to trust people who have been employed here for the best part of twenty years.

Whatever he tries, he shouldn't rely on the patient taking any of it lying down – she hates all of this stuff with a vengeance and complains of the heat even if the window is closed when it is raining – she needs her fresh air and will not be deprived of it. She is, in general, a very difficult customer, whether it's me looking after her or anyone else. To suggest anything different is just showing his ignorance. We are aware he is new, but that excuse only works for so long, and if he knows he's new why doesn't he understand to rely on us old hands a bit more and support us where we need support? Especially since we were only obeying his orders. It's not our fault if he orders us to do things that are impossible, or which require us to do unusual things.

In any case – she's back in her room and shows no sign of getting better.

I called my colleague over and asked him for his opinion. He made some joke or other, the exact wording of which I can't remember, but it was something in poor taste. However, in that infuriating way he had, he indicated something in the inscriptions that I had missed.

May Geb be gracious to you

On the day of burial the catafalque is dragged by men and oxen to the tomb site, accompanied by mourners who beat their breasts in sorrow. The dance of the *muu*-dancers is performed at the door.

THE IB OF LUCIA JOYCE
LES ATELIERS DU VIEUX COLOMBIER, PARIS, SUMMER 1927 (CONT.)

She is surrounded by white, as if she is within a white balloon, the extent of which is vast, practically infinite, since there are no edges of it for her to reach.

If she walks or runs or gallops across its inner surface she will never meet an obstruction. But this is only an illusion brought on by cold and the snow cover. Eventually she comes to a single plank left at an angle between 45° and 60° to the ground leaning against the wall, and she sits under it.

If one spreads out one's fingers – perhaps do it now… no need to stretch, lightly is fine – the plank is as wide as the distance between your thumb and the outer edge of your little finger. If you cannot be induced to do the things you are asked to do, then imagine five, six, seven or eight inches depending on the size of your hand – then that would be the width of the plank, which is not, no matter what size your hands might be, wide enough to protect a dying girl from snowfall.

Even if it were wide enough, the cold wind would find no impediment from it, nor the snowfall on which she sits. Just as this insufficient shelter seems to be all that she has, that too is taken away by a person from the other side of the fence – to be used to make their own shelter, no doubt. It's too late anyway – she has fallen into a reverie, this girl – the kind of reverie one falls into immediately preceding death, where the wishes one has are granted by God in the only way that remains, as a kind of hallucination on the themes of one's desire, such as a drowning sailor experiences after capsizing at sea.

She sits and her black coat turns white with snow. The night that surrounds her turns white as her brain is deprived of oxygen; she has stopped troubling to breathe. She has entered a waking REM state in which she will live out whatever time is left to her.

Bearing this in mind, she takes a match from the box and places it between her molars on the right side of her mouth and then takes another and attempts to light it. It is wet and should not light, but it goes alight regardless – phosphorus is a marvellous element, particularly in a dream. It can be induced to do anything, light-bringer, and no slight dampness will put it off, but it is not hot, or at least not hot enough. She cups it in her hands and attempts to receive warmth from it sufficient to save her life. It dwindles even as the matchstick blackens. She crunches down hard and lets the bitterness of the other match head slick in the back of her mouth. She lets the saliva carry it across the back of her tongue, down her throat, and grinds the rest in splinters. She fills her mouth, her sinuses, her oesophagus with the flavour of phosphorous, and pricks iron blood from her ears, from the Eustachian tube, where the splinters pierce.

She takes two more matches since the first two didn't warm her and the one she lights she takes to warm her lips and before her eyes it becomes a sparkler. Iron filings are spooned into the flame of a Bunsen burner, the appearance of molten metal, all the light of it but none of the heat, sparks hitting her lips, hitting her cheeks, but even these bear no heat. The burning is restricted to the metal from which the sparks jump, and which scars the fingers if one grabs it, leaves white lines in the black dirt, and which should be discarded directly onto the wet ground once it has burned out, or handled with gloves, although not wool or cotton, the fibres of which will catch.

As it dies it blurs, and the third match, once lit, it is a Christmas tree, blurred and haloed, around which gifts are traditionally left for children to discover in the morning with the cheerful lie that there is a man who will provide presents in the expectation of absolutely nothing. Perhaps sherry, perhaps a mince pie. Carrots for his reindeer. He will not bear down on you amidst the wrapping paper and scrape your neck with his stubble and hurriedly rearrange his dressing gown at the sound of creaking footsteps on the stairs. He will not take on the appearance of someone who expects a little favour, to say thank you on this festive morning, and you've done it before so you know what to do.

And you are grateful, although not to him, that there is a Father Christmas. The proof is in the brilliant toys he leaves and not in the taste left of sherry.

God knows it's possible to ignore those things, isn't it?

Become someone for whom those things did not happen. Thank God for that transformation.

The match flame transforms again, into a shape prompted by the dissolution into formlessness of a Christmas tree, its colour remaining, its dimensions, the proportions one might recognise when the glasses are removed, but not the tree anymore. It's not Christmas anymore, even as you reach for it. It is that bleak night time between Christmas Day and Boxing Day where the effort that has been made to act proper in front of relatives has been relieved once they are gone, or asleep, and that relief has to be experienced somehow in the bear, and the bare, and the new teddy bear, and in the bearing down.

She sleeps through it, dies through it, lying in the snow. Cheek to the pillow, head amongst the matchboxes, hair amongst the matches, splinters in the corner of her mouth, slivers in the jaw, shiverless in the cold.

When she wakes it is to another world entirely, another place, another self, a wall of blackness, but warm in the absence of snow. She dances her limbs free of stiffness and comes to a wall of hanging silk, white again, but the whiteness acceptable now. She parts the silk sheets like ghosts, running open-armed into them, dissolving them in her eagerness.

She falls into a toy shop and she is herself the size of a toy, so that a ball is huge to her, and boxed dolls are approximately equal to her in height. They are terribly severe, at this scale, very stern of face and proud of their beauty in a way which excludes the possibility that she possesses any of her own. This arrogance is acceptable when it is worn by someone twelve inches high and made of porcelain, but in a full-sized being who, she presumes, is of the same existential order she is, it is a little intimidating. It is enervating, and to make it worse there are two of them (and who knows how many more in the store room) and they can affirm their own beauty to each other at her expense, leaving her without anyone to affirm her in opposition to them.

Regardless, they are beautiful, and this world is beautiful, and perhaps a small place, cowed, in a world like this would be a beautiful thing to have.

Their dresses are white silk, hemmed in black.

There is a ballerina here, also, skewered through the coccyx on a spike, dancing around her impalement as if it were not there, as if it had never happened. The burning and tearing are borne in good spirits, which is possible, thank God, for her, since otherwise a wound of that kind would be fatal. It may even be that this wounding is the thing that allows her to be the beautiful thing that she is, because can a girl spin endlessly and dance so committedly a single dance to a single tune for all her days if she doesn't bear that wound? Would an unwounded girl have the discipline over the self that the bearing of such wounds requires necessary to ignore the pain that occupations such as 'ballerina' demand of the child?

It is just an idea, one of many that runs through the mind of a frozen match girl as she dies and her soul finds ways to make sense of the bitter little life she has been given.

And here is the spinning bear.

And here is the policeman, reborn as a jack-in-the-box.

And here is another doll, beautiful again, barely applying powder to her cheeks, the rotation of her shoulder scarcely enough to bring the powder puff in contact with the wooden skin. When she combs her hair there are only three teeth to the comb and her hair is a single undifferentiated mass which would not accept a comb, or a brush. Her ministrations to herself have the desired effect, though, for she is undoubtedly beautiful, though the girl wonders if she could save herself the effort and still remain as beautiful.

There is a spinning top, erratic and persistent, striped and coloured when still, but flickering and indistinct once put into motion. The speed at which it rotates is barely comprehensible; there is no landmark that the eye can find, no spot on which eyes can fixate. If there is, it is beyond the discrimination of the eyes of a dead girl – instead everything is a drunken blur distilled into a single object.

If one attempts to grab it, it races off in an unpredictable direction at the merest touch of a fingertip. No doubt someone of enormous acuity of vision could see enough to pick out the angles of the objects that interfere with the spinning and, with rough calculations made on the back of a beer mat, could determine where it would go next, but there is no such person in this world. Nor is there any calculus, nor vectors, nor science. There are only the vague incoherencies that mark the longings of a young girl. It is enough for her that this thing exists in whatever state it exists in, and whether it sublimates between one state and a higher state is a matter for her God, and it is yet to be determined who that God is, or what his intentions are.

She stares at the spinning top, imagines the ballerina spinning, then the carousel, then the ball and bear. Into this shop window, this Santa's grotto, comes a train, comes Father Christmas and his sleigh, comes a wall of skulls and a wooden duck. It is a parade of grotesques which are also neither one thing nor another; they are both childish and fevered, bearing the marks of her innocence and also a febrile anxiety that all is not what it seems. There is the pernicious edge that all pleasurable things take on in the understanding that they may be the outliers of experiences that will tend to be much worse. They are merely introductions, first acts for crimes against the person. In short, they are bait to which the girl is drawn in the hope that she will reach a hand out for them. Then her wrist will be grabbed and, when their function is fulfilled, they will be withdrawn, only to be returned *post factum* as a means of denying there was ever anything terrible committed – see, the world is a wonderful place after all, just the place for children, and if these pretty things exist nothing can be as bad as you are making out can it? And stop your crying, I'm not all bad. And stop your crying, or I'll give you something to cry about, you ungrateful little so-and-so, you're ruining Christmas.

Then there is the drumming and drilling of soldiers – wooden little men who are utterly incapable of atrocities by virtue of their size, and hence are the perfect presents for children. They contain both the idea of death and murder, but also the shininess of brass and miniaturisation, so that the child can feel herself both a part of a world in which these things are done, in her name, for her good, but also be in control of those things. Then later, after the lights are out, or when under the threat of an invading army, those things that happen will be seen to be in the normal run of things. This understanding will induce in her a confused paralysis that may be misconstrued as acquiescence, even when the perpetrators know that it is not.

Drumming and drilling and bayonets, fusiliers rigidly addressing themselves to their flutes, the music of battle, too high-pitched to evoke fear, but laying the tracks in the mind, in the self, in the behaviours that will eventually allow an army, friendly or unfriendly, to reap the benefit as they move in across France and she is confined to her bed, strapped down in the absence of her guardians.

These soldiers circle like a carousel, too quickly to distinguish one from the other, like the blocks of colour on a spinning top, too quickly for the eyes, and they present arms to whom we also cannot see, because these soldiers block our line of sight, or perhaps it is the fog of war. She cannot tell to whom these soldiers answer – Napoleon, probably, or to Alexander of Macedon. Or to someone else who is only a name in a book, but by virtue of the typesetter troubling to arrange the letters in such a way that they spell out his name he is enshrined in the history of all things that happen and will happen.

He is someone worthy of having arms addressed to him.

They wear the conical hats of dunces, but inverted in shape and colour, perched so the point must exist somewhere within the frontal lobe, lobotomising these men so that they will be able to do the things Napoleon asks of them without question. The tip of the hat embeds where the facility for ethical action was once located. It lodges where the understanding that we must answer, first and foremost to those around us and use our own discretion in matters of violence is. We should not simply do that which our betters order us to do, but these helmets are proof against that fact, that collection of neurons. You can see in their blank expressions that this is the case, and so who knows what these soldiers will do when ordered – absolutely anything.

And here is a bear drinking sherry on Christmas day after Mother has retired with a migraine.

And here is a rabbit emerging from a hat.

And here is an individual soldier, this one with a floppy cap and brass buttons carrying a curved sword. Is he different then, this one? His cap is impossible to use as a lobotomiser, his sword has succumbed to some influence that reduces its straightness, some eastern element perhaps. If the orient and occident are so opposite, as the war suggests they must be, is this influence away from the absence of empathy and towards love? Not too much to render him impotent, but enough to curve his sword?

Now he offers her his hand, touches her hand, and certainly he does not ask permission, but neither does he grab her by the wrist and pull. Nor is this initial touch merely the prelude to violence; he seems to offer her the choice – would you like to come with me? And as a soldier this choice-offering is already significant. If he wished to make use of her, he need only do so.

No trickery is required.

Unless he is of that class of men who can only receive pleasure in the knowledge that psychological pain is suffered by the partner in the activity.

Such men offer something good, only to snatch it away. They promise respite, only to go at it harder, hammer and tongs, with glee in their eye and spittle on their lower lip where the hair grows.

Not this soldier though, and when she allows the touch there is the spontaneous generation of triangular hills, formless sheep, and hunger where previously there had been only the spiritual functions remaining to the dead girl. Hunger is a kind of hope to her, a hope that the death and passage into a realm where earthly matters are irrelevant is not irreversible. Instead, here is the need for food, which only a live girl feels. Here are sweetmeats, and wine and roast turkey, and all the things that soldiers feast on after battle and that are provided for the common weal on feast days. Here are crackers and party hats and thimbles, and jokes that raise only weak smiles and groans, but which nonetheless distract people from the satisfaction of their unholy desires at least long enough for some minor sense of relief to settle in the bones of children, even if this works against them in the end, when it is all overturned again.

And, indeed, here comes an end to the fun before it is even begun. A spoilsport makes himself appear in the shop, amongst the toys. He is raven-limp, washboard-chested, diamond-legged, helmeted, skull-bearing, and the knife she has taken in order to carve for herself turkey, or ham, or a piece of pudding, this he objects to.

—Put down the knife.

He says this and then:

—I am death.

And we see where this has been going all along, and should we be surprised?

It may well be that the reverie at the end of life takes the desires of the victim as its theme, but which god would control it if not Death?

Should the living God control it? Of course not.

God's remit, if he can be said to claim one, is life, eternal and fleeting, and the monitoring of the events of it. Death he delegates to a secondary figure, and of course it would be he that oversaw the air-starved delusions suffered by dying children as they freeze. The movement of events will be towards his introduction. The story of the dream mimics that of life itself. All events lead, some more and some less causally, towards the end point at which life ends.

And so it proves, since feathered Death leers close now to the girl, unhindered by the soldier, of whom Death has no fear. Death has seen him on the battlefield and knows him and understands that this soldier cannot bring death to Death, unless it only be the death of others. In this he is a colleague, a compatriot, a partisan for Death's cause, which is to bring an end to all things.

All toys die, all carousels cease, soldiers are killed in action, and they go into the sky and dwell there for eternity, and it is to the sky that the spoilsport chases the girl, the soldier vouchsafing for her, despite that being a promise he is ill-equipped to keep.

They take horses, one for the two of them, and one for the spoilsport. Here the two (the lovers?) will always be at a disadvantage against the spoilsport: they are burdened by each other, by the sense of attachment and of love, where he need only think of himself, and the execution of his work. Death's unburdened horse is not handicapped by the weight of their togetherness, and Death loves his horse and cossets it, whereas the lovers are too concerned with the safety of each other to pay the horse the attention it deserves. They already impose on its good nature by both riding on its single back. Death can afford to let the horse run at its leisure, but the lovers must spur the horse forward if they hope to escape, to force it to run past its inbuilt tolerances and against its specifications. Thus, in love, there is a cruelty that is not present in the spiteless prosecution of the death wish, which may only be seen to be cruel from a distance, the picture close to being one of indifference at worst.

There is no practical way for a horse to remain in the clouds, let alone for it to be ridden there – the horse is naturally a creature of the plains and is not, by any stretch of taxonomical law, a bird or flying mammal, unless it be a mythological creature such as a Pegasus, or the winged ox of St Luke, or the winged bull of Gilgamesh, or a harpy, or some other fictional invention. So the presence of these horses in the skies can only be a function of oxygen deprivation, yet there they are, for this girl. The water vapour that obscures one's vision through the glass in the windows of a shop or bar is here sufficient to facilitate an attempt to escape the inevitability of death: it becomes solid clouds.

The fact remains, though, that all games must cease. There is in the universe an inbuilt tendency for spoilsports to end a child's games, and force them back to the world that *is*, rather than the one they might wish for.

Yet that is not to say she should not fight for her wishes. This the soldier does on her behalf, that being within the skill set of his profession. Though it might seem contradictory for him to raise his sword against Death, for whom he has always been a faithful servant, he does so in his love for the girl.

Impromptu that love seems, and so utterly selfless it can only be the fancy of a child whose experience of men has always been that they are utterly selfish and indifferent to her pleasure or suffering. It is not entirely convincing, even to the girl, and perhaps that is why she falls, suddenly sensing the phantastic provenance of his actions, and the scenario he is reacting to. It is enough to distract her anyway from the very difficult business of remaining on a horse that flies through the clouds. Its gait is no doubt affected by the lack of solid footing. It tires. It has been ill-treated. It is, perhaps, not the easiest creature to ride.

She falls. Even in a world like this there can only be one outcome of a fall from this height, or what purpose is there of being high, if it does not entail death for one who comes suddenly from high to low and meets the ground?

Once dead, Death gathers her up, and to be doubly dead like this – dead in the snow and dead in one's own experience of the processes of death, is to be dead indeed, since there is no place to go except on to the realm of the dead. If she were hoping for an Egyptian afterlife, or an Assyrian afterlife, or a Greek afterlife, as the iconography of her reverie might suggest, she does not find it. Instead there is a green hill far away without a city wall, where our dear child is represented to us by a crucifix.

There a tuft of hair, caught on the splinters from the cheap wood, and a lack of care taken in the sanding, or no sanding at all, the effort being wasted on her, and the wood raw from the joiner's yard, or the timber yard, just right for the catching of threads and hair and the scratching of skin.

A crucifix is both a symbol of death and life, since it was from here that Christ was risen. And now a tree grows from the dead girl's crucifix, from the womb of it, and the hair that adheres to this womb is transformed into a bush of pubic hair from which white roses grow and the petals of these roses, now mature in death where they were buds unopened in life, fall ripely like snow. Then snow falls like petals and, around the corpse of the child, shawled women gather to witness her death. They are like those that witnessed the death of Christ, except that to these women the girl is an idiot, not a saviour, a moron who deserves her death, since, as they say to each other:

—Only a fool thinks she can warm herself with matches.

The Egyptian system of writing is complicated – sometimes pictographs are to be read symbolically, sometimes an alphabetic substitution is employed, sometimes combinations of signs have specific meanings or functions, and sometimes the images are simply descriptive. Amongst the other writing there recurred at intervals an object like those depicted in the much later tomb at Kom Ombo and which are understood to be medical instruments.

My colleague had made one of his characteristic intellectual leaps and suggested that if this object was a scalpel, or something similar, and these priests were charged with carrying out a medical procedure which the deceased was resisting, then this might fit the paintings, though what function that could have in the tomb decorations was something he could not guess.

And give you your head

At the rear of the
procession, the
household slaves bring
the canopic jars,
dragged on a sledge, and behind these come
the personal effects, the bed and the chair.

THE SHUYET SHADOW
OF LUCIA JOYCE
NEAR L'ÎLE DE PUTEAUX, PARIS,
1934 (FOR EXAMPLE)

Many generations of men have made their living creating objects. This is so obvious that it is not worth saying, since the definition of the word 'object' is broad enough that it includes everything, almost, that there is. Except a soul cannot be considered an object, nor can anything of the class of ineffable things, such as 'rights' or 'happiness', so if that's what you are thinking, then revise that idea.

Still, some narrowing of the field is necessary if this statement is to be useful, so let us instead say that many generations of men have made their living from the creation of, and sale of, physical objects of this or that sort, the value of which is determined by their utility. You will argue that there are classes of objects that are sold with no specific utility, such as jewellery, from which many generations of men have made a living, but the counter argument to this is that those objects possess a relative utility, and surely you are not arguing that beauty is without utility in the world?

This is by the by, since many generations of men have made their living from the creation of objects of utility, and this does not preclude the existence of many generations of men that have made their livings from the creation of objects the utility of which is not immediately obvious (history is full of objects which we do not recognise the utility of, and the modern world is full of objects that historical man would not have recognised at all, never mind anything else).

This is also by the by, since the question is, should a man be responsible for the use to which his objects are put once he has made and sold them?

If a man buys scissors, for example, from a maker of scissors, is the maker of scissors responsible for the use to which they are put? If he heats metal to the requisite temperature and then hammers it into blades, or if he casts metal in the shape of blades and finishes them on a lathe, or on an abrasive wheel, or if he utilises a drop hammer to make a scissor shape, or by any other method makes an object recognisable as a scissors, is he responsible when a man buys it and then drives it into the stomach of a bystander?

You will say no, since the function of a scissors is not for it to be driven into the stomach of a bystander, but rather is to cut paper for the making of decorations at Christmas, or to follow the chalk marks on a piece of cloth and so cut the back, front, and sides of a girl's dress, so that they can be sewn into something that she might wear. However, if a scissors can be driven into the stomach of a bystander is this not then something that the maker of the scissors should be responsible for, since there is nothing preventing him from rounding off the ends of the blades so that they are incapable of puncturing the skin?

The question is not a simple one to answer.

To try another example: what if, rather than a scissors, which is an object that a dressmaker might use, the blacksmith makes objects that a doctor might use, such as a scalpel, or a speculum, or something with some unspecified function the designs for which are supplied to the blacksmith by the doctor? Doctors are respectable men and they do not wish to be questioned, so it is possible, you will agree, that a blacksmith might well not know to what use an instrument is to be put, allowing the burden for the responsibility of its use to be put on the man who commissions the making of that item. A blacksmith can reasonably assume that a respectable man will not commission to be made objects that will be put to disreputable uses.

Also, if we are speaking of generations of men, what if one's grandsire was the blacksmith in question? What if, finding himself with very many orders for a particular item, an ancestor of a modern man alive today specialised in the creation of bespoke articles for men of medicine, and retooled his workshop, trained apprentices, and in every other way decided to capitalise on his success, and created whatever object he was asked to create by men of medicine? Would he then be responsible for the uses to which the object was put, and could his children, grandchildren and great-grandchildren be expected to be responsible for them?

Methods of production improve with time in a manner analogous to the processes of evolution, and soon a hundred objects, a thousand, can be produced as easily as one once could be produced. Also, when there is one thing in front of the eye this appears very specific and unique, with ten, less so, with a hundred it is hard to concentrate, and with a thousand you become blind to them, as if you were saying 'lettuce' a thousand times – soon the word loses its meaning. Try it – the word will become nothing before long, and you will lose patience.

As methods of production improve, and sales increase, and increasingly large numbers of men rely on the creation of these objects for their living, and the owner of the factory rarely visits it and hires a manager/board of trustees, and retires, and all the functions of the blacksmith's forge are forgotten in the mists of time, there is a legal obligation to provide a dividend to shareholders. Questions of responsibility over the use to which objects are put are derogated to the executive functions of the state, and statements such as 'I just make them, I'm not responsible for what people do with them' become very rational indeed – impossible to argue with, even, under the law. So, at that point, if all the scissors of the world were used to stab the stomachs of all the bystanders of the world it would not be the maker of scissors who was to blame, even if without scissors there would be no scissoring.

Again, the question of the proper use to which objects are put comes to the fore – without scissors, after all, there would be no pretty dresses for little girls, and no Christmas decorations, so let us imagine something like, for example, the curette, which is an instrument which can be used in a variety of ways in a variety of procedures, but which is primarily used for the scraping or debridement of tissues in the human body.

It is an innocuous looking instrument, and would certainly not raise an eyebrow if designs for it were taken to a blacksmith and he was asked to create one, nor if one were seen in a factory, and less so ten, or a thousand generations later. Even its name is innocuous – there is something about French, when read by an Anglophone, which predisposes one to think of romantic and pretty things, something that cannot be said of German, for example, which is an aggressive-seeming language when one does not understand the meaning of the words.

Should the makers of curettes, then, be responsible for the uses to which curettes are put? This would depend on what uses those are, so let us give examples. Should the maker of the curette be responsible for its use in the treatment of cerumen impaction in the external ear canal? A man receiving treatment for poor hearing who goes to his doctor and who, perhaps ten minutes later, leaves able again to hear a pin drop on the desk in his study will not, habitually, write a letter of thanks to the company that manufactures the curette which removes his earwax. Another man has a sebaceous cyst; a somewhat more drawn out procedure is carried out to treat it, during which a variety of instruments are used, including a curette, and throughout which he is tugged hard on the scalp, and it is all very tiresome. Does he write a letter of complaint to the manufacturer who supplies his doctor? He does not – he might grumble, perhaps look up the address of the General Medical Council, but that is all. A last man takes his daughter for the removal of a foetus which has improperly lodged itself to the wall of her uterus and which threatens the birth of a feebleminded child.

What should he do?

The answer is nothing, since he has no reason to thank anyone, nor any remedy under the law if he has a grievance, since the formation of a company with limited liability protects the makers of objects from the consequences of their use, providing there has been no dishonesty in the sale. If a company made a thing that was then used to kill all the unborn children in the world, even if they had sold it advertising this function, it would not be subject to censure, since it is the responsibility of the purchaser the use to which he puts an object, and the world can continue as normal, the livelihoods of generations of men secure, and the market for curettes unaffected, it seems, and also all other objects, regardless of how they are used.

I looked at the other images with this in mind, and while there were many things that did not fit this explanation, there were certain elements that might have done, including one panel which depicted a table in the Egyptian style – a two-dimensional representation of its surface and the things laid on it. On the table were laid herbs, jars of oil, and what passed in the period for medicines, especially honey.

And join your limbs together

Shabtis, in the form of statues of workers who will carry out tasks for the deceased, are brought.

DR W.G. MACDONALD
LONDON, JANUARY 1935

It is not sufficient or desirable to obtain the necessary tissues from a supplier of offal – there is always a delay between the death of the animal and the sorting of the meats that introduces decay into the organs of the foetus. Nor should one attempt to secure unborn calves through the usual suppliers – slaughterhouses and butchers who are able to meet the demand are used to providing much larger foetuses which, for the purposes of the serum, are overdeveloped (and sold by weight, which introduces extra costs that are needless in this case). It is better to develop a relationship with a dairy farmer with a sizeable herd, and make it clear to him that good money can be made from the products of any terminations, or from any spontaneous miscarriages from a pregnant cow. This should, with luck, provide a reliable supply of the embryonic tissue, though in discussion we have wondered if this means of sourcing is ideal. It may be that taking foetuses in this way predisposes the tissues to problems that we might not easily be able to recognise – nature has a habit of aborting calves that will develop mutations, for example, and while often there are visible signs in the development prior to death, just as often there are not (as is attested to by the delivery of a sizeable number of seemingly perfectly-formed stillbirths at term every year). By sourcing only spontaneous abortions and the products of terminations (which tend to be done in ill, very young, or elderly mothers, in the main) we run the risk of injecting our patients with cells that are predisposed to error *in vivo*.

Ideally, we should find a perfectly healthy cow, with a perfectly healthy gestation, and remove the foetus at four months (which is best for our purposes, since the organs are sufficiently differentiated for us to separate them, but still flexible enough to provide cells capable of rejuvenation in the patient) but for practical and financial reasons this is, at present anyway, difficult to achieve. No doubt when the treatments become widespread we can maintain our own herd for precisely this purpose and once the cows reach the end of their breeding lives we can offset the running costs (feed, shelter, veterinary bills, stud fees, et al.) by selling them for meat and leather in the normal way. Presently, this would consume more capital than we have at hand, so this will have to remain a dream for now, the fulfilment of which we will certainly aim for in the future. The day will come, I can imagine, where we will have a very pleasant clinic in the countryside and the patients can relax and watch the cows in the field and listen to their contented lowing as they recuperate.

In the meantime, we should always make sure we are sourcing the best possible specimens from whatever suppliers we use. I cannot stress how much our success will rely on this – any scrimping, carelessness, or lack of attention in the selection at this stage will drastically reduce the possible efficacy of the serum. If the efficacy is reduced, the effect on the patient will be lessened, and we will certainly not be in a position to claim that our process has superior results to the transplantation of monkey glands, to name our most obvious competitor in the field. We know from experiment that our procedure gives better results, so we need only allow that fact to become known for us to reap the rewards (for both us and our patients) that many of the shameless quacks we see operating all around us reap. But that does rather rely on us getting the best quality foetuses.

Always check the development of the hooves – it is around four months that these become distinct, firm and yellow. The skin of the foetus is a light pink, and a little transparent – it's possible to see the ribs, red muscles, and blue organ sac through the skin – so the yellow of the hooves is very noticeable. Too young, and the hooves remain transparent and you find that the organs are not sufficiently developed to separate easily; too old, and the organs become too specialised towards bovine function for our purposes.

The foetus should be less than a foot long, certainly, and if the testicles have descended into the scrotum, or the teats are developed (a little pinch here and there with the forefinger and thumb can save a lot of time) it is past its best and should be turned down. Similarly, if there are hairs on the lips, and eyelashes on the face – these are both signs that it has spent too long in the womb.

Even once bought, the specimen should be examined carefully. If there is an unpleasant odour when opened this is a sign that there has been too much decomposition. Unborn calves should be almost odourless, just as a slab of meat would be – they have not been in the grass, there will be no faecal matter, and the foetus should be more or less sterile. Have no qualms about returning it at this point – if the seller has lied about the freshness of his wares this is certainly nothing you need to feel embarrassed about and he should provide a refund.

If everything is as it ought to be, then go ahead and separate out the intestines and the lungs and discard them – we are after the organs of secretion primarily, so also see if you can locate the thyroid (in its neck). We have discussed routinely cracking the skull and removing the material inside, and certainly this is something worthwhile – the pineal, pituitary and hypothalamus are in there. It is not terribly difficult to do, no more effort than shelling peas, but there is a tendency for fragments of bone to come with the brain, and this can be a problem in the preparation of the serum, so only do it if you can be sure of a clean break – if there's any doubt, discard the head and contents along with the skin and bones. One day we might come up with a neater solution to this problem, but at the moment err on the side of caution.

Whatever remains, wrap, place in a cool dark bag without anything in it that might disturb the contents while in transit – in fact, just use an empty doctor's bag (we have one or two in the office) and bring it to us as quickly as you can.

Once puréed, filtered, and added to normal saline, the serum can be used in treatment via needle injection into a muscle mass. That is if one can get the patient to co-operate. It is unethical to administer treatments without informing the patient as to what the treatment is, but there is a group of patients for whom this serum would be helpful that seem incapable or unwilling to be helped regardless of how slowly one explains it to them. It might be easier in these cases to simply enter the room and, in an unguarded moment, slip the needle into wherever one can find. Otherwise, one might outline the reasoning behind the treatment, how the treatment is manufactured, the quality control procedures in place, and what benefits the patient might be expected to receive, and still receive a kick to the shins when it comes to the injection. Whether this is down to the familiar anxiety we all feel over the needle, or whether psychotics, neurotics and schizoids are naturally prone to disruptive behaviour, we don't know, but it's certainly something that should be taken into account.

You should always talk to the attendants prior to entering the consulting room – they will know if the patient is the kind to cause a fuss, and if they are, or if you get the impression that they might be – sometimes these attendants are a bit reticent to bad-mouth their patients to outsiders – it's perfectly acceptable to have the patient restrained in a straitjacket, or by two or more attendants in advance of entering the room. In my opinion, based on personal experience, this should be standard procedure, and not just for the wellbeing of a man's shins! Needles are fragile things and can easily break off in a girl's thigh if she decides all of a sudden to rear up out of the chair and aim a kick. Then there's the issue of removing the needle before she embeds it into herself, or tears the skin running into the wall or door; any number of accidents can be caused if she's not in control of herself, as they often aren't. And then, unfair though it might be, we are the ones to blame, despite having done nothing but receive the blows. Certainly do not retaliate, regardless of the provocation (though I needn't point this out, I hope).

Afterwards, they need to remain isolated for a good period to let the serum do its work, and that is easier in these places than it is with someone who lives at home. It's hard work convincing a patient that he needs to leave his job for six weeks, but these ladies are in a place set up for isolation, and if they are resistant to the idea then they can be put in padded rooms where they minimise the harm they can do to themselves, or they can be sedated (which is often the way with the more intractable cases anyway). Be sure to schedule return visits regularly, and remember that monitoring is charged at the same rate as a clinical appointment. There is a printed calendar on which follow up appointments can be marked off and left with the receptionist for her to enter into the appointment book. We also have branded pens and pads if you feel it would be useful to give the front of house staff a small gift and thereby cement your relationship with them. Ditto the expenses account for lunches and drinks, though please reserve this for doctors and budget holders.

It is very important that patients are not only monitored after treatment by the local medical staff, but that the positive effects of the serum are independently noted by our staff, and also effectively and repeatedly communicated to the medical and administrative staff formally and informally. Ideally we would like for our serum to become the default treatment for all existing and incoming patients – it is what makes taking on these troublesome cases worthwhile in the first instance, from our side – and this is most likely to be achieved through recommendations from staff to the executive of the institution, and through the dissemination of information across the medical profession. Positive word-of-mouth can mean the difference between profit and loss and affects all of our well-beings, patients included. We do our bit, publishing books and papers in journals, but you should feel you have a role in the reputation of our product too, and should consider yourself an ambassador. Review the materials we have sent you, liaise with the technicians, and in all ways try to embody the values of the firm. This should not be difficult; we are doing excellent work with an excellent product and we should all feel proud of our achievements to date and look forward to a bright future.

On the other hand, if there are adverse reactions to the serum, these should be played down, and the patients removed from the list of those we treat. If all we can expect is complaints, and if the positive effects of the serum are always hidden by a mountain of vexatious enquiries and legal threats, then we should bow out immediately, especially if the patient or their family are in the public eye, or are in any way capable of influencing policy makers. There is, it seems to me, such a thing as bad publicity, regardless of what people say, and while an endorsement from a well-known figure would be helpful, the opposite also holds true. As we know, any negatives of the treatment will be likely to be from mistakes in diagnosis – the serum would never have done any good – or in aftercare, or from circumstances out of our control. There's no need to take any responsibility for these outcomes, or to suggest that there is something wrong with the product, or your behaviour, and you should certainly not admit to any error, formally or informally, but particularly not formally.

Any complaints should be forwarded to me directly and I will liaise with the patient myself – or her representatives if she is too unwell to manage her own affairs – and keep you informed of developments.

And on the same wall there was a depiction of the deceased, again in the position of fear or supplication, but this time in an empty chamber.

I am by no means as intuitive as my colleague, but it did occur to me that perhaps the deceased had been ill, had received treatment unwillingly and unsuccessfully, and, perhaps, that she had then been isolated. Perhaps the disease was communicable, and then it occurred to me that perhaps this was precisely it – this deceased's family, though high ranking, and requiring that she be buried in the proper manner, had worried that this woman's disease would be communicable not only to those living, but also to those in the afterlife, and had taken steps to ensure that she never reached it.

I went about with this new supposition, one I did not confide to my colleague, and here were scenes that suddenly might give support to the argument – here she was attended to by priests carrying the implement, and there she was censed with purifying smoke.

May Horus be gracious to you

All are weeping and raise their arms in grief at the passing of the deceased into the land of the dead.

THE BA OF LUCIA JOYCE
GENEVA AND NORTHAMPTON,
SEPTEMBER 1934 ONWARDS

One cannot imagine a horse on a small table.

The rooms are quiet and very neat. There are no windows, but curtains hanging on one wall – if one draws them aside there is a picture frame, but no picture within it. If one wishes, one can imagine a picture. Perhaps this is its function: pull aside the curtain, please. What do you see? What would you wish to see? What would you not wish to see?

Above the dado is white, and below it is yellow.

There is an armchair, quite comfortable, but there is no cushion. One might smother oneself with a cushion. Is that possible? One can certainly smother one's mother with a cushion, in a book, but can one smother oneself? Possibly not, since the last stages of smothering require pressure to be applied after the victim has lost consciousness, which one cannot do to oneself. One might take the pieces of stuffing from a pillow and stuff them into one's own throat, clogging up the pipe through which the lungs get oxygen, or jamming the stomach with wadding – this might be effective. It is certainly not a practice that doctors ever advise, and there must be a reason for that.

In a pile beside the armchair are books – not the sort of books in which mothers are smothered, but the opposite kind, in which nothing difficult or inflammatory is found – bedtime stories, and works of non-fiction on safe topics: the gardens of Italy, and the histories of countries far away.

On the table on which one cannot imagine a horse (which is not to say that if one were on the table one could not imagine a horse, which would be incorrect, but is to say that one could not imagine a horse being on the table) is a tablecloth. The tablecloth is large enough so that it covers the modesty of the table's legs down past the knees, and around the hem are pretty flowers in blue and yellow. A horse, should it stand on this table, would have several problems. Firstly, it would have a difficult time finding enough room for all its hooves. The distance between a horse's forelimbs and hindlimbs is quite substantial, while this table is only small.

Also, the table is poorly constructed and from cheap materials and does not have much weight-bearing potential – a horse is heavy, and consequently the table would break if the horse was induced to put its weight onto it.

Lastly, there is a tablecloth on the table which would slip and ruche up if the horse made even the slightest movement, so the whole thing is impractical, and hence unimaginable.

Lastly, having a horse would be in violation of the rules, since these are rooms for solitary confinement, and this table is provided to give the solitarily confined a place to eat their dinners off, and not for the placing on of additional guests, horses or otherwise. Whether no-one can see through the window when the horse is stood on the table and thereby witness the breaking of the rule against guests is irrelevant, since there is no conceivable way that the horse could gain entrance to the rooms since the same people who enforce the rules are the same people who bring in guests, horses included.

If one puts one's palms flat on the tablecloth, and then moves them around in concert, then the tablecloth moves with them, which means that the wood beneath is polished, which is the last reason that a horse must not be placed on it, since, like a tea cup, their hooves leave rings on the polish that do not come out without hiring a French polisher. Except these marks would be semi-circles, and though horses' hooves are thought to be lucky, and can be seen next to leprechauns and other lucky-to-find creatures in drawings, this would not be lucky at all. Not in this case. Not unless one wishes to be shouted at and chided as a slut and sent to one's room to await the return of the father, who knows his way around a belt.

So, if one cannot have a horse on a table, and hence cannot imagine it, and if the imagining of it would be to imagine something so impractical-seeming that it would be hilarious if one could, one cannot also imagine setting fire to it by lighting the tablecloth. Still less can one imagine inducing the horse to stay where it is on the tablecloth rather than jumping down, particularly if one is in the kind of bleak mood attendant on the desire to immolate oneself in the manner of Brünnhilde in the ending of the *Götterdämmerung*. The imagining of ridiculous things and the desire to immolate oneself are inimical, and there's no way you could do it without the horse.

One will remember there was a great deal of talk of that horse, sung in German, of course, and the delight with which it wishes to join its master in the festive, joyous flames of his pyre. Horses aren't aware of treachery, even if it is treachery brought about by a magical potion, and hence can neigh unselfconsciously with delight at the thought of burning to death on the funeral pyre of their master. Human women *are* capable of remembering it, and it is only by taking the example of the delighted and tortured horse, writhing in the flames righteously, that they can convince themselves that they are willing, let alone able, to burn themselves to ash. This would be an effort, even if it were to make right all wrongs and bring down heaven itself in a wall of flames. Or of red and yellow tissue paper onto which light has been shone and a fan directed at from below.

So anyone who suggests that the action of setting fire to a tablecloth was done in the spirit of Brünnhilde in the ending of the *Götterdämmerung* is, frankly, mistaken, though it makes for a nice story on paper. Silence the shrill clamour of your grief – that certainly sounds right, and it is one of the things said daily by attendants, though in less operatic language, and not sung so beautifully, or in German. Silence the shrill clamour of your grief, they say, or I'll come in there and give you something to grieve about. Silence the shrill clamour of your grief, you mardy old bitch, or I'll come in there and give you a kick in the cunt (ho-ho). Silence the shrill clamour of your grief, for God's sake, you're driving me crackers.

Anyway, that is not said *to* Brünnhilde in the ending of the *Götterdämmerung* it is said *by* her, which any idiot knows, so if that's your idea, then you've made a mistake.

This table is a great deal better for the placement of a glass of milk than it is for the standing of horses, though if one were to compound one's error and put both the milk and the horse on the table at once, milk would certainly be spilled. The laments of children addressing themselves to their mothers over the loss of their sweet milks would be certainly heard, though by the mother probably not, since she never comes near enough to hear anything, never comes within a chair's throw of the place, and no lament in the world can be heard over the distances that woman determines to keep from the source of the spillage, no matter how sweet the fucking milk.

There was a woman once called Hazel, who was very rich and very beautiful and there are men for whom that combination is utterly irresistible, no matter how much doleful and languorous (but ultimately troubled) young women love them, which is fine. It is certainly not Hazel's fault. It is not *she* that made the promises. It is not *she* who made herself a secret. It is not *she* who left herself for herself and left anyone else wondering what it was about themselves that made them unloveable. Nor was it she that grieved, understandably, at being jilted. Nor was this compounded by her parents' overreaction to the whole thing, as if she was now a churn of soured milk that somehow they had been lumbered with and which would be impossible to fob off onto anyone. She did not find herself falling in with the wrong crowd, vulnerable, and being made to do things, horrible, and now kept as some dread secret lest the world collapse around them and everything they'd all worked for.

Can't you see?

It certainly wasn't Hazel's doing, though curses on her regardless for drawing him away from her, using her glamour, and turning him away from his true love. And she was a married woman already.

If one intended to make a pyre from the legs of that table, and splinter up the wood of the table top, then it would be a tiny fire. Every year, thousands of hedgehogs are burned on Guy Fawkes Night since they seek shelter from the cold and try to hibernate in the bonfires awaiting burning. This pyre would scarcely worry a hedgehog at all… perhaps a baby one. If one were a Roman, whose intention it was to encase a hedgehog in clay, cook it, peel away the clay (thereby removing the spines) and then feed on the unusual meat within, this pyre wouldn't be fit for purpose at all, and one would find oneself disappointed. To imagine a disappointed Roman, all in his toga, and a hedgehog, all covered in clay, is silly, and are silly thoughts the kinds of thoughts that go through the heads of people who intend to murder themselves by setting themselves alight?

It doesn't seem likely.

And all this before you add the horse.

Northampton does lie on a river. It is the river Nene, and while the Nene is not the Rhine and could never be mistaken for it, it does share some of the same letters in its name. If one opens the curtains on a glassless window and attempts to see the Nene through it, then one cannot see it. Nor can one see the Rhine, unless one crosses one's eyes and, in the chaos that this makes in the brain, the right eye seeing left and the left eye seeing right, and the two sides muddling together so that neither side is clear and in the wrong place anyway, then one can superimpose a brief and simplified image of either river in the gap that leaves. If one has seen either river. This does make it rather difficult to then turn back and do what needs to be done to the table before one builds the pyre on which one intends to burn the corpse of one's lover, induce his horse to immolate itself, and then immolate oneself on that pyre, even if the tiny blaze could provide enough heat for so much immolation.

There would be no point scorching oneself; it would just add insult to injury. If one were to survive an immolation with a nasty burn to the skin of the calf, an irritated and fractious horse, and an unburned corpse, this would be insulting. A modern cremating oven must be capable of reaching temperatures of 870–980°C, which is 1,600–1,800°F, and then remain between these temperatures until the body is reduced to ash. The idea that the fuel available from the dismantling of the little table on which a solitary confinee has their supper in a windowless room would be sufficient is frankly ridiculous.

The image of a pyre gathered on the banks of the river Nene is also ridiculous, and Northampton is so far from heaven that even if the pyre was the hottest pyre the East Midlands had ever seen, the idea that it would reach to heaven and there immolate an entire pantheon of gods is also ridiculous.

He was very handsome, though, and very sweet. His accent particularly, and so charming and clever, if anyone were to be burned on a magnificent heaven-destroying pyre then ought it not to be him? Who better to be the kindling with which such a blaze is ignited, and the greedy and selfish gods punished for their greed and selfishness? He had neither of those two traits, willing to marry without a dowry and almost willing to overlook the charms of a wealthy and beautiful heiress in favour of a sken-eyed and maudlin waif who would go on to live her life in a room with a blank picture for a window and an impossible horse for company.

By gathering the whole tablecloth together and then hanging it out as if it were laundry day between outstretched arms and then bringing one's hands together and folding it not evenly, but only vertically, it is possible to make a roll of fabric that can be laid on the table in a circle; that much one *can* say. That much is an undisputable fact. One match between the back teeth and the other in the hand, once struck, this circle of cloth can be made to burn, though it might take a few tries. If a new match is required, crunch down the old one, chew, and take another from the box, or the book, or from the pocket where they are always to be found amongst the lint, waiting for when they are needed, but not making a bulge that anyone will notice.

Safety matches are no use.

Once it is burning, one can use the chair on which one usually sits and eats whilst staring at the curtains, to give access to the table, where one can stand within a ring of fire, if one so wishes. Again, this is without a doubt true. You may try it yourself, if you wish.

Do so now.

Take cloth (you may not have a table cloth to hand, but anything will do) and do what is described above. You see? It is easy. So that much *is* true. If you own a horse, induce it to immolate itself. If you own the corpse of a lover who has died, attempt to cremate it – you will find that *these* two things are impossible, so you will have to satisfy yourself by standing within the ring of fire.

By doing the above you will insulate yourself from the world, for the setting of fires of this sort is a kind of magic, and now, if you have done as you were asked, you will be surrounded by a magical fire that can only be breached by your true love (providing they are not already dead). When that person comes, if they still exist and are within a distance that makes it practical for them to come to you (and you have not made it impossible for them by putting the door on the latch, or telling them you have gone back to your own country and are not to be found in your usual haunts and that you love another woman, I'm very sorry, and that you always have, I'm very sorry, and that it is entirely your fault, and that anyway you felt that pressure was being placed upon you, yes, but not just by your father, by you and your constant knife-edge balancing act between sanity and insanity, between happiness and unhappiness, and much as you love them, can't you see it would never have worked and this is better in the long run?) if you have not done *that*, then your true love will be able to come upon you in the state you are now, perfectly preserved and hopefully they will have matured to the point where they do not make ridiculous statements like the foregoing, but will have developed some fucking spine. Your perfectly preserved youth will be their reward for having come so far from their childishness. If one can say that about them then perhaps they would truly deserve a horse that would immolate itself on their behalf, cheerfully in the joyous flames, and also a wife who would joyously fling herself on his pyre, and in doing so set a fire that would rise and burn the very heavens asunder and kill all the gods on the banks of the River Nene in Northampton.

But perhaps a tablecloth is insufficient for this. The table is too small to support the weight not only of a horse, but also of a faithful wife who wishes only to preserve herself for a lover who is worthy of her. As the table leg wobbles in its poorly constructed jointing, the glass of milk topples and rolls, falling off the edge having wet the tablecloth enough at that spot to put out some of the fire. It falls to the ground where it shatters, and she falls with it, shoulder first, and lands so that she dislocates the joint and causes a tear in the rotator cuff and minor abrasions. She also sustains cuts to the skin of the face, which must all go in the report, I'm afraid, and yes, that does rather undermine the plans we had to give her a more relaxed regime, which, as you can see, she is ill-equipped to manage in her current state. The doctor will not take her in Geneva when he finds out about this. Yes, we must make the report. It would be negligent of us not to. We understand your reservations, but, for a few inches this way or that, you could be looking at a dead daughter and not one with a few minor cuts. The jugular vein is only a finger's breadth away from where the glass penetrated the flesh. Well, it is your choice, clearly, but he will not take her. Our only solution would be to return her to you, and we know that is not a viable alternative at this stage in her cure. What cure? Well there is no need to be rude. We are doing our best, but she's very difficult.

Indeed, it was possible if one began on the north wall and followed the images across to the final image of her isolation in the chamber to track a rough progress through various failed treatments.

And give you your head

At the door to the tomb, the *sem*-priest performs the ritual of the opening of the mouth, by which the senses of the dead are returned to the mummified corpse.

THE REPRESENTATIVE OF THE COMPANY CHARGED WITH EUTHANIZING
INTRACTABLE CASES IN VICHY FRANCE, BRITTANY, NOVEMBER 1940

They are hard to convince, these French. Whether it is his stuffy, German-inflected accent, or the lingering smell of war that adheres to him, they do not take his words to heart.

He removes his tie, and undoes the button. The sense of relief is so strong that he reaches for his medicine as if in pain, but leaves it on the dressing table once his body understands that he is not.

Perhaps it is the burns.

They are all so superficial in their attitudes: the way they dress, the attention they pay to their hair, the way they hold themselves (a kind of practised loucheness that speaks of hours in front of a mirror), even the manner in which they smoke their cigarettes, the arm held long and loose, drawing it up in a wide and lazy arch and then letting it fall back as if they lose interest in the whole limb once it's done its work. He is tight with scar tissue on his left side, and needs to hold the cigarette between his teeth and drag hard to get anything out of it since he can't make a seal with his damaged lips. He is probably ugly to these people, and they let this affect the way they understand what he is saying to them.

Whatever it is, he is having no success.

He leans on his elbows, head in his hands, but this does hurt and he sits back up. There is a half-finished bottle of wine on the bedside table, and he goes to it and runs his finger around the inside of the glass that originally held his toothbrush, but which now has only dry red grains of bitter tannin from the night before.

One glass, no more.

Perhaps they cannot get past the sense that it is he to whom mercy should be shown – that is a common idea, he imagines. He can see it operating in the backs of the minds of the sympathetic, even in his family. Wouldn't it have been kinder if he had died? Unfair to make this brave man suffer, wincing as he takes a puff, always tugging his neck away to the right, as if he is trying to free himself from the constriction of the rippled, white skin. Unfair on them to have his wonderful bravery tempered by the requirement to look at him all day, and fight the revulsion that people naturally feel for the disfigured. Should they have to imagine what it is like to burn? Have the embodiment of it haunting their everyday, at breakfast, at lunch, at supper? Coming across him by accident with his shirt off as he shaves and the bedroom door is ajar?

And the children. Is it easier to have a father who is a dead hero, or a living monster? Unfair questions, bitten back, but they play out behind the eyes of these sympathetic people. The unsympathetic? They spit and walk by.

Or do the French secretly feel, as he does, that his work is unfinished on the battlefield? If there is life in him, even burdensome life such as he still possesses – his treatments must run into the thousands – wouldn't a true man use that life to revenge himself and his country rather than haunt the corridors of places far from his home, trying to convince people of things they do not wish to be convinced of?

He sits on the bed, arranges the pillow so that it bisects the headboard vertically, and shifts himself into a half-lying, half-seated position. His boots will smear polish on the quilt, but he does not remove them. They stand like two gravestones at the end of the bed, headstones at his feet. Is there a culture that buries its dead so that the stone is at the feet?

Whatever they think, these doctors and nurses, they are enemies of the new state; this is what he determines to think. This route through the problems he faces is his strongest option, since it allows him to suggest, without saying as much, that they must adopt these new policies independently, as men of science, as rational people, since this is the way things must be now, regardless of any squeamishness. He has the authorities on his side in this line, whereas all the other moves put him on the defensive, some fatally so. This way of thinking makes it *their* lives that are at risk, *their* jobs, *their* statuses, and that is nearer the truth anyway. Who is most likely to suffer: the decorated war hero, or an intransigent French doctor in some clinic far from anywhere anyone cares about? This strategy returns some of the power to him, evens the field, and if pretty girls look down at their shoes when he enters the room, or frown, or put their hands involuntarily to their mouths, then pretty girls should also be in fear of their lives when they see him, and should consider what they are willing to do to save those lives, and the lives of their loved ones.

Unworthy thoughts: he is not a monster, whatever they think.

But he knows people who are, and the fact that he doesn't have these nurses and secretaries on their knees in front of him doing precisely whatever he wishes them to do is something that should count in his favour. Do they not understand what goes on in wartime? He could tell them stories that would sicken them, but isn't that the sad truth? If an ugly man wants his arsehole licked by pretty girls like this, or his balls sucked, then his best option is to have them do it at gunpoint, having executed their homely friend, since restraining himself from doing it would never induce them to do it out of gratitude. Or to bring their whole city to its knees and, when the only source of food is in his control, pay them with carrots to undress for him.

More unworthy thoughts; he would like as not save these girls from such a fate, if it was within his power. If he came upon a soldier who was about to claim his spoils, wouldn't he stand between them? That is the kind of man he is – not a homosexual, as the other men claim, but a man who feels things from the position of the person suffering, and for whom this stops him feeling any pleasure in it. He is not a saint, but he is not a devil. Having suffered himself, he has a keen sense of the suffering of others. When he sees it, he determines to end it. Why should people suffer if there is no need for it? Sometimes the cure is worse than the disease, but sometimes it is not.

In Danzig he saw them pulled out into the garden and shot, and while some of them didn't understand, and so could not properly feel fear, there were others who very much did fear it and who ran, or fought. That is no way to show mercy. If one has to chase a man down like game and shoot him four or five times as he struggles, that is not mercy; that is barbarism.

Perhaps he will take his boots off after all.

He finishes the wine in a gulp, puts down the glass and bends his right leg at the knee. This is not painful, but when he reaches with his left arm, that hurts. He winces, then frowns, then grits his teeth, then grunts, one action after another as he stretches to reach the laces. It is this pain – very ordinary, very banal, on a scale small enough for the mind to encompass it without resorting to fantasy – that allows him to feel the pain of others, to understand that it cannot be caused indiscriminately, needlessly, by soldiers who do not understand pain in the way he does. They are only used to inflicting it, or ignoring it. Give a soldier a job and he does it in the most efficient way he can. He will take a gun and shoot a man through the back of the head – that is nothing for which he can be criticised, since it is what he is trained to do. So one should not give jobs of this sort to a soldier, which is the point he tries to impress on these people: do not give soldiers a job when doctors are better placed to carry it out. A doctor will know what to do to prevent suffering; that is his oath.

He cannot move the left leg from this position, so he grabs the hem of his trouser and drags it up toward him. It is not that the leg is paralysed – it is not – it is just that the muscle tissue is not complete and some directions are impossible, so he has to move it like a puppeteer moves a puppet. He is used to it now, so it does not occupy his attention.

In the corner of the room there is a medium-sized canister of pure carbon monoxide gas, and there are five more in a wooden box in the car. At the end of the week he'll open up the box and replace this one in the space that it left, if precedent is anything to go by, and drive to the next clinic up the coast.

He finds there is a surfeit of sea air in this work, and mountain air, and naturally occurring salt springs, as if any of these things could offer a solution. The food is excellent, though, as is the wine.

His boots stand empty beside the bed as he undoes the belt at his waist. His trousers are tweed and while he doesn't notice during the day, when the pressure the belt exerts is gone, the fabric no longer presses hard enough at the skin of his waist to stop the fibres from itching. He keeps his nails short, but unless he is careful he will draw blood as he scratches. This will leave open a locus for infection, so he pulls his good right hand away, places it under his buttock and itches with the ring finger of the left hand, the nail of which never grew back. This is not satisfactory, but it is safer. Better this way.

What is the satisfaction one receives from scratching an itch anyway? There is a feverishness in it, it seems to him, a frantic animalistic quality, a masochism rewarded with a strange kind of pleasure that would allow you to stab down to the bone through your bandages with a knitting needle if you let it. Some things are so irritating that you can damage yourself in the punishing of them. Which is why you must resist.

There is no doubting that revenge is enjoyable, or that righteousness lends itself to fervour, or that a lynch mob can become cruel, and if we know this, then why do we allow it to happen? It's better that we find a way of becoming detached, and so do what needs to be done without resorting to self-defeating savagery. Revenge, once satisfied, leads to guilt; righteousness, taken to extremes, tends to mysticism; a lynch mob becomes indiscriminate.

Not so the doctor. The doctor has diagnosis and cure in which no pleasure is evidenced. What doctor finds pleasure in the performance of his duties? Perhaps in the outcome, but never in the treatment. If there is pleasure it is in the satisfaction that comes from the cleverness with which his duties are executed, the precision.

Eventually he takes off his trousers altogether, lifting himself off the bed and pulling, resettling and pulling again, twisting and pulling one more time and there are the two legs, one gnarled and shaved back like the first twig a boy whittles on a camping holiday with a knife his father has given him, and the other perfectly normal. Later, at dinner, if chicken is served, or a rack of lamb, he will see a drumstick, or the bone sticking from a chop, and be reminded of his ankle. He will pause, but otherwise conversation will continue as normal.

Perhaps tonight will be different.

There is no need for anybody to be shot – that was the trouble in Danzig. It is difficult to convince anyone that shooting is a just course of action, which is why it was a mistake to give the job to soldiers. An owner will wince at the shooting of a lame horse, at least the first time, and how much worse would that be for a mother re. their daughter, or a son re. their father, even if mother and son (possibly daughter and father) know that it is for the best? It is mercy to put an end to suffering, this much we all know, so it is only necessary to find a method that is acceptable to everybody. The application of gas is something we are all used to, from the dentist, for example, and recently for mothers in childbirth. Precedent is useful, too, in that the equipment already exists to deliver the procedure – it is a matter of attaching a face mask and turning the valve. Anyone who has seen it done could not object to it – the patient becomes drowsy very quickly and soon dies without any sense of suffocation or panic, or any ill effects at all. If the patient understands what is about to happen to her, a sedative can be given orally in advance of the procedure, or intravenously in extreme cases. He has the equipment in his bag, including the anaesthetics.

It is only then a matter of determining for which of the inmates the procedure is useful. Talk of ballast on the state and lives unworthy of living is counterproductive, he has found. To people with a very strong sense of civic responsibility it plays well, as it would to the Spartans, no doubt, but to those of a more individualistic turn of mind, possibly like the Athenians (though he isn't sure of this) it is better to talk of an end to personal suffering. If it comes to it, the state can be brought up, but it provokes in the French a wilful resistance to authority, and he wonders if they disagree just to spite him (and Germany by extension).

Suffering is the way to go.

Which doctor cannot have looked at his patients – the intractable ones who will never be cured – and wondered whether there is any point prolonging the farce of their treatment? The fees are important, of course, but eventually the clinic becomes full of intractable cases and there are many more people in the community that the doctor might usefully be able to treat if those who will never recover weren't taking up the beds. No one is suggesting that people who can be cured should receive the treatment, it is only those who live out their lives in suffering that might benefit.

This, it seems to him, is an argument that has no counter. Should people be made to suffer forever? Can a doctor allow patients under his charge to live long lives of pain on his watch? Of course not. If they do not agree at this point they will not agree. He will have to leave, replace the canister in the box with the others, and make his way up the coast. As he leaves he will point out that legislation will soon make this procedure compulsory, as it is in Germany, and he will leave them a leaflet and his card so that they might contact him then.

His jacket is hanging where he left it on the back of the door. His habit is to put his clothing on a hanger as he removes it, and the jacket looks, from a distance, like a microcephalic, the hook of the hanger the pinhead. He picks up his trousers from the floor, folds them, and places them on the bed next to him.

If he had a larger car, or a van, he could bring the projector with him. There is a film of the procedure being carried out on a number of patients, to show the potential use cases. There are no microcephalics in the film, but there are other incurables – syphilitics, schizophrenics, epileptics – and he would challenge any man of science to watch the entire film and not come away convinced of the efficacy of it, the kindness and mercy of the method, and the logic of the rationale. Should a child be left to live her life in absolute misery when there are alternatives?

Roughly a third of the patients in any sanatorium can benefit. It is even possible to gather the patients together in a room and, while they sleep, administer the gas so that they do not even know the procedure has taken place. Very few alterations would have to be made to a standard hospital ward to make it suitable – the blocking up of any ventilation shafts and the making of ingress for some piping. Absolute airtightness is desirable, but not necessary.

In his bag he has some pro-forma that he will leave regardless of what they say at dinner tonight. They have a column for the insertion of the patient's name, the length of stay at the clinic, the diagnosis (all of which can be filled in by clerical staff) and then two further columns 'is this patient likely to be cured?' and 'recommendation for euthanasia', both of which can be ticked or crossed by the doctor. This is all that needs to be done; the rest can be taken care of by specialist staff of his office in consultation with attendants and administrators. Removal of the patients post-treatment can either be arranged by the families at their expense, or by the authorities, but no expenses need be incurred by the facility in either case.

Now the elastic band on his underpants is cutting, so he opens the drawer in the bedside table and takes out a tub of moisturising cream. He pulls down his pants, turns onto his good side and, with two fingers of cream, begins massaging the thick skin on his hip bone.

It is coming up to six o'clock.

In some of the images, a recurrent group was visible – perhaps they were the family. In the first scenes they faced her, but later they turned their backs and held their hands away from her until they no longer appeared and her only contact was with the priesthood and the scorpion goddess Ta-Bitjet, wife of Horus son of Ra, the blood from whose conjugal deflowering is proof against poisoning (since Horus was almost killed from scorpion stings as a child).

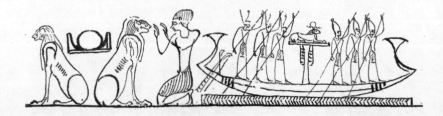

And join your limbs together, that you may endure

The deceased speaks — 'I have been given my mouth so that I may speak with it in the presence of the Great God.'

THE BA OF LUCIA JOYCE
PORNICHET AND NORTHAMPTON,
JANUARY 1941 ONWARDS

It is coming up to six o'clock. When is he going to get up?

It is imbecilic to lie beneath the earth. What is he doing under there? What is there to do? Watch through the soil the goings on above?

If he is the centre of the world, and he is beneath the surface at a distance of six feet, then he is only a distance of six feet from any point on the surface. This much is demonstrable in calculus and hence must be true if the propositions are true, which they all are (check them). Therefore, it is irrelevant whether he is interred in Zurich, or Dublin, or Paris, or Trieste, or on the banks of the river Nene. He can never be more than six feet away, and why send a letter? Don't they have telegrams in Switzerland? They have them in France. In France it is even possible to find a friendly acquaintance to deliver news on one's behalf – one telephones that acquaintance (one who lives closer to the recipient of the news than the one who has news to deliver) and asks politely whether that acquaintance wouldn't mind awfully popping in to tell someone. That is if the someone doesn't have a phone of their own, or isn't under the care of some person or organisation that possesses a phone that may be rung very easily, and if you have a sore finger just ask to speak to the operator; they'll put you through.

Or send a telegram.

To open a newspaper – something that Lucia is encouraged to do, after all, it is not good to dwell on matters internal indefinitely, there is a world outside the confines of your own skull, outside the walls of the garden, on the other side of closed eyelids, keep in touch with current affairs – and discover news that you ought properly to have heard from the horse's mouth is distressing. Can it be dismissed as a mistake?

Editors of newspapers make mistakes every day – there is even a section in the newspaper which lists and then apologises for the various mistakes that have been made in the previous day's edition. If you ever have any specialist knowledge of this or that matter and then you read an article in a newspaper on the same topic you are always amazed at how inaccurate the content of these articles is. They often have even the general gist wrong. So why would anyone believe a word of it?

In the garden there is a small, round, cast-iron table painted white. You can easily run a finger around the edge of it – one circle – without stretching. It is not solid, but latticed. While the index finger of the right hand cannot quite make it through the holes, the little finger can, up to the second knuckle, but you must take it out before the finger goes red, then blue, and eventually white.

Beside the table there is a cast iron chair, too heavy to lift easily if you wish to shift position, but if you call over someone to help, it can be done. If you ever observe another woman who has sat on this chair, if she is wearing shorts in the summer, if she has sat there for some time staring down the garden, then, when she gets up, you can see the pattern of the lattice that makes up the seat of the chair on the backs of her legs in red. This pattern is the same as the pattern on the table.

On the table there is a porcelain cup and a saucer in which mint tea is cooling, and there is a pastry, untouched. There are cigarettes and matches. This is in the summer, though. At that time of year there is a newspaper there, too, to one side. In the winter you can stare from the upstairs window at this table, and remember the backs of women's legs, and the smoking of cigarettes, and the weight of cast iron, and compare it to the tray you place on your lap as you sit on the edge of the bed, and on which there is no room for the paper. That is placed on the writing table all the way over on the other side of the room facing the wall on which there is a picture of another garden in which there is no iron table and chair, nor any women, but which does have a pond.

—Have you read the paper yet?

There are all sorts of thoughts that go through your head that need not be expressed despite the urgency with which they are felt. Ought not, in fact, be expressed if there is any hope for a manageable existence in the world. If you are addressed even in the politest terms, it can produce thoughts that are violent – violent in form, violent in content, violent in style – these thoughts ought to remain thoughts, and not come out into the world as actions.

—Not yet.

—Well, remember, there is a world outside one's own head and it's always wise to keep abreast of current affairs.

So much is certainly true. If you imagined it was not true then the number of times you have heard this repeated, the weight of the words as they pile up over years, would force you to reappraise your denial of these facts. Why else would they be said so often?

A bed is a very comfortable place, and if you stretch out your legs and lay the tray on your lap and sip at the coffee which is served today in a shallow bowl around the edge of which swallows beat their wings, provided the pillows are sufficiently plumped, it is a very pleasant experience. You do not have to strain to see the garden; the window is right there. While there is no snow, the sky is white and grey and heavy, and there is every possibility that there will be snowfall by the evening. Then, when you move to the window after supper and look out, the lights from the rooms below will illuminate the untouched snowfall in squares of flickering orange and yellow. The silhouettes of the trees will be heavy. If you do etchings, the white lines are very important, and these trees will look like that – white lines contrasting with the black silhouettes to give an effect that...

—I'll be back in a little while for the tray.

What does the absence of something look like?

What does the lack of a telegram on a tray look like?

If the tray is wood, it looks like wood. If the tray is melamine, it looks like melamine. And what does the absence of something sound like? If it is the movement of an attendant in the hall and quiet conversation in the next room then it sounds like that. If it is the sound of blood rushing in the ears and the pause between the beating of the heart then it sounds like static, like a poorly tuned wireless, like the numb, waterlogged sensation in the inner ear when one receives a blow one is not expecting, right across the cheek with a flat hand, but which also drives air at the ear drum and perforates it if you are unlucky.

How does the absence of news feel? Like nothing, in the experiencing of it, but later, when one looks back and thinks, after the storm has passed and the snow has stopped falling and morning is here on the twenty-third, but of which month you aren't quite sure, then it feels very unusual. It feels like idiocy. It feels like betrayal. It feels like an innocent time that has been proven to be a lie and the pleasures of which must now be shied away from forever. No such pleasure would have been possible if the news had been delivered: it would have punctured it like an inner tube is punctured by a glass shard from a discarded bottle knocked from a window sill in the early morning. If you imagine by a cat mewling to be let in that makes you one sort of person. If you imagine by an angry lover trying the locks that makes you another. You are punctured either way and flat and useless. You are a burden to be repaired before normal service can be resumed.

The newspaper is there on the writing desk, and you've always thought that there was something perfect about a nicely folded newspaper, something redolent of civilisation's triumph over chaos that war and death and tragedy can be rendered so affectless. Somewhere you've heard of butlers ironing newspapers before presenting them to their masters and this is very good. It is not sufficient to take the suffering of others, reduce it to ink, and present it in absolute order in columns on a page; you must also find a way of making one man serve another man to the extent that he will spend his time heating an iron on the fire in the early morning. He will lick his finger and hear it hiss when he applies it timidly to the flat, then let the metal cool until it will not scorch or make the ink run, and then make perfectly flat what is already flat. He will then process to the other man's room with the paper held in front of him while all the time he could be eating, or shitting, or paying these attentions to the people of his own life.

You have always thought this, Lucia, but when you open that paper today, if you ever sip the coffee, now cold, to completion and replace the bowl with the swallows on the tray and remove the tray from your knees and place it on the bedside table and take the few steps over to the writing table where the paper is folded, if you ever do that, you will not be able to think it again. There are things you can read in that paper that will make affect of the affectless, and no amount of flatness of tone, or style, or coldness of delivery will render those words painless for you. For you alone. This should not be the first word you hear on the subject. What option do you have but to consider it a mistake?

Your father is dead.

In the spring there is a surprising amount of rubble in the garden and the windows have been boarded up. As the dandelions sprout on the lawn two terribly skinny gentlemen come and take first the cast iron table and then the cast iron chair. You can watch their slow and halting progress if you press your cheek up to the glass by the gap between the boards and turn your gaze as far to the outside as you can. Even though it's warm, your breath mists the glass, and when they put the table down to catch their breath and to rub their hands you use your tongue to draw in the condensation – you attempt a flower, but the tip of the tongue is a clumsy paintbrush. It's no better than a child could manage.

A baby.

There are no newspapers now, except the one you remember, and no pastries, and no mint tea. What little you are given is often stale, even the water, which leaves your throat dusty, and your stomach flat. This is a blessing because there's nothing worse than feeling full when you are empty, is there?

—If you hear anyone, anyone at all, you will stay absolutely silent, do you understand? .

There is a difference between understanding and acquiescing. There is a difference between doing what you are told and agreeing to do what you are told. There is a difference between staying silent and having absolutely nothing to say. In that difference you occupy yourself with memories – the lattice-work patterns on the backs of women's legs.

—What is there to say?

The images on the newspaper and the gathering of rubble in the garden, the generation of seed heads on the dandelions and the noises in the street, the haunted expressions on the faces of the attendants and the dusty water, it all means something. What that something means is impossible to say.

There have been no visitors for as long as you can remember. There have been no phone calls and no telegrams and no letters. If you have visitors it is possible to express the things you have to say and cross-reference them with what you expect their reactions to be against the reactions that they actually make. You can then listen, very carefully, to the things they say in reply to the things you have said to them, and clarify what is going on in the world. If there are no visitors this is very difficult.

Days and months and years, possibly, seasons certainly, drift past in ways that are both extremely fleeting and excruciatingly drawn out depending on how much attention you choose to pay, which is increasingly little since there doesn't seem to be any reward for it.

If death was possible, would it be desirable?

Your world has become very small, not that it ever extended much beyond your range of vision and hearing. The range of experiences that are experienced within that range of vision and hearing is itself restricted – the boards, the corridor, the bathroom, the newspaper – so much that the absence of things is very much more significant in its draw on your attentions than the presence of things. Where is x? Where is why? Y can't we go into the garden?

Keep your voices down.

In autumn, the faces you recognise are replaced with faces you do not recognise and they do not recognise you. To them you are an object which requires remedial work – cleaning, delousing, feeding, accounting for. There are questions to which the answers are lost, or of significance that is not obvious, or to ends that you already know are dead, and beneath the ground he is watching you.

You pick up the bowl with swallows and it is warm now against the oncoming chill. Though the garden is filled with leaves and rubble, a wooden table has been placed there and a wooden chair. They are both constructed from pale, untreated wood, but which is sanded. When you run your finger around the square the wood does not splinter. Though the edges are rough, the flat of the table is smooth, not solid, being made from slats of wood which would stripe the arse if you sat on the chair with shorts, though it is too cold for that.

If you smoke indoors the room soon fills up, and you can't open the window, and quick! turn off the light. The atmosphere in there gets cloying. It is better to sit in the garden and smoke, and perhaps sip wine and make conversation with beautiful younger women, and watch the swallows swoop and dart and keep low to the grass.

Keep your head down.

It is even better to sit by the river and watch the boats. Even better to be on the boat, watching the shore and smoke until you are sick. If you eat very little, and what you do eat you spit into your handkerchief, too many strong cigarettes can make you retch when taken with wine, though over the side of a boat, who cares? Who's watching? He doesn't care.

Indoors, though, if you move a picture to the side, one with an image in it, to see what's behind, it's not what you think. Instead it is a patch of paler colour, as if someone has come in with a brush and determined to paint behind everything you have hung on the walls a lighter, less brown shade. Even behind the mirror, cracked now since it fell from the wall in the night. When you woke there was a lot of noise in the corridor, a lot of anxious whispering and running around. There was the sound of broken glass being swept up, as if all the mirrors in all the rooms had fallen at once. Had they leapt down from the walls in a concerted effort to break themselves?

But, of course, no one has tried to exert their influence over the colour of your walls. It is you, you realise, who has painted your own yellow walls brown with the endless cigarettes, one after the other, the smoke of which gathers in the back of the mouth and makes the scars sting in a way that you mistake for pleasure. A tobacco chewer mistakes the cuts they make on the gingiva, and the sting of the salt, the relief from the lack of having chewed tobacco, for pleasure. Isn't all pleasure like that?

A misrepresentation to the self, by the self?

If you wear a cardigan and a jacket, if you wear a scarf, in the autumn you can smoke in the garden and listen to the sounds of a celebration off in the distance. What are they celebrating? There is no way of knowing, but is that relevant anyway? Let us imagine that Ernest Hemingway, the famous modernist writer who will go on later to commit suicide by gunshot to the head, has returned to Paris having defeated the Nazis. Keen to share the victory with someone whom he knows will appreciate it, he has driven a convoy of Americans to Sylvia Beach's bookshop *Shakespeare and Company* on the rue de l'Odéon. He has liberated her from the snipers who have been harassing and killing passers-by. Her bookshop published the book *Ulysses* which, despite being inferior in all respects to *Finnegans Wake*, is the book for which its author, James Joyce, is best remembered.

That might provoke a celebration the like of which you hear in the distance as you smoke cigarettes in the garden. It is not that celebration, which is taking place many miles away in Paris, but it is the same kind of thing – gunshot, laughter, cheering, furious near frantic behaviour borne of years of fear, now relieved. You can listen to that and smoke, and though you do not recognise the new attendants, and many of the others are gone or aged a decade overnight, you can smile to them.

When people celebrate they will come up to you, even if you are withdrawn and affectless with a blanket over your knees and your cigarettes and matches held in place so they will not fall. They will grab you by the face and kiss you, on the lips and perhaps on the forehead.

They will ruffle your hair.

If you do not respond they will laugh and another will come and put his or her arm around you and carry on a conversation very loudly in your ear. They are right; you should be involved in communal celebrations of this type. You are not dead. But you are in a withdrawn and affectless mood, so cannot reciprocate.

They are so cheerful that your lack of affect will not dampen their mood, and this is one of the few times you can remember where it is fine to sit and not be engaged without anyone feeling they have to up the stakes, or gee you along, or to root out the source of the trouble, or to give you increasingly high doses of serum, or barbiturates, or injections of seawater, and instead they just let you be in your state while they are in theirs.

Sometimes at Christmas, after a lot of drink.

Which is not to say that it is pleasant to be affectless and withdrawn, but is to say that it is fine to be taken as you are. It is easier, certainly, than being expected to demonstrate that exact degree of excitement and public display of shared emotion that the people around you evidence. That is something very difficult, since you feel nothing and are a very poor actor, and no-one you know has been within miles of you for as long as you can remember. If only Ernest Hemingway could come and liberate you at the head of a convoy of Yanks, or Samuel Beckett, or better still James Joyce could rouse himself from the place he lies beneath the soil in Zurich, watching, and make his way to the west coast of France where fireworks are being set off, and instil some life into both of you, the great genius.

Or the brother, or the mother, or any of those who had taken such a lively interest in the affairs of the family when the patriarch was above the ground. Though what impetus is there now? For people who do not believe in ghosts?

It is only for you that he watches on, the others can relax in the relief of the tension of the obligation to meet the needs and desires of a mind like his – such difficult work and paid so poorly! If he palmed off the responsibility to breathe life into you even when he was breathing, why should anyone else take up the burden now he is dead? The champion, the defender, no – you should stay where you are. The immediate threat from the Nazis has been alleviated by Ernest Hemingway, and the bookshop is liberated. Why would they come now when they did not come before? When there was a real threat? When doctors ended the lives of those not worthy of life.

From then on the priesthood took over all important symbolic roles.

May you receive it, your Hemset, your god

The family take the coffin into the tomb which they have decorated with spells and images of the world within which the deceased will live for eternity.

DR W.G. MACDONALD
AROUND RUISLIP, 15TH MARCH 1951

Ruislip, on the river Pinn, was Dr W.G. Macdonald's destination, and he drove there with an uncomfortable mixture of reticence and haste that marked a journey that was begun too late in the hope that it never had to be made at all. He waited by the telephone and watched the clock, his ear attuned to the first bell, and his eye to the progress of the hands, and there was always the possibility that it would be cancelled. Perhaps the plane would be delayed by mechanical failure. Perhaps his passengers had a change of heart and decided to remain in Paris. Perhaps the pilot had become ill and a replacement had to be found. Waiting for news of any and all of these possibilities allowed time to move past the point when it would have been prudent for him to set off, considering traffic and the possibility of minor delays, past the time when a good driver with a fair wind could have expected to arrive punctually, and into a red zone where anyone would be lucky to arrive when they had said they would arrive.

Now he looked at his wristwatch and he was already late. There were still five miles to go. At least.

He was outside Rickmansworth.

There was nothing in the trip that should have been so off-putting, and there was nothing back at the office that was so deserving of his attention. Perhaps it was just inertia. He had a general sense that not doing something was preferable to doing it, on some days – if it was raining, or overcast. The thought of ringing for another cup of tea was much more attractive than putting on his coat and walking down the stairs. Getting the car started and going to fill it with petrol, and taking the back routes to a place in order to avoid the traffic – it was all such a bore. There was a weight in it that seemed to crush his chest, especially in comparison with a cup of tea and the crossword. Perhaps a biscuit. Or simply sitting and not moving, even his head, so that his vision blurred out of reality and he was left with his own thoughts. It was not that this was pleasurable in the slightest – indeed, it often felt like sadness – but on some days, and in some weather conditions, it did rather seem appropriate. Or at least not doing it was a chore.

Laziness, really.

He was not a wonderful driver, either. Some men take great pleasure in driving, and in cars, and in the accessories available – leather gloves, flasks, caps, that kind of paraphernalia – but he was ambivalent to it at best. He had learned to drive late, and although he had been driving for decades now there was still that sense that he wasn't properly part of the scene, that it wasn't for him. There was the constant threat of a problem with the engine, or of a tyre to be changed, neither of which he was equipped to deal with. Journeys of any length felt like a dangerous gamble to him, where the possibility of accident, or worse, embarrassment was always hovering.

He didn't like talking to the class of man that one had to go to in order to get cars fixed. They seemed to have the measure of him in some way; even when they were polite he could feel them thinking poorly of him. Can't a man repair his own tyre? Doesn't a man know how to fix a carburettor? What do we have here, then? A man who can't… et cetera.

There was always someone directly behind him on these country roads, too. Everyone else was very keen to go faster than he was comfortable going, and this was all to do with being manly. In the hospital no one questioned him on this score – his learning and professional qualifications were more than enough for the nurses and secretaries. Good afternoon, Doctor. Yes, Doctor. They recognised his seniority; but out on the roads, in the streets, he felt small and somehow feminine.

All nonsense; he was tired and overthinking things. Why can't a man be reluctant to take a trip without it being some psychological issue?

He was behind a tractor now. He tapped on the wheel, and the wrist-watch was right there, letting him know that he was now ten minutes late.

So what? What would happen if he was twenty minutes late? An hour? Hardly the end of the world. He was on his way, he would arrive eventually, and then there would be no amount of tutting that he couldn't apologise his way out of. After all, this was a courtesy, to collect a client from the airport – they could always have taken a taxi.

Perhaps it was her, then. Her bearing was irritating – again, that sense that he wasn't a person worth recognising. She was very wealthy and whatever qualities he possessed, she had him there. Inherited, too, so she was used to thinking herself better than those around her, ever since she was a child, probably. He could imagine the haughty glances given to the stable hands and waiters and cooks of this girl's childhood – she was American, so they had a *Gone with the Wind* quality to them, these daydreams – and he would be in a long line of recipients of her innate privilege. She was stern to look at too, the centre line of her hair very defined, like the sea Moses parted, and her mouth in a constant downward droop at the corners. How old would she be now? Old, anyway, and not the kind of woman, even when young, that one could either intimidate or charm. What does that leave for a man, in terms of social interaction? Kowtowing?

Perhaps that was it, then: he didn't like to be less than the highest authority in the room. His feelings of wellbeing depended on that fact, and now he was loathe to put himself in positions where he had to answer to someone greater than he was.

Nonsense; he was continually in meetings with the board, all of whom outranked him.

Yes, but not in his own field.

The tractor pulled over into a layby and he went past, waving thanks to the farmer who utterly ignored him. Wasn't waving the driverly thing to do? Surely it was…

There was the other business, of course. They had a history. There had been a time, long ago, when he had put a great deal of faith in certain treatments that had then turned out not to be as effective as he'd hoped.

Not entirely ineffective, but very close. In the long term. And expensive. He had advocated the use of a treatment derived from the cells of foetal calves, as an alternative to the monkey glands which were extremely popular at the time. When it became clear that monkey glands were ineffective he should have ditched his claims for the bovine serum, but he did rather try to milk the situation (no pun intended). There was a gap in the market, briefly, before the field was debunked, when a shrewd man could have offloaded a great deal of expensive stock to people desperate for an alternative. Unfortunately, his product became tarred with the monkey glands brush, and it all got a little sticky (no puns intended).

Was it guilt, then?

No. More embarrassment and, again, that sense that one's authority has been, or will be, undermined.

Still, here she had come, back for more, so clearly she had some faith in him.

Or was it coincidence? Or was her hand forced by some other consideration? Or something else?

It was all so tiring. Why had he agreed in the first place?

Batchworth, Batchworth Heath, then right before Northwood, and there was Ruislip Heath over which planes were landing and taking off.

He wasn't an aficionado of planes either, though there were some he knew – the Vickers Viking he recognised, since the name had a pleasing alliteration, and there had been an incident that was in all the papers where a Frenchman had committed suicide by blowing himself up with a bomb in the toilet. That plane had taken off here, just like the other ones were doing now, and landed back too, with a gaping hole in the rear and one fewer living Frenchmen aboard than when it had taken off. The consensus was that, as a means of ending it all, this was a peculiarly selfish choice of method: why not blow yourself up down on the ground, where no-one else would get hurt? Or slit your wrists anywhere private? Or drown yourself in gin when you get home? He could understand that point of view, obviously, but secretly he thought there was something grand about it, something memorable. Why not make a big show of it? Perhaps this man was killing himself precisely because he had been a non-entity throughout his life, and this was the thing that would put him on the map. It was certainly memorable. Who knows, perhaps there was someone waiting down there on the tarmac in Paris who was relieved and delighted to hear the plane had turned back.

It's an ill wind, after all.

The trouble with thinking things that distract yourself from a future event is that while it does relieve the gnawing of rats in the stomach, suddenly you are presented with that thing you have been dreading as if out of nowhere. Here she was in front of the car, waving him down: the old woman. She was with her charge, the girl he had failed to cure (now a middle-aged woman) standing in front of the entranceway to the airport building.

He had no choice but to give two cheery honks of the horn, even as he took a sigh. He didn't recognise either of them – at least he didn't feel a sense of recognition. In fact, was he getting muddled? Was this a different old woman altogether?

He came to a halt and applied the handbrake, put the car in neutral, and turned off the engine. Was that the right order? There was no time to think because she was up to the passenger side door, opening it.

—Where should I put the bag?

A pun occurred to him, but very briefly, and he indicated that there was room in the rear since the bag was small. It is amazing how quickly a separation of years suddenly becomes as if nothing, and having this woman bark at him brought it all back – the conflict over his methods, his fees, his attitude, his demeanour, the old woman's meddling which had resulted in a great deal of anguish all round, and now he was not at all surprised that this meeting had met with such antipathy from him. His stomach, it appeared, had a better memory than he did, and now the old woman was indicating the bag, and that he should come round and collect it, which, of course, he did.

—Is there anything in it?

The bag was as light as an empty bag is; when he picked it up with the strength required to lift something heavier it flew comically into the air. The old woman didn't smile.

—Don't worry. I will provide clothing and essentials later, if you can concentrate on your job.

There were none of the politenesses that one might expect, nor much chat at all, so he took from his jacket pocket the schedule of fees and passed it to her. She took it and made a great show of searching for her reading glasses, patting herself down from head to toe and back again, before opening the clasp on her handbag and taking them out from there. When she read the list she scowled before meticulously folding it and placing it in her bag with the glasses.

—Expect me early next week, she said, though to whom she said it was unclear since her charge was already in the passenger seat and she was looking in the opposite direction.

Would that be it? At least it had the merit of being brief. Brief enough, in fact, for the exchange to be seen as a storm in a tea cup and perhaps nothing to be so affected over anyway.

He made his way over to the driver's side door and opened it, and out billowed cigarette smoke as if he had opened the saloon door of a packed bar.

—You should stop that filthy habit. Doctor's orders.

The more I thought about it, the more I was seduced by this idea (against my more scientific understanding that I was making connections where they did not properly exist, and ones which were so filled with supposition that they were almost worthless), and it seemed to me that a crime had been done against the laws of the people who had made this tomb. The desecrators of this place had taken upon themselves the role of Osiris, the god of the dead, and made judgement of the deceased's actions where that is properly to be done at the ceremony of the weighing of the heart.

May your Ka be gracious to you

The coffin is lowered into the stone sarcophagus, and the canopic jars placed at the foot of it. The personal effects are brought in, along with offerings of food and wine.

STAFF OF THE INSTITUTION
NORTHAMPTON, DATE UNKNOWN

Doctor's orders to an attendant don't get questioned.

You do what you are told.

When an attendant is told to strip his charge, and to mummify her in sheets and towels soaked in cold water, that is what he does.

So the patient is stripped and the towels and sheets are doused in cold water. Then the patient is re-clothed, head to foot but not the mouth, in the winding cloth. We use linen wrappings from overused or stained bed sheets that are no longer fit for purpose. We use cotton towelling that is past its prime, balding in places, torn into strips and wetted. We bind from the fingertips to the elbow, and from the elbow to the shoulder, then around the neck and under the chin. We go over the forehead and around the eyes, and across the bridge of the nose. One man holds her still – not so difficult with the frail birds, but never easy – a flinging arm to the bollock can stymie the process, but this is not so much of an issue if pre-medication has been ordered. A nurse can apply it via vein, and the cotton wool ball will be kept in place by the winding cloth.

Like a baby, a patient will cease her crying when swaddled. Her arms are held tight, her legs are prevented from movement, and the room is dark. If we shush in her ear like a mother, the patient almost always calms. It is a reflex, though it doesn't always work for mental cases with episodes of frantic behaviour; here we combine it with cold water. Cold de-saturates the nerves, drawing their heat into the liquid. It prevents over excitation.

Once our charge is restrained on a canvas stretcher or hammock, we draw a continuous bath of cold water into which the patient is lowered. They object to this, even if they are swaddled. They try to release themselves from the straps – we restrain them at the ankle, knees, elbow, wrists and across the forehead. Restrained, they are prone to drowning and hypothermia, so we keep a close eye on them.

First, the attendant notes their name and the date and time of their arrival at the top of the sheet – if there are any assistants in the process, the names of these people are similarly recorded, and if they are unable to sign their own name then their name is signed for them by a supervisor.

With a thermometer, the temperature of the water is recorded. We bring it up to the eye, but avoid placing our fingers on the bulb, which will only record the temperature of our fingers and not the water. We note the number in the space provided on the sheet. The water must be neither too hot nor too cold. The addition of cold water should correct the latter, hot water the former. We never use a kettle – that runs the risk of scalding – but hot water is added every fifteen minutes. If the patient evacuates in either manner, then we begin again; the water is allowed to drain, and fresh water is provided.

We watch carefully at all times – if there is another call on our attention then we find someone else to attend her promptly. Otherwise we risk the patient drowning.

She is unable to make any movements by herself; she is so tightly bound that even if she slips a little under the water she can't right herself and drowns. To prevent hypothermia, we check for cyanosis, excessive flushing of the cheeks, excessive blueness in the cheeks, or a loss of either colour in the cheeks. We take the pulse every time the temperature of the water is checked to ensure that there are no problems with the heart, and that the patient has not died. If the patient shows extreme reactions beyond what might be expected of them, then we drain the water, and take her on the stretcher to one side while the supervisor is called.

We note the patient's mental state – write on the sheet if she cries, laughs, sings, goes silent, or makes any attempt to end her own life by stopping breathing. What she sings, where possible, we note, also how she sings it – in tune, atonally, with relish, or sarcastically. Hallucinations, both auditory and visual are noted, such as 'patient proclaimed that her father was watching her (despite his being dead)' or 'patient listened intently to noises that were not there with a strained but ecstatic expression'.

When the supervising attendant's shift concludes, we note when he leaves and the arrival of his successor is also noted at the same time. No shift is considered to have ended without a new shift having been begun.

If for any reason the patient is removed from the water, the reason for this removal is noted. The patient's wishes are not sufficient reason for them to be removed from the water. The time of removal is noted on the sheet and the patient is rubbed vigorously with a good dry towel until they glow with health. This prevents them remaining cold and wet.

And what does the patient think while immersed?

It is possible, perhaps likely, that the cause of the disturbances that are seen on the ward – the throwing of chairs, the setting of fires, the surly and dismissive attitude when presented with figures of authority, the withdrawn and reluctant persona, the refusal to eat sufficient to maintain a minimum healthy weight, the attention seeking behaviour, the unhappiness, the poor hygiene – have, as their source, a psychological cause rather than a somatic one. Possibly there is a psychosomatic cause, or a purely psychogenic cause.

Under immersion, the patient brings to the fore all those things they have purposefully forgotten or have repressed.

Like a child left locked in a school gymnasium as a form of punishment, detained after the end of classes and then forgotten either purposefully or by accident (and then the caretaker has left and locked up and no staff will return until the following morning) these forgotten experiences run around and make difficulties. They scream the building down, which echoes through the corridors. So loud is the tumult in the locked and empty school of the mind that these experiences disturb the behaviours, even without the patient sensing the sound. As the neighbours to the school building are disturbed without knowing the reason for the child's detention (she threw a board rubber toward a teacher) or the name of the child, or even whether she was a child, or instead some kind of spectre, or trapped animal, or something unidentified but terrifying, so is the patient disturbed.

So, the patient might profitably think to open the doors on the pains which they have forgotten and remember them in the knowledge that the disturbances themselves are lessened when suffered directly. They cause fewer aberrations of behaviour than those which the noisy screamed echoes of the pain cause. So pain, during hydrotherapy, might be an appropriate subject to turn the mind to.

If the logic of this suggestion does not find hold in the patient (because, most likely, they are mad) then a willingness to turn the mind in toward a subject suggested by the physician can be provided using certain drugs. The painful experience can then be iterated repeatedly by an attendant while the immersion in water is taking place, immersing the patient in her pain simultaneously, and thereby providing short term relief from the symptoms of her overheated nerves, while addressing the longer term tendency for the patient to shriek her pain silently in the locked and empty school gymnasium of her mind.

The attendant might repeat 'do you remember the time when…' and here would be inserted a painful experience revealed by members of the immediate family, or culled from previous interviews with the patient when she was less unstable, or taken from the police records. Failing the above, plausible and likely painful experiences can be selected from a list that can be provided by any reputable psychiatrist.

While wrapped in cold bandages, or whilst restrained on a stretcher, or while crouched in a tiled room and doused with a hose, the patient might think of those things she wishes not to think of. They are too many to name individually, but there are classes of such experience into which these ones will fall: the class of experiences had whilst left alone for prolonged periods as a child; the class of experiences had while harshly punished for minor misdemeanours; the class of experiences had whilst serious misdemeanours are punished by the induction of pain in a helpless loved one (a pet rabbit, or chinchilla, for example) up to and including the point of its death, and for which the patient is made to feel guilt; the class of experiences had while the father indulges himself sexually, and for which the patient is made to feel guilt; the class of experiences had where the mother punishes the daughter's primary and secondary sexual characteristics for being more beautiful than the mother's currently are, and for which the patient is made to feel guilt; the class of experiences had when induced to do one thing in the expectation of praise, but for which punishment is then given; being laughed at, cruelly, for those things that the patient was previously induced to feel pride in; being mocked in front of third parties for matters told in expectation of strict confidentiality; being beaten whilst pleasure is ostentatiously displayed by he that delivers the beating; being burned with a cigar; being pricked with needles to the tune of a favourite nursery rhyme; being shaken very hard; miscellaneous.

Whilst dwelling on difficult and traumatic experiences is in itself difficult and traumatic, if the experiences themselves, or the experience of them, or the memory of the experience, or the sensations and feelings induced by the memories as they are experienced in the present can be integrated with the self as it exists in the present, this is the key to resolving the painful effect of the inducing incident. It is in the repression of this material that the flaws in her behaviour exhibited by the patient in the present are amplified. So, let her scream, let her suffer, let her shiver – all these are demonstrations that the self in the present is developing methods of dealing with what should have been dealt with satisfactorily in the past. Once the melodrama is over, there will be a person more able to cope with themselves and their history than she was before. Just as the attendant dries her body and rubs into the skin a glow of health with a new white towel, so will the physician at subsequent interviews bring a blush to the mood of the patient, by pointing out to her how much stronger she now is in the face of thoughts and preoccupations that would previously have seen her crouched in the corner of the room, or tipping over the side table, or refusing her soup.

Once emptied, we scour the bath with Vim powder and a hard brush. The enamel is pitted from long use, especially around the plughole, so no elbow grease is spared. We circle the brush whilst pushing hard enough to bow the bristles, keeping a firm grip on the wood. For this job, plastic gloves – yellow or pink – are used (if there are none in the store cupboard we make a request on the inventory sheet) to protect the skin of the hands. If bleach splashes onto our lips, or eyes, or mucous membranes during the process, we immediately rinse them in an adjacent sink.

When the bath is clean to our satisfaction we begin again and repeat the process – the debris left by the patient is often not visible to the naked eye, and consequently we are not best placed to understand when it has been removed. Even if our effort is probably redundant, we make it regardless: better that we expend ourselves uselessly than germs and micro-organisms are left to flourish in areas used for medical purposes.

We rinse the bath and gloves after use, and place the gloves in the store cupboard.

Once the patient is returned to her ward, we put the observation record in her file and reestablish her usual routine as soon as is practically possible. Regardless of the efficacy or otherwise of the treatment, the conditions in the ward as they were prior to the treatment must be maintained – this allows for a continuity of routine for staff and patient, and also allows any improvement/degradation of behaviour to be observed against the baseline control established by day to day life in the ward. In the event of any unusual reaction to the procedure, we note this and add the note to the file – the doctor attends to the matter at the next available opportunity.

They had sealed the deceased's mouth so she could not speak, and so could not proclaim her innocence of any sin.

May your god be gracious to you

The tomb is sealed and the deceased begins her journey to the afterlife.

THE DENTIST CHARGED WITH REMOVING LUCIA JOYCE'S TEETH
NORTHAMPTON, DATE UNKNOWN

He is called out to an appointment, ushered through to the room, introduced to the patient, and the nurse opens the mouth.

It is a right mess at the back: abscesses, crumbling away, significant degradation to the bone structure, x-ray like a bath sponge, vacuoles on a cell diagram. A strong breeze and this lot would be out like tiles slipping from the roof and smashing in the drive. Like slate pieces chipping his paint work. He'd sand it back, prime it. New layer of enamel and several hand coats of wax, buffed to a shine.

They're virtually out by their own accord, as if the teeth want to flee this tube of flesh, and make a life for themselves alone, outside. These hard objects are disgusted by the softness they find themselves surrounded by. Couldn't a canine make a better go of it alone? It couldn't do worse.

He gets the nurse to open her up wider and inserts a dental prop.

Show him a strong tooth. Show him a structure that will take the teeth of a pair of workman's pliers. He'd have it done before lunch. His knee on her chest, brute force, one at a time, and ride back to the saloon to play poker and drink fingers of whisky in the company of petticoated whores from the rooms upstairs.

Painless Parker.

This is more like archaeology. He'll have to pick out the tesserae from which this corrupt mosaic is figured, unpick them from the shattered superstructure. Tease them out from the glue. It'll take much longer.

If only he could chisel away the maxilla, grind into the mandible and get it all away. Start again with new stone, cement it into place and slip the flap of skin over to cover the evidence. A sculptor would do it that way. Unhappy with the results of his apprentice, he'd show him how it was done. Let the master see the fox, let the hounds watch the hunt. One heavy hammer and one sturdy blade and the whole skull would be gone from the vomer down, ready to accept a perfect replacement, carved in the workshop in awed silence.

No.

She won't wear the nosepiece: too jittery, too nervous, too barking like a dog. She writhes in the chair, keening and whining like he is going to torture her. Even with the wrist restraints she manages to get the mask off, whipping her neck round and thrashing. No need for hands, no need for thumbs. Opposable digits are not required for her mischief. It could be achieved by a fish, thrashing about in a net, hook in her mouth. She'll tear the cartilage to pieces and die slowly in the shaded deeps beneath a weeping willow. She'll drift into stagnancy where the river bank is weak, damaged. Out of the current, out of eyeline and earshot. Working against her own better interests.

—I'm not going to torture you.

One and half grains of pentobarbitone and he'll see her in an hour.

He arranges the bone curette, rongeurs, root tip elevators, probes, mirrors, and explorers. Unless she takes the nitrous it will be intravenous thiopentone. He can't work on a woman like this, not safe with all the movement, all the incoherency. His tendency to slap must be resisted, the urge strong though it might be to undercut her hysteria with a blow to the cheek, a cuff to the side of her head. A punch directly to her eye socket. An elbowing. A kneeing. He could cut through all the nonsense and let her see the lay of the land. Done hard enough he'd provoke the same effect that several quid of analgesia could achieve.

He does it through the vein instead: chemical cosh, fast acting and legal. No bruises except one so tiny there's no noticing it. No need to account for it. No talking it off, no living it down. He smacks her with the syringe.

Spare the, spoil the.

Now she's out, the nurse can put the nosepiece back on. The elastic is tight against her hair like a laurel wreath. It's like a permanent wave; it's like a crimp.

She breathes slowly, eyelash unresponsive and docile. If it was up to him then all life would be like this – quiet and peaceful and dreamless while what was best for them, but painful, was carried out in their absence. He'd strap them into a chair and get about the business of fixing what their inadequacies had brought about in their bodies. He'd anaesthetise the lot of them and do what needed to be done. Then, when they awoke, numbed and blinking, it would be to a world in which things were better than they are, where things were manageable and correct, where the damp roots had been removed from the earth where too much water had caused them to rot. He'd prune the dead wood back, pinch the yellow leaves between fingertips, compost the death and decay in the darkness, out of sight: piles of detritus transformed beneath a blanket into good productive loam ready for the fork, ready for the shovel, integrated with the land to make new growth to the proscribed plan.

He finds it necessary to cut a semicircle in the gingiva, so the lip is drawn up in an emotionless snarl. The assistant holds it in place with instruments, suctioning the saliva and then the blood, so that the scalpel can slice above the incisors. He makes an inverted arch which can be folded up and held. It is reflected into an aqueduct, black and red in the gloom of her mouth. The nurse brings forward the lamp and it all glistens like berries gathered in the autumn and washed.

He swabs, she suctions, he melon-balls the bone away.

In Kew Gardens there are plants that bear seed pods that, when held between finger and thumb, explode pepper corns all over. He sees a tooth like that stuck near the throat. It is difficult to deal with that tooth and not run the risk of choking her.

Despite the injection, despite the constant flow of gas and air, she moves as if she is unwilling still. She gives a long [no(o-o-o-)] shouted from the bottom of a well. Her muted echoes of dissent can be ignored.

He uses iodine swabs, suctioning. Black thread stitches the wounds where necessary. The body has an amazing ability to regenerate some areas; the mouth being one of them. Why, he wonders, not the rest? Why do we not regenerate as a skink does? New arms, new legs, new organs? The history of medicine might be subsumed into that of horticulture, relieving the physician of the jeopardy of his trade. Snip it out and let it regrow. Open wounds and let the body regenerate them. Pull out teeth and, rather than taking casts and making new sets, wait for a week and see the buds of them appear. Watch them grow *in situ* until the new are as good as the old.

Not the will of God.

And what does the patient think while her teeth are removed?

That the mouth is like a vulva, the throat the vagina, the valves of the oesophagus the cervix, the dentist the gynaecologist, and drills and needles and clamps, and shafts for which multi-faceted interchangeable heads are available are themselves interchangeable. Needles in the gums, needles in the soft palate, needles in the hard palate, in the gingiva, in the interdental spaces. Iodine swabs and powder sprinkles into the wound like salt, seasoning. Pump and clamp. The curette, curettage, applicable at both ends. The scraping out, the removal. Adenoids intact here, but the process is the same – things which must be removed. The teeth wish to be born, so here it is the reverse: the child too long where it is no longer required, these teeth requiring a life of their own. To be out of a mouth from which nothing listened to emerges, which consumes nothing to fulfil them, whose guardian takes insufficient care of them. She is incompetent in that way. Scars across the back of the throat and the sides of the mouth. Splinters in the flesh. Loci for infection.

To the dentist, all mouths are the same. The mouth of Napoleon would have seemed the same to his dentist as the mouth of one of his soldiers, no doubt. The mouth of a film star the same as the mouth of a lunatic to her dentist. Still, there adheres a certain quality to the work he does for the rich that is not present in the work he does for the forsaken. Perhaps it is the glamour of the environs in which his work takes place. Certain places in central London have a subliminal influence over the mood, the mood over the thoughts, and the thoughts over the mouth as it appears and is experienced. One opening into the flesh, while biologically and anatomically identical in its type is felt to be a 'better' mouth than another one for which one is paid to minister to in Northampton, in a home for the diminished.

The mouth itself seems to be diminished.

Or perhaps the dentist to the wealthy is himself filled with a sense of his own value that comes from the status of his patients, whereas the dentist to mad old bitches feels himself, for the period in which he is obliged to work on their mouths, a mad old bitch himself. Has he failed in his life to have to attend to them? He's not fucking Christ, after all, to wash the filthy feet of every piece of human scum that crosses his path.

Is he Christ?

No. That honour belongs only to Jesus Christ, and, in a lesser way, to his priesthood, to the church. A dentist is not a priest, so perhaps then he resents this work, thinking of the class of person his colleagues tend to. The men with whom he shared digs during his education, men he sees occasionally at reunions and festive times of the year, men who drive cars that are larger than his, have wives that are prettier than his, have wives who are more attentive than his, have wives who are not found placing their lips on the generative members of men who are not their husband, by mutual friends who say this only since it is a burden on them to have to keep the secret, and who, if not gleefully, then with a certain self-righteousness, do not claim he should have performed his own marital duties with more vigour if he wished to prevent his wife from taking the semen of other men into her mouth and then spitting it into her handkerchief before placing the lot of it in her new handbag and clipping together the clasp.

The rongeur, the rat chewing through bone, gnawing on it, required when there are immoveable roots. When the tooth and the bone are reluctant to be parted, mother and daughter, too close a relationship, too similar, they must be separated from each other for both of their goods. The whole situation must function. The world must go on as it needs to, even if the two of them are trapped by their attachment into a formation that cannot be allowed to continue.

When both are in opposition to the needs of their environment, in opposition to each other, there is only one route that can be taken through – forced removal of one from the other, for all our sakes. She cannot go on living here, when the two of you fight like dogs. You are driving her mad, and she will kill you in the end.

What does the rational man do? He removes his emotions from the matter and applies a utilitarian argument. He creates an equation, makes of the real an algebraic representation. He assigns values to the terms, and by following logic comes to the correct solution – remove the teeth, separate mother from daughter, create new teeth, and come to terms with the new regime dentures require – sterilisation, a change in the manner of moving the mouth, the avoidance of certain types of food.

He may not like the process by which the bone is scraped away, but he does it nonetheless. Now the equation is on paper and the decision has been made. Isn't that the job of the professional man? – to come in, dispassionately, and do the work that has been assigned to him, without pointlessly going over all of those issues that led to the decision being made in the first place? He comes in and does those things that need to be done. Should he be censured after the event? Should he be made a pariah because he removed a woman's teeth? Of course not.

She might say that teeth ought not to be removed (if she said it, she would be an idiot, but she might say it), that a lunatic has no proper grounds for consenting to such a procedure, and that any such procedure would be an assault, just as if a man had taken a spanner to a woman's face. But this is to forget that a lunatic has given up the rights to herself by becoming a lunatic in the first place, and has been placed under the care of the state. The state has the responsibility for her health, and also therefore the right to decide what is best for her, regardless of whether she consents to it, finds it a desirable state of affairs, or wants it. If that is not enough, then take it up with her doctors. Take it up with her MP. Take it up with parliament, with the Queen – such is the legal situation, and the man who operates outside that legal framework lays himself open to prosecution, and should a man be punished simply for doing his job?

Dentures are very good now, so much better than a mouth full of rotten teeth, both practically and cosmetically. They can be removed for cleaning, they do not break easily, they are at least as good at the work of mastication, and if it was not for the fact that they can slip around the mouth and irritate the gums, then many dentists would recommend them in the place of poorly maintained teeth any day of the week, so he stayed long into the dark evening.

And then left her to rot without the necessary protections.

I looked over at my colleague and, knowing that he was not the kind of man who would share my feelings on this matter, I resolved to go about my plan alone.

This woman had gone into the afterlife friendless and I resolved to address that lack.

Your ka being in front of you

The spells, rituals, talismans, and texts protect her from crocodiles and snakes, and provide her with the strength to pass the seven gates, cross the fourteen mounds, and enter the twenty-one portals.

TORIA THURSBY
NORTHAMPTON, 13ᵀᴴ DECEMBER 1976

In the winter it is almost always dark. The sun sets before the evening meal and doesn't rise until after breakfast, so there's no need to close the curtains. If you are feeling under the weather they don't make you come down to eat, but they will insist on having lights on in the rooms if it's dark, so if you want to watch the transitions you have to wait until their footsteps in the hall go silent and then get up and flick the switch off. This is harder work than it ought to be, but preferable to sitting in artificial light, no matter how long it takes, or how your fingers ache. Edison gets a lot of credit for the invention of the light bulb, but is it really such a boon? The light they give is so monotonous and harsh, overwriting everything with a grim whiteness that makes mirrors of the windows. Your candles provide enough to read by, if they are close to the bed, and you can snuff them out without having to drag your old bones up. In the dark a window pane is a marvellous thing – as minutes pass it changes: a block of colour you only gradually recognise, shapes that grow out of nothing and then the most beautiful subtle colours, different in the morning to the evening, different in each season, an infinite and unnameable progression in the eye that is exquisite.

When day returns there is the tree, and the bird's nest, and the distant tower blocks.

If they catch you lying there in the dark they tut and flick the switch, which can be a shock if you aren't prepared for it. We can't have you stewing here in the dark, and the sheets straightened and the pillow plumped, and there you are, your own face in the window, so much older than you remember it, so much older even than your memories of your own grandmother.

Do you really need to see that? Or the framed pictures that you have seen a thousand times and which were not terribly inspiring in the first place. You've never liked Constable, have never been to the mountain photographed in the painting's opposite number on the other wall, and the replacement of the infinitesimal gradations of the day's progression with these mass-produced and poorly executed excuses for art, the same in every room, irritates you.

Even if you aren't feeling on top of your game today, you still have to get up. There are the routines that the institution relies on, that you rely on, you realise, that must be adhered to, particularly the medication. You must have something, even if it is just beef tea, since you can't take your pills on an empty stomach, and if you don't have the pills then you will regret it in your joints, and in the headaches, and in the static that builds in your eyes and ears through blood pressure, so you force it down. It makes you feel better – it is warm and takes the edge off the nausea that you hadn't realised was building – which is another irritation, as if your body is in cahoots with them, siding with them, acting out their prophesies regardless of how much you want to resist admitting they know best.

Except about the light – you know you are right about that.

Anyway, you are needed. You allow yourself to be washed and dressed, a process that they have perfected over years so that it is almost possible to ignore it. There was a time when it was mortifying, but now she hums and does it all and you stare over her shoulder and think of something else – tennis, sometimes, plays you have seen, memorable events with minimal emotional content – and then you are standing there ready and she is backing out of the door, carrying linens, or yesterday's laundry and you are alone in your room and can make preparations for the day.

Your friend will be anxious, since you did not come down for breakfast. They will have told her there is nothing to worry about, but she will be worried nonetheless. And why shouldn't she be? It is perfectly rational to be worried for a seventy-nine-year-old woman's health, and perfectly rational to assume that nurses will not necessarily tell her the truth, especially since she has a history of reacting poorly to bad news. They shouldn't chide her for being worried; if anything it's a good sign: it shows she cares enough for something to matter, which is a problem for a lot of the others. Better to be worried for a friend than to sit in a chair all day and do nothing at all.

She will also have hidden her pills. When she is anxious, she hides her pills at the back of her mouth, behind her dentures, and when the nurses aren't looking she spits them out into her hand and shoves them down the side of her seat. There's no point in picking her up on this, it only makes her defensive, so you'll need to get her up on some pretext, retrieve the pills and reintroduce them to her as if for the first time. It's little tricks like this that your long life has prepared you for – how to deal with difficult characters – and though it feels tiring to you on occasions you also know that it is one reason to keep living, something that perhaps only you can do for this woman. To be needed cuts years off your age; it spurs you into action, and it's those helpless cases that die young and miserable, the ones who will do nothing for anyone, don't see why they should, who dismiss everyone around them, that haven't really understood what life is all about – it is about being needed, it is about doing things for other people, and that's what makes your life worth living.

That is what you tell yourself.

The hall and stairs are hard work, but you refuse to use a walker, and you don't trust the Stannah: it is infantilising. There is nothing wrong with hard work; better that than to take the easy route out and atrophy entirely, and if it takes you a few more minutes to get downstairs, are you really in that much of a hurry?

Your friend is not at the bottom of the stairs, wringing her hands, which is a good sign. You had dogs for most of your life; some are relatively independent and can entertain themselves if you need to run an errand, but others wait behind the door, whimpering and digging at the threshold, and she tends towards this latter sort, though not irredeemably – she just needs distracting. She has one of those portable radios and an earpiece that allows her to listen to Radio Three in the common room, so perhaps that is what she is doing now: listening to Wagner, if she is lucky, with one finger in her ear and a transported expression. You can't tolerate Wagner – so melodramatic and overblown, lacking in subtlety; a lot of fantastic nonsense told bombastically – but you keep your opinions to yourself, lie a little, take the earpiece when she offers it to you and nod appreciatively at the aria.

Is that cowardly? Some people would think so, but then people are so opinionated these days; they've forgotten the importance of considering the feelings of others. If it gives her pleasure to think her pleasure is shared, then where is the harm in that? And if it's cowardice to make an old woman happy, then you are content to be a coward.

Midway down the stairs you realise that you have forgotten to bring your reading glasses. You turn, and the five or six stairs to the top stretch ridiculously up, like the never-ending flights in an Escher drawing. You laugh at your own pathetic frailty, comparing these steps to the walks you did as a young woman, a middle-aged woman, an old woman, even: wind-bitten across the broads, no distance too far providing there was a drink to be had in front of the fire in a pub at the end of it.

Forget it, not worth the effort now. In fact, she can go to fetch them for you. She likes to be given little jobs when she's in the right mood, and you can express your gratitude to her effusively, something she likes even better.

You grab the bannister and forge downward – up is too much, but you can still manage down, for God's sake, and at a lick when your blood is up.

Downstairs smells of breakfast – fried eggs, burned toast and Ready Brek, which is superior to porridge in the opinion of the other residents. It's fine since you never liked porridge anyway. You feel a little wobbly… no, that's not quite it… the floor feels too solid; your heels generate too much resonance when they meet the floorboards. That's not it either… this is why one should wear slippers and not insist on outdoor shoes. It's okay to take advice occasionally, acceptable to let others know what is best… or is it? Isn't that the beginning of the end, when you start admitting other people know better about your life than you do? Is the problem in the knees, then? They jar as you walk, no matter how softly you try to tread. You should stop being ridiculous. If you had anything real to worry about you wouldn't pay so much attention to these minutiae… if you were being chased by a tiger.

Out of the door ahead of you come two nurses either side of whatshername, the one who has occasional fits – epileptic, not temper – and you press yourself back against the wall so that the dado rail is in the small of your back. They go past and you hold your breath – it's a fact of getting very old that you can sometimes lose control of your bowels, but you all agree not to talk about it, or to notice when it happens. When those of you who are not afflicted in this way feel the urge to be disgusted, as you do now, you squash it – relatively easy if you've had children and grandchildren, not so easy if you have not – in a spirit of comradeship, and as a sacrifice against the future, when you dearly hope people will pay you the same courtesy. In here it's the least of one's troubles, and if the maladies keep themselves to the physical, then everyone is happy.

She isn't in the common room, but the chair she usually sits in is empty. You go over and sit in it, as if this is what you've come here for, and even though that isn't the case, you are appreciative of the chance to sit down, though that strange sense of disjunction is noticeable here too – you feel too light, as if you have been filled with helium and are now on the verge of lifting off. You grip the arm rests.

The room is full of old women; some are already back to sleep, others are chatting in confidential huddles, one is ruminating like a cow, churning her teeth loosely in her mouth and periodically pouting. The radio is on in here, though not Radio Three – it is the local station, something it announces at every opportunity between the news of traffic signals malfunctioning and the minor intersections between the national news and the people or places of the region.

Which is where?

You reach down into the tightness between the seat cushion and the sides of the arm chair and, sure enough, there are pills: capsules, more accurately. You once knew exactly what she was taking, the counter-indications, the closeness with which their advertised effects matched their intended uses *in vivo*, so that you could discuss it all with her, but that is something of the past, now. What has changed, you can't pin down, but the particularities of these concoctions is something she simply accepts, and she has turned her attentions to other concerns. Which is not to say that she wasn't concerned with these other concerns before, but now they are more all-encompassing. Since the brother died.

In some ways it is a relief for you – it is very much easier to explain why people do not visit when they are dead.

Excuses must be made for living people, very complicated excuses which require a great deal of knowledge of family history, and a certain amount of resourcefulness in the answering of difficult questions. On the fly, often. But you care deeply for her, and would not have her suffer the grief that the death of a brother brings just for your convenience. Or a mother. Or, back into prehistory, a father.

And there are other problems.

You palm the capsules and bring them up to your chest. You are wearing a baby blue cardigan, and it has a pocket on the left breast, and you mask the fact that you are slipping the pills into this pocket by simultaneously removing your handkerchief and coughing into it. Such slight of hand is rarely seen outside members of the Magic Circle, and you are very impressed with yourself, so much so that you smile. Perhaps that was a career missed… along with all the others.

You rise, creaking, and the blood leaves your head entirely. You have been warned about this – postural hypotension – and yet you consistently fail to take it into account. Now you wobble, halfway between standing and sitting, supporting yourself as best you can on your arms, while the world becomes entirely white, as if everything real has bled milk into everything else and become one snowy mass with no form or substance. The sound of your breath is very loud in your ears, and your heartbeat thumps in your throat.

Is this it?

It isn't it. When you stand up the body sometimes has a job getting blood up to the head, and if there's no blood in the head there's not enough oxygen. It can make you feel faint. So don't stand up quickly, or you risk a fall – the doctor has said this, in increasingly weary tones, for years.

Eventually the heart cottons on and pumps a bit harder and then it all comes swimming back.

You straighten up. If she isn't in the common room, then she's probably in her own room – it's too cold to be out in the garden.

If that had been it, then what? Stroke has carried off more of the women in this place than you can remember, either to the grave or to a cheaper institution, where they can sit out their days in an efficient immovability that no longer requires psychiatrists, or therapists, or anti-psychotics, or any of the specialist facilities – a stroke victim who used to be troubled is like any other stroke victim: not much trouble to anyone.

It could have been a stroke. It could have been any of a number of things – you don't bother with the ins and outs – it's not the kind of subject there's any point dwelling on – but you know enough to realise that women of seventy-nine can go of anything. Would she accept it? That is the problem.

She is in the garden after all. You didn't think she was, but as you pass the window on the way to the other staircase, there she is at the bottom, by the compost heap, wrapped up in her waterproofs with a blanket over her shoulders. If you want the French doors open you'll have to go and get someone with the key, so you go round to the kitchen instead, which is how she must have got out.

When her father died, the nurses told you, she wouldn't believe it. She's spoken about it to you since, how he watches her from the grave, which is morbid, but not entirely unexpected since she wasn't invited to the funeral. The mother never came to see her, after that, and she can't believe she's dead either. Same story with the brother. Your father would tell you, when you were a child, about faith, and what it meant – it is no small thing to believe in something you haven't seen and not everyone has it in them.

She does not have it in her.

There she is, staring into the trees. What does she see there? It can't be much – it's hardly a forest; there's a couple of ashes, a privet bush, and then a creosoted fence. Some rhododendrons.

When you die, will she cry?

Or is it too late for all that?

Will she pine?

Who will rescue her pills from the side of the chair and get her matches from the kitchen? She has this silly habit of chewing on match heads, when she is not smoking. Who will pass her the handkerchief so she can spit the splinters into it and then empty them into the WC later, when no-one can see? Who will listen to her stories? She has a hundred of them, strange people she has met, some of whom you recognise from books you've read, all the things that have happened to her, which no one knows about, all the places she's been, her strange ideas, her dreams.

Who will listen to her at all?

You shouldn't think such nonsense. Seventy-nine is no age, and you're in better health than she is. A country upbringing and God-fearing abstinence from the indulgences of life are a fine basis on which to predict an extended old age, whereas smoking two packets of cigarettes a day, eating match heads, and standing in the garden in the cold weather is asking for trouble.

But, then, what will you do when she is gone?

We went about our recording of the tomb. Later we filed the claim with the consulate. Still later, we hired professionals to photograph the tomb decorations, but when it came to the removal of the sarcophagus, I found ways to prevaricate and obstruct progress. I feigned illness, I ensured I could not be found when the time came to sign papers, I sent to England for funds when I had ready access to them in Egypt – I even argued unnecessarily with Mr Pfeffer, provoking him with curses until he resigned and left in a huff for Paris. I did everything I could to ensure no movement was made.

And your god being behind you

She names the portal-keepers: he who eats snakes, the burner, and the one who eats the excrement of his hinderparts.

STEPHEN JOYCE

It was dark outside and when the gentle shake woke him, and then the calm whisper, he saw them first by reflection in his window. There was a rectangle of light, his father silhouetted in it, and then the outline of his nonno leaning over him. In the first moments of being woken from his dream there was a disjunction – he couldn't quite tell whether they were in the room with him, or on the other side of the glass. Also, where had the dream world gone? Walking beside the river, leaning down to feed fish who were half-emerged and gaping for bread. But fish do not come up onto the bank and beg for scraps, and fathers and grandfathers do not hover outside the windows of an upstairs room – the fish would drown in the air, and the people would fall to the ground.

He rubbed his eyes with the sleeve of his pyjamas.

His nonno's hand was on his shoulder, and his lips were at his ear, and from far away there came the mournful tones of the air raid siren, wailing at the sight of incoming bombers and the fires they set in the homes and streets of the city.

—Up you get. Quick as you can.

He said quick, but there was no hurry in his voice. The boy turned to face him and sat up in one movement, moving with the fluidity that only the very young can demonstrate. Nonno leaned in to him and the boy reached out in reflex, his body expecting to be picked up and carried from the bed, but Nonno did not lift him. He embraced him instead and squeezed. The boy put his head over Nonno's shoulder and yawned across at his father, who was slow to smile, but did it in the end.

—Where are your slippers?

Nonno was speaking to himself, not waiting for the boy's answer, sweeping an arm beneath the bed and pulling them out, one at a time.

In the far distance there was a concussion, dulled by miles, sounding like a faint hit of a bass drum, the fur on the head of the drumstick dampening the sound, but not so much that it didn't shake the glass in the window frame.

His papa turned, but he didn't leave the rectangle of light. He raised his hand and placed it on the door frame, and sighed, and the boy blinked and swallowed the sleep away, knowing that his father's muted reaction wasn't what one should expect of the real in this situation, but having nothing to account for the disparity except the closeness of sleep and the bleeding into the world of the logic of a dream.

His nonno turned him around on the bed, evened out the legs of his pyjamas and slipped the slippers onto his feet. Then the old man stood and offered his hand to the boy.

He took it.

Even then there was no great urgency, as there had been in the past. Instead of today's calm and measured quietness there had been bellowing, and slamming of doors, and the sense everywhere of anger and fear. The sleepiness of everything was of a harsher sort, of the jolting out of one world into another, the reluctance of the mind to accept a fate harsher than the one it dreamt for itself in the warmth beneath the blankets, and an overcompensation for this felt in the veins which surged with anxiety and a jittery eagerness to be in motion.

There was a flash, like lightning, that painted his papa and Nonno's faces with harsh highlights, contrasting wedges of colour that edged the lines that travelled down from the corners of their mouths and across from the edges of their eyes. He had been backstage at a pantomime once and had seen the performers removing their make-up – white face paint makes a similar effect when you smudge it with a sponge, before it is all off and the principle boy ages in a second, then makes herself youthful again with a damp flannel.

It was a few seconds before they heard the noise. Just like with lightning, if you count until the thunder comes it will give you an idea how far away it hits. Perhaps that was it; there's no need to panic if they are miles away. Panic is counterproductive. Proceed calmly to a place of safety.

He walked with his family out of his room, out of their rooms, and into the corridor. Here there were people panicking, but panic of this sort is oddly private, and each family panics by themselves, acting out their role in a little play that is much like their normal behaviour, except compressed into moments.

There is little conversation between groups who meet in corridors, and even ritual nods and liftings of hats are held in abeyance. Small children will stare at each other, while doors are locked, or forgotten possessions gathered, and he looked at the boy from across the way, but neither of them made any fuss, or spoke. Indeed, their expressions were utterly flat – there was no time to express anything, only to obey the important commands of the adults. This boy's parents were engaged in an argument about keys, where his own papa had already locked the door, and as they left them behind and went for the stairs, he gave the other boy a little wave, which was reciprocated following a glance at his people to ensure they weren't watching.

Their rooms were on the fourth floor and the lift was so slow that it wasn't worth waiting for it, so they passed by the iron cage, which was empty anyway, and took the stairs. His papa took them two or three at a time, at first, but when it became clear that his nonno couldn't match the pace, he waited with one hand on the brass rail for them to catch up. The boy could have done it – he could have done better, in fact. On mornings before the adults were up, he would take cushions from wherever he could find them and pile them on the mezzanine between floors three and four and jump from the stairs down onto them. He'd start at the first step and jump, which was no jump at all, more of a step, and then the second, which was still not taxing, nor the third, nor even the fourth and fifth.

The sixth, though, was higher, and by the seventh or eighth, a certain degree of courage had to be mustered before he could throw himself down. His record was twelve, but this resulted in him flailing back and cracking his head. The inevitable crying brought his nonno out. He didn't scold, but he did gather up the cushions and take them back before anyone else found out. They were dusty, something which later caused comment, but his nonno winked at him and the mystery was never solved.

—How's Nonna?

There was the briefest of pauses, but neither of them replied. This is the way of adults; they find it very hard to do more than one thing at once. If they are talking on the telephone, they cannot also help with a paper aeroplane. If they are reading up on the requirements for the arrangements of permits to travel and visas, they cannot also reach for a high glass or cup so that he might pour himself some milk. If they are swearing and cursing to people in one room, they cannot also be wiping his nose.

So, if they are making their way down the stairs, they cannot also answer questions.

Coming up the stairs, in the opposite direction, was a man in uniform and he put his hand on papa's shoulder and ushered him down, saying something in Swiss German that he didn't understand. The man didn't touch him or his nonno, only nodded to them, but once he was past he started shouting. Hurry up, or something like it. As the man ascended the stairs the soles of his shoes squeaked like mice, and when he turned the corner his heels clicked together. He wore green socks.

Nonno let go of his hand and gripped him by the shoulders. With his hands here he both used him as support and steered him around the corners of the stairwell, following papa. Nonno was heavy, but the boy was getting stronger as he grew, and he felt that it was something he could manage, this weight, albeit slowly.

They were overtaken on the way down the stairs by a grey-haired man carrying a doctor's bag that he clutched to his chest like an infant. His chin was tucked over the handle and clasp, and so tightly was he holding it there that he had to look up from beneath his brows to see where he was going. As he rounded a corner he slipped, and even then he did not reach out with his hands, but let his shoulder hit the wall rather than risk dropping the bag. The man clinked: there was glass inside his bag, probably, and whatever was in this glass would be valuable. Nonno had taken him to see a western, once, where a man had ridden in the back of a wagon with a crate of nitro-glycerine on his lap; every bump on the road had this man sweating. The grey-haired man was like that with every step he took, though, like the man in the western, speed was of the essence and a certain amount of carefulness had to be sacrificed to avoid death by Red Indians. He was soon out of sight.

By now the last remnants of sleep were gone and the sharpness of every-thing was obvious all around: the growing shriek of the sirens as the ground floor approached, the cold night air encroaching from the open doors into the contained heat of the hotel, angry voices from corridors he did not look down. Still, his nonno's hands on his shoulders were safety to him, his papa's broad back was too, and now he felt hungry. When a child is asleep he does not feel hunger unless it is represented to him by something else in a dream. He can dream of pillows in place of bread rolls, or axes in place of chops, and by some logic, either visual or verbal, this will satisfy the stomach. When he is awake no such trickery will stop the rumbling if the boy is calm enough to eat, and despite everything he was calm enough.

—Will there be breakfast in the shelter?

He turned to look at his nonno's reaction without slowing his progress. The old man's face was in an intermediate expression, somewhere between puzzlement and resolution, and it stalled there until he had to look forward again or stumble on the stairs.

—Possibly not.

Now here came another man, moving stiffly enough that they were side by side for a little while, shoulder to shoulder, and the men behind him had to wait to get past. This man was dressed very nicely in dark tweeds and smelled of lemons and flowers, some hybrid cologne that made him seem sophisticated in a way that was impossible to account for. His cufflinks were silver squares stamped with a diamond pattern, and his shoes were perfectly polished. If the boy had been thinking carefully, he would have realised that the man was immaculately turned out, more so than any man had the right to be, disturbed from his rest in the middle of the night. That said, he might not yet have gone to bed, or might have risen particularly early, to make a morning meeting somewhere a train journey away, for instance. What time was it anyway? If the boy had looked before leaving the rooms, he would have seen that it was twenty-five to four.

This man's hand was burned and scarred, the mottled red of his skin contrasting with the white of his cotton sleeve, the weight of its fabric, its starched stiffness, the perfection of cloth against the failure of his flesh. The boy looked up and his face was like it too, on the left side. The right side smiled down at him, but the boy could not manage to smile in return – the effort was somehow too much.

The burned man turned away and with an effort of his own that showed in small lurches into the railing, drew ahead of them, past Papa, and away. His cologne drifted in his absence, and the other men coming down the stairs behind him, anxious in having been restrained in their pace, picked up some of the scent of it, except too little to be noticeable.

When they eventually reached the bottom of the stairs the lobby was empty except for the owner. He was in a long night gown, like something from a comic short. He didn't have a night cap, limp down his back, with a pompom at the end, nor did he have huge loose woollen socks (he had heeled brown leather slippers), but he gave that impression – a ridiculous emergence into the public realm of small comforts that should properly remain private.

—Cellar is full. Nothing to worry about. Word is that the raid is over Friesenberg.

—Can we get something to eat, then? For the boy?

—I'll see, sir.

He turned, and when he was facing away he shook his head, as if to suggest that no one Swiss would think of asking for food at a time like this.

They stood in the lobby while the owner went into a back room, and through the glass doors the night played out on the street. There were restaurants and pensions in both directions and into and out of the segment defined by the edges of the doors passed men of all classes, walking, running, out at a time when they should properly be indoors, awake when they should be asleep, in the living world when they should be safely contained by their own unconscious minds, traipsing the streets they make for themselves there.

There is something of the dream world in the real as it is at twenty-to-four in the morning during an air raid, even if a boy is fully awake and has his awareness sharpened by hunger. There is the absence of some of the things we take as constitutive of reality – there are no cars on the streets, for example, and there is no light except that which leaks from poorly blacked out windows, since the streetlights do not operate after dark here in wartime. Men act in a way that is peculiar to situations like this, too – they will come out in public in their private clothes, as one might in a dream, and tiredness will affect their behaviour so that they act in ways that are not entirely like those that dominate the waking world. Perhaps they are not thinking straight, or perhaps this is what they would always do, given the chance, but they allow their hidden natures, their desires, to surface, as happens in a dream. They will clutch vials of serum to their chests, and protect them like infants.

Outside in the street, on the steps down to the cellar of the hotel opposite, there was a man with a cow. Despite the noise from the sirens, and the bass drum concussions of bombs falling in the distance, and the constant shouting of men with very important things to say, loudly, this cow's distressed lowing was the loudest thing. The man had a rope around the cow's neck and no matter how hard he pulled the cow would not go forward; it set its legs apart – four corners of a huge black and white rectangular cuboid, almost impossible in the straightness of its lines, especially at the back – and would not obey its master. He went round to the rear and pushed the right angles her thighs and hips made, but it had no effect other than to make her swish her tail in his face, something that enraged him. He looked around on the street, and, finding a broom leaning outside the restaurant next door, he began hitting the cow, first across its backside, and then, when that didn't work, on the backs of its legs. The cow moved then, and the man dropped the broom and ran to the rope. The cow was in motion and the man sought to direct it, jamming his feet against the third or fourth step down into the cellar and leaning back, but instead the cow moved steadily off, dragging the man with her, out of the segment of street the doors gave view of, and into the war beyond.

—There are pastries, but they are not fresh.

—Thank you.

They left the lobby through the back door and the owner watched them all the way, until, as they passed the threshold, a man all in black, thin as a bird, with his hat under his arm drew the owner's attention to him with a cough.

—Sir, if you find you have the need...

The man in black passed the owner a business card, which identified him as a funeral director, though the writing was too small for the boy to see. The owner had no pockets in his night shirt, and, anyway, what kind of time was this to be touting for business? What was the world coming to? First, foreigners asking for food in an air raid in the middle of the night, and now one of his own seeking to make a profit from the dead.

The owner sighed and admitted to himself that both these things were practical for them, if impractical for him, and he put the card on the counter beside the small silver salver on which mints were piled, and now, for the boy, the pastries were a more pressing issue, lacking the smell that freshly baked goods had, but visually stimulating his appetite even without it. He didn't see either the man leave or the owner retreat into the private areas since he was looking up at his nonno, and tugging his sleeve.

Nonno made him wait until they were standing on the steps down to the cellar before he passed him what looked like a horseshoe, coated with toasted almonds.

—It's full. You'll have to find somewhere else.

He had had these horseshoes before, and inside he knew there would be jam, and perhaps crème pâtissière.

—You'd turn away a boy and an old man?

At the bottom of the steps were two men in white uniforms, grubby at the cuffs and neck. If the trousers had been checks they might have been chefs, but their trousers were white too and while the jackets weren't clean, they also weren't smeared with food. A chef when rushed, as most chefs are, will wipe his hands not on the towels he carries in his belt, but down the sides of his jacket, occasionally across the front, or on the front of his apron. So, if he is working with sauces, gravies, or coulis, the colours of those things will stain his clothing – these men had none of that.

—Don't worry, they're bombing the Jews today, so this is a formality.

—Then why not swap?

One of them shrugged.

Whatever concussions and flashes had set off the sirens were memories. The cow and the undertaker, and now these two – orderlies from a spa? Dentists? Obstetricians? – and, most of all, the horseshoe pastry were things more recent in the memory, or right in front of him.

The wind changed direction and the siren quietened, the worst of its noise blown somewhere else in the city.

Nonno sat at the top of the steps and the boy sat with him. His father stood, but this didn't prevent the boy from biting into his pastry. If it was stale, he didn't notice since it was sweet – raspberries and vanilla custard.

Sometimes, during an air raid, a bomb will land on the offices of a newspaper, but that is not the only time when it will snow burning paper.

A bomb might land on a public library, or a printer of wedding invitations, or a stationer. It might land on a manufacturer of the paper itself, or the place where wood is pulped and later dried in sheets. There are many ways in which it might begin to rain burning paper.

So, to see white snowflakes, their edges on fire and blackening, is not indicative of a dream, or of the breaking down of reality. An incendiary bomb might set fires in a paper warehouse, burning up through the supporting structures until the roof collapses and the swirling plasma, the release of gases from wood, the action of the wind through the broken windows, might send gouts of half-burned paper up into the atmosphere where they might fall, burning, across the neighbouring districts.

Who knows which equations determine the distances that paper might travel? The boy did not.

When he looked up into the sky, his mouth full of pastry and custard, and raspberry seeds sticking in his back teeth, he was amazed to see snow falling, burning, to land at his feet. The snow turned to infinitely thin curled black crisps of nothing, which became smudges when touched with the toe of his shoe, but he did not question his eyes.

Snow is white and cold where it lands, but this was hot and black; snow does not smell of anything, but this smelled of smoke and of used matchheads; snow is wet, but this was utterly dry, so dry that it could not sustain itself under any pressure at all, and became ash when you blew on it.

Mostly it fell in pieces smaller than a postage stamp and was black before it hit the ground, but the larger pieces were edged in red, a thin line that snaked and contracted against the white, lessening and replacing it with black until it met in a piercing dot of light that disappeared immediately.

One piece fell the size of letter paper, and on it were obituaries of notable persons who had died the day before, laid out in columns, some with pictures. The boy recognised no-one and the fire burned through the paper too quickly for him to read it, even for him to understand what it was he was reading. Anyway, why would a nine-year-old boy pause to read, which is hard work for him, when all around it is snowing fire?

His nonno pulled him in, fearful that this fire would hurt the boy. It might have, certainly, if the fire had caught the edge of his clothes, or landed in nearby flammable material – a pile of litter, an oil slick from a leaking engine, or kindling stores leaning against the wall of a shed. If it had landed in his eye, this might have hurt, too, and required him to wear an eye patch, like a pirate, while he recuperated. His father was less concerned, or braver, and the boy himself began to laugh, as if this was enormous fun, to see burning snow, falling from the sky.

And it was.

In the street across the road there was a man taking pictures of the sky, pointing his camera directly up, where there is usually nothing to interest a photographer at night, unless he also has a telescope. It must be a relief, to a photographer, to have no-one to direct, no-one to communicate to – and fail – about his wishes for this or that shot. The red and white against the blackness of the sky simply is. There is no need to coerce it into being something else.

If he wished to make a film of this event, he could stay exactly where he was until the phenomenon subsided, at which point he could pack up and leave, certain that he had done his job and knowing that nothing need be added or removed in the edit, except perhaps music.

When it was over the boy swallowed his mouthful.

—Can we go to the circus later? Or the zoo?

This city was full of pleasures that a boy might enjoy, even during wartime. A circus was not one of them, not in winter, but a zoo certainly was – there was an excellent one in the Fluntern quarter of the city, and while one could not go there and see a man place his head inside the mouth of a lion, or make it jump through a hoop, there were lions there. There were also elephants, and all of the creatures a committed and well-resourced collector of specimens could ship back from the exotic places of the world.

—Not today. Perhaps another time.

—What about the museum? That's educational.

There was no denying this, surely? Wasn't education such an important thing for a child who moved around so much that schooling was often impractical? How else would he learn of the Egyptians? Of mummies and gold masks and wall paintings? Of the Ba, the Ka, and the Akh?

—Another time.

Abruptly the sirens stopped, and, though they had been quieter, the absence of them was like ringing in his ears, his attention brought to the space they left in his mind. His father pulled him up by the arm and the three of them stared at the men now filing out of the cellar, shaming them, since danger was passed and their cowardice was revealed by the face of a small boy with jam around his mouth and an old man, both of whom they would have preferred to die in their place, had it come to it.

First came the men who were not chefs but attendants in a clinic for nerve cases, then came some non-descript men of middle-age and middle-class with nothing to distinguish them from any other men of their type, then came the man who was burned on the left side, but who smelled of lemons and flowers, and then the doctor, clutching his bag to his chest in which were vials of serum derived from the organs of foetal calves, and then the maker of delicate mobiles, and the man who loved another woman, and the man who was raped by a dog in a fantasy, and the dentist who removed the teeth of old women, and the men who bear down on one at Christmas, amongst the discarded wrapping paper of one's presents, and the intern who burns one's letters and photographs on the lawn in the hope of impressing his employer.

When they were all out, like the animals who left Noah's ark, Stephen said:

—Nonno, where are all the girls?

To which he replied:

—Who needs girls when you have me?

And he pulled him to his chest.

It was my dearest wish that this body should remain undisturbed, and every night I would pay those we had already paid to guard the tomb entrance to allow me down into the tomb alone, when my colleague was asleep.

May you receive your head

And reaches the Hall
of the Two Ma'ats.
She speaks the names
of the parts of the
doorway, and is greeted then
by Thoth, god of wisdom.

THE BA OF LUCIA JOYCE AND THE MAN CHARGED WITH HER BURIAL
NORTHAMPTON, DECEMBER 1982 ONWARDS

Green on brown, the grass grows like mad once the hole is dug, then filled in and allowed to settle. Back at the beginning they would do it by hand, taking it in turns, chatting, punctuated by tea in tin mugs, the boiled water communicating with the callouses on their palms through the conduction of its heat through the tin handle, forcing rotation first clockwise and then anti-clockwise. Now at the end it is done alone with a Massey-Ferguson 50B.

The plot is in the extension, so no trouble getting between the old stones, and tea can wait till the work is done. Either way the result is the same: once the earth is tamped down, some loose is left on top and a bag of compost split on top of that – only time the shovel is required, and then just to cut and mix – a bag of grass seeds sprinkled over. They sprout before they hit the dirt, and when it rains you turn back and there it is, green on brown, obscenely fertile, mockingly alive. Parasites on the corpse, mow them later with the Murray 11, cut it back, weed out the dandelions. While you're kneeling on the grave you are face to face with the dead, give or take a plank of wood and a volume of soil, an infinite number of worms and microbes. You can look them in the eye, give or take an eyelid. You can speak to them, give or take a resident soul.

It's not hard to picture yourself down there, when you are kneeling on a grave, especially before the stone is laid. You can't lay a stone on a freshly dug grave – it takes some time for the earth to settle – in its place a plastic marker with the name of the deceased is put there, or wood. Wood gives the impression of lolly sticks, the inscription the joke. Children can use lolly sticks to make all sorts of toys, slipping them together and making them hold without the use of glue.

Do corpses get lonely, under the earth? Worms and beetles and microbes are no company, and the body is arranged in such a way that it faces upward. Even if its eyelids are open, and the opening of the mouth performed, and a plank and a volume of soil removed, it only ever sees upwards. Perhaps they should put the body on its side, so at least it can see its neighbour, alternating corpses lying on opposite sides. Though who wants to spend eternity staring through closed eyelids and soil at a stranger?

Once the stone is eventually placed, when the land has come to equilibrium, the grass around it has to be removed and a patch of turned earth maintained.

They are all alike now, all these new graves in a line, their occupants staring up at the sun or into the night. This patch of brown next to the green looks very neat. It is possible to feel, in this neatness, that everything is right in this place, that to join in the line, to have neighbours either side who are doing the same thing you are doing, marching in step for eternity, is correct. Only if this neatness is maintained, which cannot be done by a tractor, or a ride on mower, but can only be done by an old man on his knees. If you want a tin mug of tea at 9.45am then you can damn well have one. What are they going to do, sack you? At your age?

Is it going to be lonely, under there?

There are families who maintain family graves, and not only the very wealthy. There are tombs and sepulchres and pyramids and mastabas (though not much recently) where whole families are interred. There, multiple generations of people who are not complete strangers to each other lie in death in each other's company, for eternity.

Some of the notable dead took their families with them, their wives and cats and bushels of their corn mowed down and preserved. Others waited in the presence of their sires and dams and grand-sires and grand-dams for their wives and cats to come when they were ready. It's also perfectly possible to buy adjacent plots of land in a graveyard with the intention of interring your corpse, and the corpse of your loved ones, in close proximity so that you will not be lonely for eternity. All for a very modest sum (subject to availability). The turning over of agricultural land to alternative uses is a boom industry, and if your chosen cemetery does not have space for your requirements, there are many new cemeteries opening every month on land previously owned by farmers who can no longer make a living from agriculture.

It's possible to take an existing grave and, using the shovel, dig up the earth until you reach the coffin. Carefully remove it, dig down further, re-inter the coffin and then place another coffin, within which the spouse who lived on as a widow for forty years is placed, on top of her husband. The idea of turning the wife face down in the coffin so she can see her husband again is distasteful and must not be suggested. The idea of the husband staring at the back of his wife's head in perpetuity does not occur to anyone.

The Massey-Ferguson 50B should not be used to dig down to the coffin even if it seems as if it should save time. There is something disrespectful in the use of heavy machinery for such delicate work, and if you dig too deep you'll dig into the fragile and mildewed wood and disturb the bones within. Once the coffin has been removed, a hole is just a hole and, if there is room between the grave stones, it would save time to use the digger to excavate the extra soil.

Don't drive it too close since the ground will be unstable.

It's not acceptable to bury a widow who has remarried in the grave of her former husband against her will, even if that clause was present in the former husband's will. The authority over the eternal resting place of that woman's corpse passes to her new husband on remarriage, should he survive her. If he then dies it returns to the widow herself (via the executors of her will).

She is doubly widowed (there is nothing suspicious in this).

In this case she may choose which of her husbands to be buried on top of (or neither) though the wishes of the surviving relatives must also be taken into account, since they will be footing the bill in any case (from the estate). They cannot be induced to pay for things of which they do not approve: I'm not having that bitch on top of my dad for all eternity; are you fucking joking?

In the cost of these plots a certain amount is reserved for maintenance, although this is generally borne by the owners of the cemetery. A tidy and well-presented cemetery is a form of advertising, and no one is going to trust the corpses of their dead to a place that cannot even hire old men to get on their hands and knees to pick dandelions from the turned earth around the gravestones. Dandelions must, in any case, be removed by spring, at which time they generate vast numbers of seeds and make the job much more difficult than it would normally be.

What if she doesn't want you with her, though?

What if he doesn't want you with him, though?

What if they don't want you with them, though?

It is easy to image a situation in which the doubly widowed widow wishes to be buried with her first love. He is her true love, her love who, through her subsequent marriage, was always in the back of her mind. Photographs of whom she would often consult once the washing was done: the wedding album in which she was a much younger woman in white, and he was yet so handsome.

Yet, it is equally easy to imagine that this first husband, separated through, let us say, war, has a grievance against the wife who survived him. Not in the early years, when she grieved properly for him and was seen always in black and lost a lot of weight and could scarcely be induced to laugh, not even at Christmas gatherings. She would turn down the sherry. In the later years, though, she cuckolded his corpse with this new husband, even going so far as to take him into her mouth, which he insisted on, he knows. But still, spitting his semen into a handkerchief and placing that handkerchief into her new handbag.

It's a bit rich now, coming to him and disturbing his eternal rest, he who is very used to being alone, thank you. He doesn't want some cock-gobbling old bitch sitting on his chest for all eternity: there's no way that old whore is getting near my dad's grave; I don't care what the fucking will says.

Old men who tend graves (when they are not taking yet another fucking tea break, what do we pay you for?) can imagine any number of circumstances in which the presence of one person's corpse in close proximity to another's is not to be sanctioned. Not only those corpses the survivors of which talk loudly over the graves in question about while he is face to face with the dead. Snipping dandelions off at the stems before they can develop parachute balls and disperse their seeds from the seed heads.

A brother and sister should not lie together if, in life, they lay together. That would be asking for trouble, such as when Set tore the body of his brother Osiris into fourteen pieces and distributed them by throwing across the ancient lands of Egypt. From here their sister Isis retrieved them all, except the phallus which was eaten by the fish of the Nile. This is why you should never have fish for supper when visiting that country on holiday, nor ever drink Nile water. Not because you have some puritanical reservation about having cock in your mouth, but because to put the cock of a god in your mouth is considered extremely rude by those who worship that god, even if the cock has been eaten by fish, digested, and passed into the waters of the Nile in the days of prehistory.

One must not be rude when one is a guest in another's country.

Though, as anyone with a passing knowledge of the science of homeopathy would know, the extreme dilution of digested Osiris phallus in the waters of the Nile would make Nile water almost infinitely potent as a medicine (though the medicinal effects of Osiris's phallus have not been investigated, let alone proven, unless that knowledge has been lost).

Isis made for the reconstituted Osiris a golden phallus to replace the one the fish of the Nile consumed. She took the form of a swallow, beat her wings, and induced the emission of semen, which she did not place into either a handkerchief or her handbag, but rather used to create Horus, their son, in her womb (though the method of transmission is mysterious).

So, then, one should not place brother and sister in close proximity, even if one or both of them are dead, without expecting funny business, and consequently having to deal with the creation of sons in the sister's womb either via the removal of foetuses, or the raising of feebleminded children.

Similarly, no one wants to spend an eternity with someone who, in life, was tiresome or difficult to manage. Who would wish to endure the presence, for example, of a person who threw a chair at them? Regardless of the circumstances under which the chair was thrown. An old man who pours his grouts into the turned soil behind a headstone can imagine many – the loss of Northampton Town to Southend United, the loss of Northampton Town to Aldershot, the victory of Northampton Town over Port Vale being only a sample. Even if it was the culmination of long weeks of baiting by the person at whom the chair was thrown, the throwing of chairs can make anyone reluctant to spend eternity beside whoever it is that throws the chair, no matter what bonds of blood might otherwise tie them together. When combined with the foregoing, is it any wonder that people just want some fucking peace for once? For all eternity? Buried with their husband and son? With their wife and son? With their mother and father? With the second wife?

Similarly, there is no particular need to mark the gravestones of those who throw chairs and pour grouts, and who come home late after the football having had a skin-full and who don't want to hear, again, of how inconsiderate they are. They don't care how much interest has accrued, or how the men from various places to whom the chair thrower owes money have been knocking on the door while other people hide behind the settee.

It was so embarrassing.

They just want to go to sleep, forever, in their own bed, with their own wife, without an eternity of fucking earache. The chair wasn't that heavy. Can't you just stop crying? You'll wake the neighbours.

So those people do not deserve to lie forever in a box in the soil beside the people they loved in life. They should not expect to do so, since eternity is an awfully long time. Without the proper preparations made, and the rituals observed, and tomb decorations commissioned, one might find oneself suffering those same indignities one suffered in life throughout the infinite afterlife. Better to have no chair throwers there, to have them separated by seven hundred miles (by road) where they can remain quiet and unriled.

Build a place in their absence: a shrine to those who were once disturbed and are now no longer. Build a statue of them, effete and unperturbed, smoking a cigarette, at which sacrifices can be made to ensure the long and happy afterlife of those buried. Neurasthenic, anaemic, bespectacled and bookish pilgrims can gather at this graveside, having first gone to Dublin and been disappointed not to find the resting place there. They can read the list of those who lie in that grave, never to be disturbed by the disturbing party, since she is neither in Dublin, nor in Zurich, nor in Trieste, nor in Paris, but in a place where no-one would wish to be, by the river Nene. Northampton is so far from heaven that whatever fires she sets will never disturb the higher heaven in which these people live. They are so precious, so delicate, that if voices are raised in the afternoon this is a serious problem. If friends come to call they must be silenced. If suitors are to be found, they must be vetted. If brothers are found with their hands up her shirt and down her knickers then it is they, delicate flowers, who must be protected. She must be taken to the doctor, where foetuses are removed to prevent the necessity of rearing feebleminded children: you've always allowed her to be so free and easy and look what it's caused; she's like a bitch in heat and there must be boundaries.

It's not as if there wasn't any room in the end – at first, certainly, the adjacent plot having been filled, but later? The city fathers provided room enough for second wives in the grave of honour, but none for daughters.

And there I made to repair the damage that had been done, to the best of my abilities. In the space where her face had been scored away, I painted it, using her death mask as a reference. In the places where the spells of protection should have been, I copied scenes from other tombs, overwriting what had been there and making palimpsests of the originals. Amongst the rags of her bindings I placed amulets from my own collection, particularly my pride – the heart scarab, onto which I carved the name I had chosen for her. I even added scenes of a happier life, so that she might at least have these as memories.

I am not a skilled painter, and there was only so long that I could hold off my colleague. There came a night when I could delay no longer and, amongst the flawed and desecrated remains of this tomb, I performed what I could of the ceremony of the opening of the mouth, in the hope that she might at last make her journey into the afterlife.

Before I left I took the *shebti* statue I had stolen for my daughter and I laid it at the foot of her sarcophagus, so that it might work on her behalf in the underworld.

Your mummy is set up for Ra in the court of your tomb, you being given over to the scale of the necropolis.
May you emerge vindicated.

She makes the protestations of innocence in front of Osiris and the forty-two gods of Ma'at, hailing each of them by their name and denying all sins against them. Her heart is weighed.

THE MORTUARY PRIEST
TRIESTE TO NORTHAMPTON,
1907 ONWARDS

Conditions in a civic hospital in mid-summer are not ideal. Even in a
world which has air conditioning, this system might be broken. Even in
a world which has public health care, this system might be underfunded.
Even in world where there is medicine, this system might be half-hearted,
or conducted with institutional malice.

Paupers – if we count ourselves among their number, if we know what a
pauper is, if we wish to recognise their existence – are not deserving of the
considerations we might imagine if we try to bring to mind ideals. Often we
are spoiled by the lives we have lived to date, so that if we try to imagine
less than ideal conditions then our imaginings on the topic fall short of
the real. We have been cossetted like lap dogs, and don't understand how
terrible things can become, and don't care anyway: stop going on about it;
you're boring me.

So conditions on the ward are trying, especially if one is kept in for
a week. The recognition of the others around us changes from a generic
categorisation of people by the degree of their illness, gradually, through
having nothing better for the mind to focus on, to a particular and exhaust-
ing form of empathy – specific and imaginary to a degree for which we do
not have the energy: if only we could get some sleep; then perhaps we'd
stop crying.

What about a baby, though? What does a baby know of ideals? Does
it care if it is too hot? A baby is used to the womb, where it is always
hot. Does it care if it is stifling? It is stifling in the womb, and very
tight on space. Is a baby troubled by the sounds it hears: the coughing
of a consumptive, or the moaning of a diptheric, or the muttering of a

rheumatic? A baby cannot differentiate sights and sounds and apply to them any meaning, since a baby is pre-linguistic. It is consequently incapable of thought (on which meaning relies). It instinctually demands its mother, and will show signs of distress if separated from her, but this is well within the normal range of its experience. Babies are taken from their mothers and lain with all the other infants. There they set up a chorus of wailing it is possible to shut out by closing the door. In this way they are silenced and cause less nuisance on the ward with their incessant keening misery.

Once they are behind the closed door they can be observed through the window, often by staff, sometimes by patients, and occasionally by uncles. They come and take from their pockets a cheap cigar (usually a panatela, rarely a corona, never a perfecto), since they are paupers and cannot afford anything too pricey. Tobacconists ensure they have stock to meet every pocket. Uncles have boxes of matches, and, gripping the cigar between their teeth (incisors if they are unfamiliar with the method, premolars if they have more experience) they light a match and bring it to the end. They puff until it holds the flame, and congratulate themselves on the generation of human mass, something that is essential to their sense of wellbeing. The air fills with the smell of tobacco, acrid or sweet, and then the match falls to the ground, black and wizened, where someone will grind it beneath their heel if they lengthen or shorten their stride.

What should be done with babies? They should be washed, fed, and given to their mother once she has the strength to take them, providing she has no pressing concerns which otherwise distract her, such as a demanding older child, or an incompetent and needy husband. If the mother is unable to tend to her baby immediately it should be placed where it cannot disturb others until she can tend to it. By all means feed it, and change its nappy, and ensure it doesn't roll off the table and crack its fucking head open, but a baby is a burden that the authorities do not have the resources to shoulder. So also a girl-child, or a woman. It is the father's responsibility to provide for the mother, and the mother for the daughter. If the father cannot do it alone he must count on his extended family, and if they are unwilling he must prostitute himself about the place making a whore of his talents until the creditors are satisfied and the bills are met. No-one must be upset, since all their livelihoods depend on it.

I know, I know, but what are we to do?

There are practicalities in the world; there are facts.

I know.

It is not ideal.

So what is ideal?

There is no point asking a baby, so I am asking you. What is to be done for babies for whom one worries? What is to be done for children for whom one worries? What is to be done for women, for old ladies, for corpses, for whom one has worried, worry now, or will worry?

Wash your hands of them all on the slightest pretext and cry foul when you hear pleas. You do not wish to have this nonsense raised in your presence. It is not your responsibility. It is none of your business.

I cannot understand what she's saying.

Such ignorance is a great luxury!

But you are not wealthy, so let's try again.

It is hot during the day and hot during the night and they never open the windows – it lets the gnats in. Her mother doesn't notice the surroundings since she has a limited range of experience: she sees into a tunnel at the other end of which is her daughter, scrunch-faced and stretching; she hears as if through a stethoscope the sparse croaks a sleeping baby makes, the slight moans and half-sounds that might evolve into crying that will wake her; she smells only the milk on her child's skin and the lack of soiling, an absence that she is alert to as if it is a something. Mothers notice all these things with an intensity that renders all the other things of the world edgeless and vague as mist.

Though the heat causes her body to sweat, and the covers to weigh heavily across her thighs, and the sounds of women and children and nurses and trolleys and water rattling pipes fall into her ears, they are interpreted through the effect they might have on this sleeping baby. Will the noises wake her? Is she too hot? Is her blanket too tight?

—Sit up, Signora; time to eat.

A tray is produced and on it is round meat, and purple-syruped fruit, and orzo with milk. The mother closes her eyes to it – it makes the bile rise in her throat – and then she snaps them open again, and yes, it was a ruse.

When a magician wants to hide the coin he'll distract your attention with a second coin, and this is what the nurse has done, because now the daughter is gone, handed off to the midwife. She is obscured behind this woman's broad, floral back, her bulging shoulders, the white split of her scalp sprouting two tight pigtails.

The mother reaches and makes to speak, but her wounds and soreness won't allow it. The capacity of her breath is reduced, as if all that pushing has collapsed parts of her lungs. She whispers things she means to bark, things this midwife wouldn't understand even if she heard them, and now the daughter is taken away. For what? Waking, weighing, pricking of the heel, snapping of the fingers by each ear.

The nurse magician's English is too poor to carry a conversation, and our child's mother has no Italian to speak of. Where is the father? He is in a bed in the men's ward laid out flat by a child's disease. The mother is left unprotected from the nurse's insistence that she eat a slice of the oily, peppered pork, and sip at the filthy chicory milk, and the daughter is taken into the hidden places of the ward where her mother cannot follow.

The magician attempts another sleight of hand: while the mother is distracted by the taking of the baby, and the chewing of meat that slicks unfriendly aniseed across the back of her tongue and leaves in her mouth a loop of thin wax paper that she has no choice but to pull from between her lips, she has drawn across the sheet and pulled up the nightie and is down between the legs, assessing the damage. The mother clamps her thighs together, but the magician nurse has her tricks, and she raises the unresisting knees and gets her information that way. She notes it in her pad and departs.

Now the mother is alone.

A row of beds in a hospital ward is reminiscent of a row of graves – it is like an x-ray shining through the soil, the bedhead the gravestone, the patient the corpse, and on both sides of the mother bodies stretch away into the distance.

The bedframe of a hospital bed is reminiscent of the bones of the skeleton – white enamel like the bleached calcium of a donation to medical science, the struts which the hands grip like the metacarpals of those same hands if they are shone through by x-rays during a difficult birth.

The absence of a child in the hours after birth is reminiscent of the early morning – lonely, but newly pregnant with possibility, and also it is a time to take stock... if only the mother wasn't so damned tired.

Down the aisle comes a pair of nurses, smiling to each other and talking and laughing. They are red-cheeked and ignorant of the bodies they walk between. Their knees are bare and their socks high on the calves. Their heels knock in unison – like metronomes – against the wooden chevrons that make up the floor. When they turn it is without resistance – they swivel at a shared right angle – since the varnish has been waxed and polished assiduously against the effects of the bleach that one of them will mop at the end of the shift, under the bed, knocking the frame and clanking the bucket.

The mother bites her dry lips, tearing back the skin on the lower one, traces the stinging strip with the tip of her tongue.

When that is done she falls asleep without knowing it.

★

She wakes to the puzzling shock of a hand cupping her breast.

It is a woman she doesn't recognise – grey and stern and desiccated, and so close, her profile at least, that she can see where the face powder has gathered in drifts in the lines that frame her mouth, and where it clumps at the corners. Her eye is like that of a chaffinch: small, so there is no sign of the white, and black. She has the child in one hand and the mother's nipple in the other and she is trying to introduce the two.

The mother is initially too disconcerted to act, but the child screws her face up against the breast and is taking such a deep breath it will certainly be released in a howl, through a mouth in which both toothless gums are presented, glistening and pink and angry. The mother's breasts are leaking at the proximity of this mouth, but this mouth will not accept them – its function is different: it wishes to expel what is inside, not bring in what is outside, and this is proper to it: why should a mouth accept alien things into itself when there is danger in such acceptance?

The child starts to wail.

The grey midwife takes this as a sign of the mother's failure, and gestures that the breasts must address the issue immediately, cursing them on the behalf of the other patients, advocating for the right to peace on the ward. She uses a language half consisting of words they do not share, and mimes anyone could follow.

The mother takes a breast, one which has fed a different child perfectly satisfactorily for months, thank you, and makes a show of jabbing it into the crying mouth, the nipple held between two fingers, and aside from briefly muting the notes, as a trumpeter might, it is no good.

You cannot make a child feed, as much as you wish that it would, and what if you do not wish that it would?

That question does not receive an answer, and here, over the shoulder of the gesticulating midwife, comes a man in a suit leading a boy by the hand.

In the absence of this arrival the mother would have made a sign that means 'bottle' and this would have been met with a weary and disgusted shaking of the head, but this boy is the mother's son, and the man beside him is her husband's brother, and such characters blanket other concerns, obviate the necessity to do anything but witness their arrival.

The mother throws open her arms for the boy to run into.

He is relatively new to the act of walking, and running is asking a lot, but he makes it into the embrace without incident. Couldn't he have tripped and knocked his fucking teeth out on the bedframe? Grazed his fucking knees on the tiles? Raised a bird's egg bump on his fucking forehead?

He could have, but he doesn't.

What is the proper age to ween a child? Opinions differ, but the mother has not yet weened this one, and this is too perfect, suddenly. Inside the reciprocation of her embrace that the child attempts, the mother sees a gap into which she can insert victory in her battle with the midwife. It is not I, she says with her breast, who is at fault, it is the baby, since, look, this child will take the breast with no complaint at all. Indeed, he is eager.

And he is, sure enough, and is soon lying across his mother, suckling, and, though it is painful for her to have him positioned like this, she smiles through it until the grey midwife departs to that hidden place where the sterilised bottles of milk are kept.

When the midwife is out of sight, the mother unlatches the boy and pushes him gently away from her stomach, now squeezed and stabbed with pains it is hard to tell the source of, but which do not feel right. She takes his little face in her hands – it is red and glowing on one cheek – and she plants kisses on it, to his delight.

The boy attended to, the mother leans back against her cushions and in front of her, seemingly very tall and masculine, is the brother-in-law. He is suited, with a shirt and tie and starch in his cuffs and collar, and half a tin of polish on his boots. He smiles at her and looks, quite unashamedly, down at her breasts, which are swollen, and wet, and entirely bare. As if she isn't already familiar with them, and is somehow called upon to inspect them herself by his staring, she looks too. They are as they always are nowadays, and he is smiling broadly.

When he speaks, it is on a neutral topic – the fact that he has brought flowers for her – and in this moment, as she directs both of their attentions to the table beside the bed on which an empty vase rests, she simultaneously draws together the sides of her dressing gown and tucks the inner side tightly inside the outer.

He has borrowed money for the hospital costs, so they needn't worry, and hence the new outfit, and doesn't it look grand? From his inner pocket he draws three cigars, one for each of them… no, obviously not the boy, and does she want hers? She nods and smiles despite herself, despite the heat and the scorching pain between her thighs and the indentations of the boy's teeth on her nipple, and the surrounding clamour of a thousand dying fucking I-Ties.

It is alright.

It will be alright, in the end, since the order to which she is obliged to kowtow is passing – the order of the nurses and the midwifes and, later, the landlords and the bailiffs – just like the order of the mothers and fathers, it is passing, and then there will be the order of the cigars, an order in which she is one of the ruling elite, and it will all be different then.

He leans across her, preceded by an invisible wave of clean *eau de toilette*, and beside the flowers he places her cigar, assuming, wrongly, that she will not smoke it if she has the boy with her. She picks it up and puts it between her teeth and he laughs because if she thinks she's going to smoke it like that she's got another think… it's no cheap muck, this. He leans forward again, as if all this is a ruse to facilitate the bearing down on her when she has only a tissue's thickness of cotton between them, and he takes it from her mouth.

From the same pocket out of which the cigars were drawn, he brings a tiny guillotine – the sort that, in the wrong hands, and with a dull rap from a mallet, can sever the little finger of a debtor – and he uses it for its sanctioned purpose: the removal of the end of a cigar. Then he passes it back to her, and even unlit when it is between her lips it tastes acrid. But isn't that right? Things that are innocuous and pallid and pleasant are things of the old regime. She will burn out that world and fill it with white, billowing, pungent, purifying smoke.

—No, signor! No, signora!

The midwife. With the hand that is not under the returning daughter's back and around, right-angled to hold a bottle to the mouth – sucked as if this is what was wanted all along – she takes the cigars from them: one, two.

He speaks in a stream of sounds both beautiful and indecipherable, and the midwife smiles at the end of it and passes the cigars back to him. She turns her attention to the mother, who must now stop her nonsense and minister earnestly to the daughter. There are mimes for drinking, and for burping, and then the midwife remembers that she has an ally and directs her instructions to him in words. He translates in an accent so broad that only his countrymen and countrywomen would understand him:

—The old sow wants to teach you to suck eggs. Smile at her and nod, and when she fucks off we can light up without any more bother.

So she smiles and nods and the woman does indeed disappear, as if he is now the magician: one with superior powers.

But, as they draw the cigars to their lips again, the boy is nagging and pulling and tugging at a bag she hasn't seen as yet, and drawing the uncle's attention away. Alright, little man, alright – there's no point in tugging it by the ears, it'll never come out of that little gap. You'll need to unclasp the clasp, as it were.

He cannot do it with his pudgy fingers, but to the uncle it is the work of a second, and here is the boy, short at the side of the bed, and he reaches up, and in his hands is a pale, grey, stuffed rabbit. Its ears are unusually long and its whiskers are sewn to its face, but he is determined that she have it.

—For baby.

The mother takes it, and she lays it beside his sister who is in her arms and is making quick work of the contents of the bottle, draining past the marks etched into the glass: fluid drams, fluid ounces.

The gift delivered, the mother puts the cigar into her mouth and the uncle leans in once more, in his hand a lit match passes across the face of the son, and hovers above the face of the daughter.

When her mother breathes in, it lights the daughter's face red in the glow.

No good, try again.

Her fists are balled, and she punches and kicks open-mouthed and wide-eyed. Her attention is on you: all on you.

You must take the flannel like this and wet it. It is better if the water is warm – not hot – but cold will do. Ring it out – it is surprising how much water a flannel can contain.

Twisted, water flows – pints of it. If it is too cold, she will cry; if it is too hot, she will scald. The flannel should be damp and warm.

Begin with the feet; they will be only a little dirty, if dirty at all, but take care to clean between the toes.

She likes it.

And then the ankles... gently, gently!

There are folds at the knee – be careful of these: germs may gather – there you go. Also they can become sore if left wet, so perhaps consider a towel.

Return the flannel to the bowl. See? Very little dirt.

Now to this area, past the thighs and up. Gently. Between us, you must part the lips, especially when the diaper has been soiled. Infection can be transmitted internally. No need to shy away; we're all girls together.

When that's clean, back to the bowl and rinse.

Attend to the folds where flesh presses flesh – that is where pain begins, and invisible sores are the cause of most tears. A stitch in time... and mother can get her beauty sleep. Under the arms and across her neck, and behind the little ears.

Never put anything inside. The body has its ways, and you will damage soft tissues.

Very well. Yes.

We understand.

Yes.

Will she ever go to sleep? From the kitchen comes the muted sound of muted pleasure – doors closed, hands over mouths, laughing choked off. It's no good though; laughter can't be stifled like that. It just makes it worse. Better. They're having a wonderful time, and this child is staring unblinking into the unlit room.

There are two choices. The first – anger – feels preferable, feels inevitable, but the mind knows it is counterproductive: no child was ever made to sleep through viciousness, and she's too young to be intimidated into silence. So it has to be the second choice – love. Only, it's hard to fake, and the clock is ticking. How long has it been? Half an hour?

The mother picks up the child, rests it against her chest so that its chin nestles into the crook of her neck and she supports it under the buttocks.

—Most terribly cold it was…

Can she understand the story, or is she still too little? She'll understand something of it: the structure, the tone. She'll understand that her mother is speaking to her. That will lull her, won't it?

Perhaps it will, perhaps it won't, but in the other cot the boy is stirring. The mother moves back towards the door, away from him.

—Most terribly cold… She says it softly into her daughter's ear, so softly that she isn't quite sure she's making the sounds, or that the sounds are louder than the child's breathing, or that the clinking and snorting from the kitchen aren't drowning them out. She shifts the girl up a little which prompts her thin warm hand to rest on the opposite shoulder for support.

— … it was…

The boy is waking. A mother knows when a child is waking, and this child is waking. When he sleeps, his mouth is open and the pillow is wet in the morning, but now he has brought his lips together and he has swallowed. Sleeping children do not swallow. They moan a little, sometimes whine, they can turn over in their beds, they can slip to the ground entirely and sleep on the floorboards, but they never swallow.

—Mamma…

A child can speak in his sleep, and it is important not to engage with him if you ever want him to go down. She moves back towards him silently, and makes to stroke his hair, but in doing so the daughter shifts a little and then sits up at the waist, unlocking her face from its place on the shoulder. As if she is replying to her brother, she makes a sound that he then recognises, and now his eyes are open and that's it, the whole thing has gone to fuck.

The temptation to rage is very strong. If the place was bigger she'd give them both a slap, lock them at the top of the house, take the key, and let them cry it out until morning, but the place is not bigger. The place is cheap and claustrophobically small and filled with the sounds of men enjoying themselves while she has to do the fucking donkey work, and, though it would give her great satisfaction to make these two little shites understand how things are in the world, she bites it back. It's the only way there will ever be an end to it.

—Come on now, you two, it's time for sleep.

From the kitchen comes the sound of smashing glass and then, as if they are in a bar, a cheer. Both children turn to look, the little one suspiciously and the older one as if there is a party in the offing that he might be able to attend.

Are they taking the piss now? Are they trying to wind her up? Isn't it difficult enough without those idiots making it impossible?

—You stay here, the mother says. She puts the girl down so that she's standing by the bed of the boy who is sitting up beneath his sheets, rubbing at his ear.

When she closes the door, it is suddenly very dark. They thought it was dark before, but the light had been coming in from the doorway, and their sleepy eyes had adjusted to it. Now it is dark properly and the girl starts to keen. The boy cannot see her, or can only see a patch of darkness that must be her, and when he reaches out she cannot see that he is reaching for her, and when his hand touches her waist she squeaks and jumps.

—It's only me! he says.

She cannot speak, but she hears him, and grabs his arm. As if it is a rope thrown out to someone drowning, she pulls herself along until she reaches the bed, and then his other arm is there, and he grabs her and pulls her beneath the covers. She crushes him to her, as if he is her mother now.

—Mamma will be back soon, he says. She lies beside him, and though they can't see a thing, they look towards where the door was.

Gradually, as they wait and watch, a rectangle appears there. At first they blink, as if it is an illusion brought on by their wishful thinking, but then, slowly, it becomes edged in pale yellow light, like the dawn arriving on the horizon.

—Shall I tell you a story? he says, but by that time she is asleep.

The box is tied with red ribbon, and though it once contained her shoes there's no way she would recognise it with its small neat bow. Whatever labels it once had have been carefully steamed off and the stock marks from the warehouse erased with a rubber. The box is not the important part anyway, it's what the box contains. Beneath the lid, wrapped in crumpled crepe paper, is a carved wooden doll, about six inches in length. It's not noticeable, because it is so beautifully done, but it was originally a piece of broom handle, quite thick and varnished and scuffed, and the paints used were the kind that come in tiny tins. Enamels.

Her uncle had found the broom, broken in the street, and it had come to him then and there. He borrowed a saw from the concierge, and took his knife and began whittling that afternoon.

At first it didn't seem as if it would work – some woods are good for carving, and some are too hard, or too brittle, and this didn't seem like good wood since it kept splintering – but once he'd carved through to the pale core beneath the varnish it was softer, easier.

The image that had come to him was of a girl, her hands clasped in front of her waist, her legs together, standing on tiptoes. She had long hair that stopped halfway down her back and a dress to her knees, and all of this could be done within the confines of the handle since there was nothing in the design that stuck out. It was beyond his skills to join pieces of wood together, but, in all honesty, that didn't occur to him anyway – to have her arms extended, or legs in a plié – sometimes an idea is fully formed, suggested by the materials available.

Once the basic shape was carved out – and this took several days – he realised his skills with the knife were limited and that he risked ruining what he had already done if he tried for too much detail, so he took what money he could spare and bought paints and a brush from a toy shop, thinking that he'd make up for any roughness with colour. If he'd had more experience, he would have known that he could mix red, green, blue and white to achieve most shades, but instead he picked a pink for the flesh, black for the hair and blue for the dress.

The painting was more difficult than he'd hoped, because it was hard to hold the doll and apply the brush without getting finger marks and smears over everything. He painted and removed the colours three or four times for this reason, which meant buying turpentine, which made his hands smell, and they all asked him what the odd odour was whenever he went in for his meals.

The solution came to him as Christmas was nearly on them, and he had almost given up – a scruffy piece of broom handle was not going to do the job at all, worse than useless – so when he thought of it he ran out and begged a nail from the concierge. Because the toes were pointed, he couldn't put it in there and though it seemed wrong somehow, he hammered the nail into the top of the doll's head. By holding the nail and turning it, the doll rotated so that he could paint the dress and the face and the hair without his fingers smudging his work.

It dried on the day before Christmas, and he pencilled in the face and the fingers and the pleats in the dress. Into the hole that was left in the head of the doll he glued a bunched up piece of the ribbon that he had bought to wrap the box with, making a flower for the doll to wear in its hair.

The doll looks wonderful now, beneath the crepe paper, inside the box secured with red ribbon, and when she opens the gift on Christmas morning, and hears the touching story that explains its making, and sees all the effort to which her wonderful uncle has gone to please her, won't she be happy and grateful?

What could be more natural than to be naked in the grass?

There are areas not far from Paris that are reachable by Sunday train, but which are still almost untroubled by the weekend exodus of the bourgeoisie who fan out in search of authentic peasant life, authentic peasant food, authentic peasant wine, and stories to tell their workmates on Monday mornings.

Certainly, these quiet places are not the most fashionable or the most convenient – they are sandwiched between wide tracts of farmland, often, and one must walk along the drainage channels away from the road to find them. On either side there will be maize at shoulder height, at head height, reaching up and blocking out the sun for a very long time, but this also ensures privacy, does it not? As long as one keeps an eye on the time, and leaves enough to return to the station before the last train is scheduled, everything is fine.

She comes out into a place even the farmer will forget until harvest, and there is a patch of stony ground that has become overgrown with weeds, and then dandelions and reeds, and then trees lining a stream. Here she slips her dress off over her head and folds it neatly, laying her socks and knickers on top of it, and then places the whole pile on top of her shoes.

Last she takes off her wristwatch.

It looks as if she has evaporated away, leaving her clothes behind, and she feels that she has. While she toes her way to the bank the elastic marks on her hips and ankles fade to nothing, and she becomes the kind of animal that is not called upon to wear clothes at all, to cover herself up.

Once – it was shortly before her birthday, not long ago – she saw on the other side of the stream a horse, or it saw her, and it seemed as if her nakedness put the creature at its ease. It carried on eating at least, grazing the stems of some plant her grandmother might have recognised, but which she didn't know the name of in French, Italian, German or English. She crouched down, her hands on the red clay between her knees, her gaze resting on the creature's flank, and it didn't take any notice of her.

This lasted long enough for her to take in every detail, and because she was a romantic girl she felt a kind of sisterhood with this horse, something that lasted all the walk back through the farmland, back on the train, and all the way home.

Would it be so bad to be an animal like this? To live in the forest? To eat only grass?

The horse had left in the end, startled by the barking of a dog out of sight, but the girl lay in bed that night and imagined what it might be like never to be dressed again.

The garden is wet from the morning's dew… or is dew from the night? The sun is scarcely risen, but these are the kind of things that you see now you have a child. An infant's internal clock is unable to synchronise itself to the working day, and your daughter desires experience of the world; she is undiluted in her enthusiasms by the quotidian demands of adulthood. Her eyes are wide and her mouth is wide and her teeth glisten like the drops of water on the garden furniture, which bead and swell on the green plastic.

The French doors click shut against the dog: he has mistaken your little outing as an invitation for a walk, despite the fact that you haven't dressed. Now he stares up at you, panting condensation against the glass. What does a dog know of betrayal? What does it know of anything, except balls and sticks and the arses of other dogs?

You turn the key, though the dog doesn't understand door handles either.

Your daughter is teetering across the patio like a stilt walker, legs stiff at the knee, heaving forward from the hips. She pauses when she reaches the steps and stoops, her hands fat against the dark concrete, white against the grit, knuckles folded against the steps, and she supports herself down the three stage mountain that gives onto the lawn: Vatican steps, a spiral staircase fire exit, then her bare feet on the grass.

She squeals and you involuntarily take a step forward. The hems of her pyjama trousers leach water, vaguely reminiscent of a chemistry experiment – a greyscale chromatography with water, cloth and the absence of water. You stop yourself from attending to her. She is safe. She wants to explore, and she should be allowed this small independence, this manageable consequence. Two minutes in the tumble dryer.

As she haltingly becomes further away, you purge your lungs of her sleep smells: the sweetness of a night full nappy, the sourness of breastmilk on her skin, the dense impenetrable musk of interrupted dreams. Those things warm the indoor air, but here in the garden everything is fresh. Fresher.

She is kneeling, patterning the knees to match the hems, and she has in her hands an earthworm: long and fat, pink and segmented, narrowing to points that seek and squirm. It encircles her wrist and she giggles in a way that brings to mind a drunk, or a dement – someone straight-jacketed and rocking, preoccupied with ideas she does not share with her doctors.

The dog is clawing at the doorway. He is frantic with love and yearning in that way that only dogs can unselfconsciously be. Keening. He pauses as if to re-establish that he truly is behind the door and not on the proper side of it. He pants, reassessing, as you stare at him, and when you return to looking at your daughter, you hear that he has understood that he was right all along and has resumed his digging at the threshold.

You do not move toward either of them.

Now she has taken each end of the worm and is stretching it taut. She pinches head and tail between fingers and thumbs in a way that is both delighted and thoughtless. The worm's Adam's apple bulges at a point two thirds along.

There is some idea that a worm, separated in two, will live on in both halves, that these will return to the soil and complete two separate lives, somehow. This has never rung true to you. You have seen the husks of dead worms in this garden. You have seen them wherever you go. Even if you had not, then where is the logic? Where would it stop? Can a worm reproduce in that way? Two, four, eight, sixteen?

There must be rules.

—Gently, gently!

She turns because she doesn't understand the word; she only understands your face. She makes her mouth into a comical 'O' and lowers the worm, still at full stretch, onto the grass. It snakes and contracts in one motion, thickening and making an 'S' in the sparse grass which is browner than it is green. Your daughter pats the worm with the flat of her fat hands, and pushes up, walking backwards, palms on the earth, hinging at the hips, upright, then away. She goes to the bottom of the garden where a privet hedge and a compost heap compete for dominance.

The dog is barking now – three strident exclamations, then a pause only long enough to make you feel as if he might have stopped, before giving three more. You let him out.

He runs first to the girl, making her wobble and put out her hands, then he races back to you. You ignore his earnest efforts to demonstrate his love, his devotion.

As the sun rises it illuminates the overcast from behind, making a pearl of the lightest possible grey in the water dense blackness of an oncoming rain cloud.

There are coats on the hooks inside. There are wellingtons arranged beside the door. There are sandals. Neither of you are wearing anything on your feet.

You go to where she is sitting now with the dog at her side. He is sniffing at something the girl is looking very closely at. It is a spider's web, glistening and perfect. At its centre is a round, brown spider, legs spread and waiting.

Your daughter, immaculately and painstakingly, reaches out her right index finger toward it. An imperfect nail clipping, still attached, juts from the edge of her finger, but it is at a right angle and the tip of her finger meets the web first. She touches a thread with microscopic precision, the whorls of her fingerprint making contact and her breathing, or her pulse, or some electro-magnetic aura of which you are not aware, vibrates the gossamer like a violin string. The spider tenses – it can sense these very slight movements since its life depends on them – and your daughter sees this. Because she is such a good girl, she pulls her fingertip gently away. She doesn't want to disturb the spider.

At one edge of the web there is a cocoon – it is not a cocoon. A cocoon contains the genetic soup that facilitates the transition between a caterpillar (an ugly creature) and a butterfly (a beautiful one) through a process that is more or less mysterious, and it is not the time of year for it. It is a gnat bound in the same thread that forms this perfect web. If your daughter wished, she could play this web as one plays a harp, trace her finger across the strings and provoke music from it by virtue of her goodness. She could unwrap the cocoon, bring the gnat back to life, and let it loose.

The dog brings its nose to the place where your daughter placed her finger, but you pull him back by the collar. She turns to look at you, and, emboldened by your smile, she touches the web again, in exactly the place she touched it before.

Spiders are attracted by vibration, but also by patterns. The spider feels a pattern in the touching, then the withdrawing, then the touching again; it understands from it that there is a meal in its web. In a flash, it darts across, and, for the shortest time before it realises its mistake, the spider touches your daughter's finger.

When a child giggles the sound should be infectious. She giggles at the touch of the spider and turns to look at you. She wants to share this with you.

You turn to the sky as it darkens. The wind picks up and, without prompting, the dog runs back to the house.

You reach down for your daughter's hand.

—Come on. It's about to rain.

Acknowledgements

Thanks to my editors Sam Jordison and Eloise Millar, and also to Alex Billington, who typeset the manuscript and designed the illustrations (which are taken from the priest Imhotep's *Book of Coming Forth by Day*, which can be seen in the Metropolitan Museum of Art, New York).

I also acknowledge my debts to the fields of history, music, medicine (including dentistry), embryology, parasitology, film studies, Asian and Middle Eastern studies, Russian studies, English studies, Joyce studies, and Egyptology (among others). I have drawn on these areas of expertise freely and without consideration for anything other than the artistic requirements of this book. Any errors are mine, and any borrowings are from standard works in the public domain.